Ocean City Cover-up

A Jamie August Novel

Kim Kash

Capri House
GREENBELT, MARYLAND

This book is a work of fiction. References to real people, events, establishments, organizations, or locales are intended only to provide a sense of authenticity, and are used fictitiously. All other characters, and all incidents and dialogue, are drawn from the author's imagination and are not to be construed as real.

Cover design and illustration by Jake Clark, jcalebdesign.com

Book Layout & Design ©2013 - BookDesignTemplates.com

Ocean City Cover-up / Kim Kash. -- 1st ed.
ISBN 978-0-9895022-3-8

For Michael

read "Ocean Gateway International Student Services" and scanning the crowd.

She realized he was looking for her.

"Fucking hell," the girl said under her breath. She popped her gum and wheeled her luggage cart in their direction.

Prologue

THE GIRL WAS STILL PISSED OFF but starting to feel better. The six minibottles of vodka were
kicking in, and she was finally getting to a good
part in Fast & Furious 4, which she chose among the
wide selection of movie options in her Lufthansa business
class seat.

Fucking business class. The girl's father cared for her
so little that he'd booked her in business instead of first.
Like he didn't know it's a sixteen-hour flight from Dubai
to Washington. She shifted impatiently, trying to get comfortable, but found it really disgusting to lay her seat flat

right next to some nasty businessman she didn't even know. The plastic pod dividing her seat from his couldn't block out the sound of his gentle snores. She clutched her Valentino purse and sniffled.

The girl's eyes grew dewy with the realization that her father no longer loved her, his one and only daughter, his princess. She opened the handbag, pulled out a tissue, and dabbed her mascara-clumped lashes.

By the time her flight touched down at Dulles International Airport, west of DC, the girl had pulled it together. Her highlighted blond hair was artfully tousled, and her lips shimmered with fresh lipstick. She'd cleaned up her mascara a little, but there was nothing like real tears to give your eye makeup that bleak, heroin-chic appearance. It looked even better than when she tried to apply it that way on purpose.

The girl wheeled a towering cart full of top-of-the-line aluminum luggage through customs, and scanned the crowd of professional drivers holding up neatly printed signs with the names of passengers they were to meet. She didn't see her name anywhere. However she heard Azeri, the language of Azerbaijan, being spoken.

A group of college-aged guys and girls were laughing and chatting with excitement. They were surrounded by a colorful riot of duffel bags and cheap vinyl suitcases. A guy who was maybe thirty, kind of cute if you're into the patchouli-and-health-food thing, was holding a sign that

1.

MY LUNGS WERE READY TO BURST by the time I hit Tenth Street, and I slowed to a walk. I stopped to hang onto a lamppost, bent forward at the waist, and tried to catch my breath.

It was just after eight a.m. on July 1. The start of week four of my Get-Your-Ass-In-Shape campaign. Every year at the beginning of the summer season, I hit the Ocean City boardwalk shops and picked out a new bikini. This year, I'd been really irritated that I couldn't find anything that looked good on me. Everything made me look fat—or at least kind of doughy and soft.

Then I realized that the bathing suits hadn't changed. I had changed. No longer could I scarf down Slurpees and chili cheese fries and stay skinny. The late-twenties pounds were showing up. I wanted the leopard skin bikini with the fringes—it was only twelve dollars!—but I just couldn't work it the way I used to. I found myself looking at sensible one-pieces, and that's when I found Jesus, right there in the fitting room at the Bikini Depot.

"Tammy, I swear by the Fourth of July I am gonna rock this bikini," I said to my best friend, who was trying on minidresses.

"Do it!" Tammy said.

"Yeah!"

"So, how are you gonna make it happen?"

I was caught off guard thinking about the logistics of exercise. "Huh. I can't afford the gym."

"So go running. That's free."

"That sounds hideous."

Tammy shrugged and pulled her dressing room curtain closed.

"Shit. Okay, you're right. I'll do it."

From that day on, I went jogging every day on Ocean City's wide boardwalk. As June progressed, my runs got longer and my belly really did get flatter. Now, one month later, I was feeling pretty good about the way I looked, but that didn't mean I liked the damn running part. I stopped for a thirty-second break, hitting the stopwatch button on my plastic running watch.

"I hate my hormones," I said out loud just as three fifty-something women strolled past.

One of them turned and said, "You think you hate 'em now, honey? Just wait." They laughed and kept walking.

I was too out of breath to come up with a response. I waited for my heart rate to come down, then did a few hamstring stretches, checking out my nicely toned legs with satisfaction.

I straightened and looked down the boards, undoing and redoing the ponytail holder on my straight, dark hair, blowing my bangs out of my eyes. I spotted what I was looking for off in the distance. I hit the stopwatch button on my plastic sports watch again, squared my shoulders, and jogged on.

Finally I reached my destination: Kohr Brothers. I got in line and did another set of stretches as I waited. Despite the early hour, the line was six deep for the original, often imitated but never duplicated Kohr Brothers frozen custard. I told myself this was a healthier alternative to ice cream, that I could budget the 130 calories in that small, beautiful cone. But the truth was, if I didn't know there was a Kohr Brothers cone waiting for me at the end of every run, I wouldn't run. I just wouldn't do it. I would buy the granny one-piece, and maybe throw in some elastic-waist jeans, too.

The three teenage boys ahead of me in line finished with their order and their lame attempt to chat up the Russian summer workers behind the counter, and then I stepped up to the booth.

"Vanilla. Plain. Small. Hurry!"

"Your run was good?" one of the girls asked, smiling and tucking her cute bobbed hair behind one ear. She asked me this every morning.

"Awesome," I said. "Couldn't be better. Today I ran all the way from the other end of the boardwalk."

"That is maybe forty blocks, yes?" asked the other, more sultry girl. "That is far. How you do?"

"Brute force," I said, pulling exact change out of the little pocket in my running shorts. The cute one handed me a cone piled high with snowy vanilla soft-serve and collected the money. The sultry one twirled a long blond strand of hair.

"Knocked twenty seconds off my time today," I said, then took the first glorious bite of frozen custard. I wiped a sticky drip on my chin.

"That's great," the cute one said. "Twenty seconds off the exact same run from yesterday? You are doing well."

"You have stopwatch on that?" the sultry one asked.

I showed her my black and safety-yellow rubber watch. "Yeah. Got it at Daffodils, eighteen bucks. Says it's a Timex, but probably a knockoff. Whatever. Really helps me track my progress."

"I have this function also," she said, extending her slender wrist and showing me a watch that looked to be completely covered in diamonds. It had small, round dials arranged within a larger analog clock face. This dial here is stopwatch," she said, delicately pointing to one of them.

"That's a fitness watch?" I said, guffawing.

"Of course. Piaget Miss Protocle XL."

The cute one whipped her head around and stared at her friend.

"Replica," she amended. "Of course."

"Piaget. Sounds like a car," I said. "Anyway, it's amazing."

"Thank you."

"One of those sure would improve my look when I'm out for my morning run."

"Yes. But I do not understand," the sultry one said. "Why you not go on diet? Would be easier than this run, run, run every day, no?"

"Are you kidding? I am on a diet. Otherwise I would order the waffle cone with cookie crumbles and double jimmies. I am totally cutting back."

"When I want lose weight, I don't eat. Easy."

"I can't not eat. I'd die. Well, I mean of course anyone would die if they didn't eat. What I mean is, I would kill myself."

"No, is easy," she said, one hand on a beautifully curvy hip. "Stop eat. Only smoke."

Well, she had me there. I quit smoking nearly a year before, and I knew that was a big contributor to this season's bikini crisis. Still, with only one or two minor lapses, I had kicked the habit and I wasn't about to go back. Couldn't afford it, for one thing.

"Easy for you to say." I rolled my eyes. "What are you, twenty?"

"Twenty-one."

"Just wait," I said, realizing with horror that I was mimicking those women who'd mocked me earlier. "Twenty-seven is a bitch."

2.

N UPDATE ON SHOOTINGS outside a teen dance club and an eastern European summer worker who was knifed to death led the day's *Weekly Breeze* news roundup. Witnesses were still being sought for the incidents, which happened last week.

I put the finishing touches on a news analysis showing an upswing in gang activity and a rise in violent crime in Ocean City. Many of those being arrested were young men with addresses in or near Washington, DC. I guess even gang members needed beach vacations.

I'm a staff writer at the *Breeze*. I broke a big story last winter involving a corrupt real-estate empire and a high-end housing project. A bunch of McMansions were built on some paved-over marshes that were the last remaining blue crab breeding ground in OC. The story got picked up by a major news agency and put the *Weekly Breeze* on the map as an independent local newspaper that reports actual news.

Donald Brightland, the editor and owner of the paper, often complained that my stunt ruined his relaxing routine of printing stories about American Legion scholarship winners and trends in beach-house decor. But he'd been smart enough to put me on salary and give me benefits after the story broke, to lure me into staying in his employ. Like I was going to leave. Where would I go? Back to my hometown of Baltimore, to freelance at the *Baltimore Sun*? Or take a crappy gig with some news service's rinky-dink Eastern Shore outpost? I saw plenty of news that needed reporting right here.

The phone rang, and I picked up. "*Weekly Breeze*, Jamie August."

"How are you doing, sweetheart?"

"Hi, Uncle Abe. What's goin' on?" My mother's brother owned some apartments in town and hired me to answer the phones for him in the off-season. I wouldn't do the job in the summertime because I couldn't stand the idea of fielding complaint calls for eight hours at a time. Let's just say Abe's buildings were in need of a little TLC. Okay, okay, they were all dumps, painted in migraine-inducing colors. "Those bright colors are my trademark. Everybody loves 'em," Abe always said. "They give my places a real islandy kind of atmosphere." Yeah. Atmosphere like you'd find in Haiti.

But he was family, and I didn't think he meant to be a slumlord, exactly. Plus, I lived practically for free in one of his eye-popping buildings—the Kitty Lou—down near the inlet, where the powerboats and fishing boats docked, and the Atlantic connected to the sheltered bay behind Ocean City. So I couldn't really complain.

"Jamie, I need you to do a job for me," Abe was saying on the phone.

"I don't have time."

"Come down to DaVinci's. I'll tell you about it over dinner."

DaVinci's was one of Ocean City's finest Italian restaurants. I knew this because I reviewed it—my extensive OC dining intel was gleaned exclusively from dinners paid for by the Weekly Breeze. It was one of my job's best perks.

Dinner at DaVinci's definitely sounded better than what I had planned: a PBJ standing over the sink. So I agreed to meet him.

I hung up and turned to Donald, who was tapping merrily away on his keyboard at the other desk in the Breeze's sunny storefront office.

"Abe's taking me to dinner at DaVinci's," I said in surprise.

Donald raised a perfectly shaped eyebrow. "Watch out, Jamie. If he's trying to get you to work him some kind of discounted advertising deal in the Breeze, the answer is no."

"He wouldn't even try that. He knows you're not a fan of Beach Getaway Rentals."

"Does he?"

"Um, yeah," I said, popping my gum. "Your article on the ten worst slumlords of Ocean City pretty much spelled it out. I can't believe you named Abe as the seventh worst."

"I dropped him down from the top five out of respect for you."

I thought of going home first for a quick change of clothes, but I didn't have time for the bus ride to the opposite end of town. I combed out my long, dark hair and considered my outfit: cut-off jeans shorts, black tank top, flip-flops. I snipped a few straggly fringes from my shorts, and changed from

14

the flip-flops to my go-to pair of high-heeled black stilettos, which I kept in my bottom desk drawer for exactly these last-minute situations. Perfect!

Donald surveyed my outfit skeptically. "Oh, hon, you can definitely pull off that look with those hot runner's legs of yours, but it's not quite... ironic enough."

"Who's being ironic?" I asked, hand on hip. "I can't get into DaVinci's with flip-flops."

He sighed. Then he stood up and removed his own belt, a white leather number studded with grommets that looked ever so jaunty with his flat-front yellow trousers and striped boater shirt. "Here, try this."

The belt was perfect with the low-rise cut of the shorts, and lent a certain '60s go-go girl style to the outfit.

"Better," he said. "Bring it back tomorrow."

3.

I CAUGHT THE PACKED BUS from the *Weekly Breeze* office uptown near the Delaware border, down to DaVinci's around Fourteenth Street. There was only standing room on the bus, it being dinner hour with everybody heading out for crabs, fries on the boardwalk, and happy-hour drinks.

A few blocks north of my stop I felt a hand inch across my thigh and cup my ass. I couldn't turn around, couldn't get away from the pervert. I looked down and spotted a grubby man's sneaker near mine. I gently picked up my foot and ground a stiletto heel into the top of the man's foot. The hand jerked away from my backside and a hoarse shriek rang out.

"This isn't Tokyo," I muttered.

"Hey kid, you're looking terrific," Abe said as I bent down to give him a brief hug. "No kidding. What the heck are you doing, Pilates? Kickboxing?"

"No, I'm doing it old-school. I'm running."

"Christ. I used to run," Abe said.

I couldn't picture it. Abe's polyester Hawaiian shirt stretched across his belly, and the bald patch under his comb-over glistened in the restaurant's subtle lighting.

I ordered a Bacardi and Diet Pepsi from the waiter, who wasn't even trying to be discreet as he ogled me in my short shorts. I couldn't tell whether he was being a lech or a snob. We perused the menu and ordered: a surf and turf special for Abe and Maryland crab ravioli for me. The waiter brought salads and blushed furiously when I looked him in the eye and recrossed my legs.

Abe seemed to miss the whole exchange, busy as he was drowning his greens in ranch dressing. I dug into my undressed greens.

"Since when do you like salad?" he said.

"Since never. But if I eat the salad, I might not have any room left over for dessert."

"You really got this sorted out, I gotta say."

"Thanks, Abe. So, what's this project you want to talk to me about?"

"First, I want your opinion."

"Really?" Abe was older than my dad. This was a milestone in being grown-up!

"Yeah, you're a reporter. You might know something about this."

"Right, of course. What's the situation?" I said, all cool.

"I'm buying a piece of property down near the inlet, not far from your apartment. It's back in the neighborhood. Old house with a shop front on the bottom level. Right now it's some kind of Internet cafe, or at least that's what they're calling it. Bunch of Russians in there. Lotta people in and out. I don't know what they're doing, but whatever it is, they're not doing it in English."

"Why are you buying the place?"

"It's a good price, and the place doesn't need much work. But I don't know about this tenant. They may be laundering money, running Russian prostitutes, gambling, who knows? I'm thinking of closing it down. All these Russians in town these days, I don't like it."

"But your apartment buildings are full of Russian summer workers. They're your livelihood," I said, a bit indignant.

"Yeah, but they trash the place every summer."

"All of them," I deadpanned.

"Of course not all of them. But a lot of them."

"What, and the American kids who used to come in for summer work treated your apartments better?"

"Are you kidding me? The American kids are even worse!"

"Then what's the problem?"

"Yeah, yeah, you may be right, but at least with the American kids I could go after the parents for damages. These foreigners, I got no recourse."

"So what's your question?" I took a sip of my drink.

"Can you do a little checking on this place, find out about the owner? Maybe you know something about this joint, or could ask around, see what the deal is."

"This isn't the only Internet cafe in town," I said. "I've seen one in a strip mall right on Coastal Highway."

"Exactly. How many of these places does this town need? I could get a T-shirt place in there, no problem, some kind of souvenir shop."

"That's exactly what Ocean City needs more of," I said, laughing.

Abe grimaced.

"I gotta know what's going on in my properties, or it could be on my head. How do I know this place isn't some kind of front for the Russian Mafia or something?"

I considered this, and my thirst for conspiracy was piqued. I admit, it never took much.

"Okay, so you want to know if this place is a legit business, and worth keeping, or whether you should kick them to the curb, am I right?"

"Something like that, yeah. Can you check them out for me?"

I considered the load of stories on my desk. Not a wise move, taking on a research project on the side. But I couldn't resist.

"Okay, I'll check it out. Give me the address."

4.

Y SALAD GAMBIT was a bust. After a tiramisu and a double espresso at DaVinci's, Abe and I said our good-byes and I waddled out to the street for a bus north. Abe had offered me a ride home, but with the heavy summer traffic on Coastal Highway, I figured it would be better to take the bus. It had its own lane. The bus lane was also the bike lane, which had led to some terrifying moments on my rusty beach cruiser, but whatever. I'd still rather bike and bus it than deal with the expense of owning a car.

The espresso had given me a nice jolt of energy, and it wasn't quite time for bed yet. So instead of getting on the bus, I decided to get a drink at the

Poolside Lounge. It wasn't my favorite spot, kind of pretentious. Plus the guys could get a little aggressive in there, and I'd already had my ass groped on the bus. But I was wired, and it was right across the street.

On the sidewalk in front of the club I fished around in my giant purse—summer-white leatherette, with studs—and pulled out a deep wine-colored lipstick. I stood under the neon sign and peered into my compact mirror to apply the lipstick perfectly, then I flipped my hair and spritzed it with a can of hairspray I always carried. What else was I gonna put in that purse? It was big enough to carry a Chihuahua—but I didn't want a Chihuahua.

I strutted into the club (is there any other way when you're wearing shorts and stilettos?) and elbowed my way up to the bar, easing between two guys sporting the thug-life look. They were advertising their underwear brand with their droopy jeans, but the letters should have spelled out Loser. I tried to silence my mental dialog, which sounded old and stodgy.

"Hey baby," one of them said as I shifted past him.

"Hey." I looked away, plastering on what I hoped was a disinterested smile.

His hand slid around my waist, stopping my forward movement.

"You lookin' fine, baby. What's your name?"

This, before I have a drink in my hand?

"Baby. Mmm mmm mmm. I wanna git witchu," he slurred. Alarmed, I turned to his friend, who was studiously not looking at us, smoothing his freshly barbered tight fade.

"Hey," I said to Tight Fade, who pretended to be distracted. "Hey!" He finally looked at me, as the first guy was draping his arm heavily around my shoulder. "Honey, I need some help here with your friend."

"Yo, yo, baby, you don't need no help from him. I got what you need," Arm Dragger said, attempting to turn me to face him.

"Seriously, I'm trying to get to the bar. You don't want me to be thirsty, do you?" I shot a look at Tight Fade.

"Yo, Dante! Girl wants a drink," Tight Fade said. "Come on, man."

"Aw, yeah, yeah, girl's gotta have a drink. Get your drink on and then we gonna get freaky," Arm Dragger said to me, releasing his grip around my shoulders but making no move to follow me to the bar and buy me a drink. Deadbeat.

Scowling, I ordered a Jack and Diet from the Asian woman behind the bar, which was set up like a boxing ring in the middle of the room. Her uniform was a corset, panties, and fishnet stockings. The outfit looked itchy. I felt bad for her, but the massive square bar separated her from the lecherous masses and she'd probably be counting close to four figures in tips that night. There were worse ways to make a living.

Drink in hand, I pushed through the crowd toward the pool deck, where a few bold girls in bikinis frolicked in the small, up-lit pool, and couples lay on the king-sized chaise lounges. I began to question the wisdom of coming in here alone.

Then I spotted the two Russian clerks from the Kohr Brothers frozen custard stand. Aha! Someone I knew. Well, sort of, a little. The girl with the cute bob haircut sipped her drink and held a sweet smile, facing two guys. One of them stood in an arms-crossed, tough-guy pose, wearing slouchy pants, a wifebeater, and gold chains. He stifled a yawn. The other wore his hair in a bushy afro, and wore skinny jeans and a T-shirt with a stencil of the DC flag. Hipster guy looked to be talking a mile a minute.

The other Kohr Brothers girl had clearly already chosen her guy. They were reclined on a chaise lounge. With her arm draped over the guy's shoulder, she held a drink and a smoke, her blingy watch hanging loose on her delicate wrist. Her other hand was entwined with the guy's hand, which was resting on her thigh. He wore what looked to be diamond-encrusted knuckle-dusters in the shape of a gun. Her tiny black dress rode high on her hip, exposing the smallest glimpse of black lace panties. One of her kitten heels hung halfway off her foot. Her heavily made-up eyes were nearly closed. The guy had dusky, light brown skin and tight cornrows. A scar traced a pale line across his jaw. The whole scene looked like a photograph on an almost-porn website.

A few more blinged-out guys were hanging around behind the chaise lounge. They seemed to be keeping an eye on the girls. Then again, most guys probably did.

Cute haircut girl spotted me, gave me a bright smile and a wave. As I approached, a huge guy with long braids and a Redskins jersey stretched over his massive belly stepped aggressively in front of me.

"This over here is Sniper Trigga's private party," he said in a rumbly voice.

"Sniper who?" I laughed. Suddenly several sets of eyes stared at me hard.

"Ah no, is okay. She is my friend," Cute Haircut said to the bodyguard. He stepped back and let me pass.

"Hallo, my friend," she called out. I approached, and she kissed me on both cheeks. "We are not introduced. I am Leyla. Don't worry, you are invited to our party!" She turned to the two guys. "David, Terry, please to meet my favorite ice cream customer."

David, the guy with the afro, turned to me with a smile and a nod. "What's up?"

"Hi. I'm Jamie August." We shook hands.

Terry looked me up and down. "Yo."

Enough. I'd had it with being sized up like a piece of meat. I eyed him up and down equally suggestively. Not that his skinny frame did much for me. He shifted and glanced away.

Leyla rattled the ice in her empty glass. "I get you drink, Jamie."

"Oh, man, I don't know. Tomorrow morning's run is gonna be hell," I said, but then I finished off the last of my Jack and Diet with a loud slurp. "Huh. Well, maybe. Okay." YOLO, baby.

"Yes. I will get you best drink. Vodka."

She said a few words to Terry, who walked away from us with a swagger that nearly made his pants fall off.

5.

WELL, WHAT WAS I THINKING?" I said to David. "She's Russian. She's going to be drinking vodka."

"Naw, she't not Russian," David said.

"She's not?"

"Nope. Azerbaijani."

"Um, Azerbaijani?"

"Yeah, you never heard of Azerbaijan?"

"Of course I've heard of it," I retorted, then felt really stupid. "I assumed she was Russian."

"Used to be Soviet."

"Uh, right," I said, scrambling to remember something, anything that I must have read in my twentieth-century history class at community college.

"Azerbaijan became independent in 1991, with the dissolution of the Soviet Union. Girl, don't you know nothin' about history?"

"It's, uh, Soviet history is not really my strong subject," I said, feeling stupider by the second.

David busted out laughing. "I'm just messin' with you. Don't worry about it."

"Good grief, how come you know all that?"

"I'm studying modern European history at Howard."

"Oh." I laughed.

"You didn't think a brotha like me was gonna know about Soviet history, did you?"

"Uh..."

"Nah, it's okay. You a student too?"

"No, I'm a reporter." I loved saying that.

"Damn, girl! That is some righteous work right there," he said. "You should be proud of what you do. The voice of the people and all that."

I was charmed, of course.

"You do any investigative reporting, exposés, stuff like that?"

"I broke the story last winter about a bunch of wetlands getting paved over for a housing development."

"Excellent."

"Mostly, though, I write up city and county meetings, keep in contact with business owners and community associations, and cover charity events and beauty pageants. I also add up budgets to see if they make sense—and usually they do."

"You trying to get out of here, get with the *Washington Post* or something?"

"They offered me a job after that story last winter, but it was basically a glorified internship, and I couldn't afford to take it."

"Yeah, DC is expensive."

"And the news business is cash-strapped. Anyway, I like being a big fish in a little pond down here. I know everybody, and I understand the politics."

"Sounds like small newspapers are where it's at."

"I think so—the independent ones."

Leyla interrupted our journalism lovefest by handing out the vodka shots that Terry had procured.

"Oh God," I said.

"Tonight it is party by Sniper Trigga. Thank you, my friend," she said, leaning over her nearly comatose friend to kiss the apparent kingpin on the cheek.

Sniper Trigga—was that seriously what people were calling this guy?—nodded and said, "You're welcome, baby. I take care of my friends."

Leyla raised her shot glass, yelled "na zdorovie," and downed her vodka. We all gulped our shots. Mine went down like gasoline. I swallowed and coughed sharply.

Only then did Leyla's sultry friend notice me standing there. "Oh, hello," she said. "I know you. I am Mina." Her eyes were bloodshot and she was having a little trouble focusing.

"Hi. I'm Jamie August."

She didn't introduce me to Mr. Trigga, so I stuck my hand out to him and said, "Hey, uh, Sniper Trigga. Thanks for the drink."

The guy's eyes lingered on my legs and then he cooly, gently took my hand. "Call me André." His eyes bored into mine as he squeezed my hand. He let go after several uncomfortable seconds.

Flustered, I said, "Are you also at Howard University?"

He chuckled. "Do I look like a student?" I heard derisive snickers from some of the guys loitering behind the chaise lounge. "I'm Sniper Trigga."

"I don't really know what that means, and since your friend here was telling me he's studying history at Howard. ..."

"I'm in the music business. And I don't know him," André said, nodding in David's direction. André's crew shot hard looks at David, who looked annoyed and a little uncomfortable. Terry snorted.

"I explain, Jamie," Mina said. "This man David—David?" He nodded in the affirmative. "He talk to Leyla. This man André, he talk to me." Helpful. Then she buried her face in André's neck, apparently finished with talking to anyone. Her white-blond hair was starting to show some dark roots.

André lifted her head and gave us all an explicit show as he kissed her, their tongues meeting in the air.

I looked away. David was already babbling on again about his theories concerning the autonomy of the various former Soviet states, while Leyla beamed. Her eyes were clear and bright, and her cap-sleeved T-shirt accentuated trim, shapely arms.

Terry stepped over and said something in André's ear, then left the group.

It occurred to me that since Mina and Leyla were foreign summer workers, they were exactly the people I needed to talk to about the Internet cafe question. I could probably also learn a thing or two about gang activity by hanging here with André. I chided myself for jumping to that conclusion. Then I reminded myself he goes by "Sniper Trigga" and thought maybe it was a legitimate plan after all.

But my head was spinning and Mina and André were otherwise occupied. So I said my good-byes.

"Hey, it was great talking to you, Jamie," David said. "Maybe I'll see you around."

"It was very educational to meet you," I said with a wink and a grin. I leaned in close to Leyla and asked, "Is Mina going to be okay?"

"She is like this always," Leyla said, her voice lowered. "You cannot do anything."

"Will you make sure she gets home?"

"Me? Oh, no," she said, cooly unconcerned. "She probably will not be home tonight. We are room-mates, so I know. She does not come home many nights."

"That's kind of scary," I said.

"No, she is party girl, is her way."

"That's crazy. I gotta say, before tonight I thought all of you guys working on the boardwalk were, I don't know, poor. I also thought you were all Russian." I realized how stupid I sounded and also realized I was probably voicing my thoughts out loud because I'd had one too many drinks.

"Not poor. This is workaway, no? Costs money, this program to get to the US for summer work.

And not Russian. Not at all Russian," Leyla said with loud emphasis.

"Dang. I am so ignorant," I said.

"No, do not say this." Leyla laughed. "When I come to America, I know nothing about. Every day I learn something new. Like today, I learn that Dr. Dre is not really physician."

André broke off his lip-lock with Mina long enough to laugh at that.

"Okay, I gotta go. Tomorrow, Leyla, I have something I want to ask you about. I'll see you at Kohr Brothers, same as ever."

"Okay, my friend."

The crowd had become even thicker as I made my way back past the bar toward the front door. I caught a glimpse of André's sidekick Terry turning away from the bar and handing a tall, dark-skinned woman a drink. She smiled, and he put his arm around her. The drunk guy who'd accosted me was still lurking around the bar. He accidentally knocked into Terry. A subtle arm movement from Terry and the guy dropped to the floor. Impressive! The woman said something into Terry's ear, seemingly oblivious to Terry's stealth defensive maneuver.

I caught Terry's eye across the room and we exchanged a brief nod. Maybe Terry would get lucky tonight after all. I sighed, realizing I had subconsciously come out on a work night looking for my own love connection—but this wasn't a Chuck Woolery kind of place.

Outside the Poolside Lounge, security had two guys pinned down on the sidewalk. One white guy, one black guy. The white guy had predictable tribal tattoos encircling his biceps, and the black guy wore an equally predictable collection of gold chains. They were shouting obscenities at each other, and several of their look-alike friends were hovering on the sidewalk behind each of them. The police rolled up with lights and sirens. I kept walking and caught the next bus home.

Oh, Ocean City, how I look forward to September, when the idiots clear off your streets.

6.

Y APARTMENT WAS A second-story shoebox in an old clapboard house near the Ocean City inlet, painted acid green. The house's name, the Kitty Lou, was painted on a wooden sign tacked over the front porch. I had no idea if the place was named after a real person. Most OC apartment houses were known to locals by their names rather than their street addresses. I called my place the Cat Box.

My front door was at the top of a rickety wooden flight of exterior stairs at the back of the house. I wobbled a little going down the stairs for my morning run, but I felt pretty good that I was out the door in my running shoes at all. At the bottom of the steps, I stood in the weedy gravel parking area and stretched.

It was a cloudy morning with a breeze coming in, one of those days that's punctuated by an evening thunderstorm. I started off in a walk, then eased into a jog, heading out on the same loop I took yesterday: north on the street and then south for the length of the boardwalk. It would, of course, culminate in the glory of a frozen custard cone. The thought spurred me on.

Day-trippers and families staying on the bay side were crossing Coastal Highway in droves, flocking to Ocean City's wide, white beach. At every intersection, moms and dads flooded the crosswalks, loaded down with beach chairs, coolers, bags, umbrellas, and beach towels, like cheerful refugees carrying their entire households down the block.

The sun showed no sign of breaking through the clouds, but that wasn't stopping the flow of foot traffic to the beach. Many people got only one week a year to go to Ocean City. Unless it was pouring rain, they'd hit the beach.

I threaded my way through the throng, jogging barely faster than they were walking—but damn it, I was jogging. I turned the corner and hit the boardwalk at Thirty-Seventh, heading south. I huffed past the Flamingo and Seabonay motels, Brass Balls Saloon, Malibu's Surf Shop and finally Shenanigan's Irish Pub & Grill. I also passed a number of old-fashioned clapboard rooming houses and private homes, which gradually became more uniform and morphed into a constant and fairly repetitive line of bars, restaurants, and shops selling T-shirts, souvenirs, ice cream, french fries, pizza, and salt-water taffy.

By now it was nine thirty and almost all of the shops were open for business. Classic rock, rap, and reggae thumped from storefronts, and the wind flapped awnings and banners.

Finally, I passed First Street. Only a few more blocks! Division Street, Caroline, Talbot, Dorchester, Somerset, and... wait a minute. Why were the shutters still pulled down on the Kohr Brothers stand?

No frozen custard? What was the point of running? The point of living?

I slowed to a winded walk and approached the stand. By Wicomico and the boardwalk, I sat down and cried. The garage-door-style shutters were still pulled down and padlocked. No sign. No explanation. Nothing.

I was feeling unreasonably emotional, way out of proportion to how one should feel when denied soft-serve. I went to Thrasher's across the way and ordered a large tub of fries. I doused them with the requisite cider vinegar and sat on one of the benches that line the boardwalk. I pouted as I shoved fries in my face and checked e-mail on my phone, which I wore strapped to my arm so I could listen to Bon Jovi while I ran. I always used every enticement to get myself out the door for this punishment.

This from the office: Body found early a.m. stuffed in a dumpster behind the Dough Roller on South Division Street. Victim was an unidentified male. No suspects. Follow up for story.

I shuddered. That dumpster was not two blocks from here. I would jog past it on the way home and take some photos with my phone. The thought did not cheer me up.

Just then Mina strolled up to the stand and squinted at the shutters in confusion. She looked up and down the boardwalk, then rooted in her blingy designer purse and pulled out sunglasses and cigarettes. As I walked toward her, she lit a smoke, then pulled out a smartphone and began poking at it with a manicured finger.

She disconnected the call in annoyance when she spotted me. "Where is Leyla?" she asked with no preliminaries. Her makeup looked like hell and she'd thrown her Kohr Brothers uniform shirt over the minidress I'd seen her in last night at the club.

"I don't know."

"She is late. And she does not answer her mobile."

"I thought you two were roommates."

"We are."

"Well, did she make it home last night?"

"I do not know. I was not there," she said.

She stared out at the sea. I felt a pinprick of worry.

"Atdirmaq," she said, taking a drag from her cigarette.

"I'm sorry, what?"

She looked at me, exasperated. "Fuck."

"Anything I can do?" I wasn't at all sure I should get involved in Mina's problems, but Leyla didn't seem the type to bail on her morning shift.

"Ach," she said. "I cannot open stand. Leyla has keys," she said, indicating the heavy padlocks on the shutters. "This is all her fault."

"I see," I said, totally irritated. I was concerned about Leyla, but I'd had enough of Mina's bad attitude. "Well, good luck to you," I said, tucking more vinegary fries into my mouth.

Mina's mouth dropped open. "But wait! I need help."

I gazed at her cooly, wiping vinegar off my chin.

"I. Uh. You come with me."

I crossed my arms and glared.

"Please." She dropped her eyes and scuffed a heel against the pavement.

"Fine," I said, my worry overriding my irritation. "Let's go." It was that or snap photos of a dumpster festooned with police tape. The Dough Roller body could wait a few more minutes.

We walked a few blocks north on the boardwalk and turned left toward the bay. She easily kept my pace, strutting in her Barbie-doll heels like they were as sensible as my running shoes. I wished I could do that, feeling the hot spots on my feet from last night's stilettos. Some girls were born to wear heels. Me, I was born to wear flip-flops. Or Uggs.

Mina pulled a heavy gold key ring out of her purse as we walked down the driveway of a handsome old wooden house on Talbot Street, which had been converted into apartments.

We headed around to the back and she opened the door to a lower-level unit.

"Is not locked," she said, turning to me with concern.

From the front stoop she reached in, flipped the light switch, peered inside, and screamed.

7.

HE RUSHED IN, while I paused in the door frame. The living room was a shambles. Cushions had been pulled from the sofa. The coffee table had been flipped over, its legs pointing to the ceiling. Bedclothes were strewn about the room, and a small chest of drawers in one corner had been emptied and tossed.

Mina let out another blood-curdling scream and charged down a short hall and into a bedroom, with me one step behind. It was the same thing here: a thorough, violent toss, with clothes ripped from the closet and the mattress and box spring pulled from the frame and leaning crazily against the wall.

In the bathroom, the medicine cabinet had been ransacked, with jars and tubes and eye pencils and lipsticks, toothbrushes and bars of soap, all strewn across the cracked but once-elegant tile floor.

Then we turned to the kitchen, pushing open one of those old-fashioned double-swinging doors. Pots and pans, utensils, and dishes were piled on every surface. A half-eaten carton of ice cream sat in a melted puddle on the table. One chair lay on its side. "This is strange," Mina said. "Why they not mess kitchen?"

"What are you talking about?"

"Rest of house, ruin. Kitchen, they not touch."

"This is what your kitchen always looks like?"

She glared at me. "We are busy people."

She picked up the overturned kitchen chair and sat heavily, clutching her ridiculous purse to her chest and bursting into tears.

"Where did Leyla sleep?" I asked, trying to cut through some of the drama.

"On sofa. Living room was hers. We share apartment, but I pay and have bedroom for me only."

I pushed open the swinging door and again surveyed the living room. I imagined Leyla opening the door without thinking twice, probably still mostly asleep, and being attacked. A dark smudge brushed across the wood floor by the front door. I knelt down to examine it more carefully but couldn't tell whether it was fresh, whether it was blood.

I pulled out my cell phone and began to dial 911.

"Who you call?" Mina asked sharply.

"The police, of course."

"No! No no no," she said, grabbing the phone out of my hand and poking me with a long, manicured nail in the process.

"Ouch! Are you crazy? Give me my phone back. We have to call the police. Leyla is missing! Somebody trashed your apartment!"

"No way. No police." She gripped my phone like her life depended on it, tears streaming down her face.

I sighed. "I don't know how it works in Azerbaijan, maybe it's much different from here. But in the United States, when somebody breaks into your apartment and probably kidnaps your roommate— you call the police."

"This is different," Mina said miserably. "Leyla is wrong girl."

"How is Leyla wrong?"

Mina shook her head and cried. I grabbed a roll of paper towels and set them in front of her, then

47

pulled out another kitchen chair. A blue canvas purse lay on the seat.

"Is this Leyla's?" I asked.

Mina's eyes grew wide, and she nodded. I opened the bag and found a wallet with a few dollars, a single credit card, and a student ID from Baku State University for Leyla Dovzhenko. Tucked into the change compartment was a cocktail napkin with the number of one David Wilson in ballpoint. The purse also contained a ring of keys, a pair of cheap sunglasses, a package of tissues, and a tube of lipstick. Bupkes.

"Shit," Mina said and sniffled loudly.

"Blow your nose," I said.

She ripped a square off the paper towel roll and wiped her nose, somehow still maintaining a death grip on my cell phone with the same hand. I'm going to have to sanitize that thing, I thought.

"Okay, Mina. We know she came home last night, and somebody took her. Who's after you?"

"I do not understand." She turned away dramatically.

"What did you mean, Leyla is the wrong girl?"

Mina remained silent.

"If you don't tell me what's going on right now, I will go and get the police."

"No! You must help me, Jamie!"

48

With a swift motion, like swatting a fly, I grabbed my phone out of Mina's hand. She gasped.

"Why should I help you? Leyla is gone, and you're doing nothing." I smoothed out the napkin with David's phone number and took a picture of it with my phone. "For all I know, you're a drug smuggler and somebody tossed your apartment and stole your fifty thousand-dollar stash of heroin."

"Ha! Fifty thousand is nothing. Would not be problem."

"Oh, hold up. So you are a drug smuggler? Jesus."

She rolled her eyes derisively.

"Then what? Is anything missing? Can you even tell?"

Mina made an exaggerated show of staring all around the kitchen. Her eyes rested on a knife block by the stove. "The big knife is gone."

"How do you know, in this mess?"

"Those knives are Leyla's. She is freak. Makes me clean when I use and put away or she gets mad."

I got up and examined the block, which was stamped with a Wusthof logo. "I've seen this brand at a kitchen store up in Rehoboth. Expensive."

"Yes, our pots and pans are shit, but these are good."

"Okay, Mina, enough about the kitchenware. What's going on here? Talk to me, or tell it to the police, sister."

Mina chewed on her lower lip. Then she came to a decision. "Okay, I tell you. No. I show you. You wait here."

She pushed through the kitchen door. I got up and tossed the soggy ice cream carton into the already overflowing trash can, and cleaned up the melted ice cream with some of the paper towels. I stacked the dishes in a more orderly fashion by the sink. I thought, why the hell am I cleaning Mina's kitchen?

Then I thought, where is she?

"Mina!" I called impatiently, pushing through the swinging door to the living room, where the front door was still standing open as we had left it. I walked back to the bedroom and then the bathroom. The apartment was empty.

I sprinted out the front door and circled the house to the street. I peered up and down the street, but Mina was gone.

8.

I TOLD MY STORY to one Detective Morrison, a tan, blond woman who appeared to be in her late thirties. She wore khaki shorts and a striped polo shirt, and looked like she was ready for a friendly game of tennis. Two hours later, I was still at the Ocean City Police Department headquarters. I sat in an interrogation room and listened to my stomach growl.

Morrison seemed truly concerned about the missing girls, and when she entered the room they'd put me in, she told me first thing that they had a team of experts working at the apartment, and a BOLO already released. "State troopers are on the lookout. I know you're worried, but I want you to know we're using every tool to find your friends."

Odd that she was talking as though both of them had been abducted, when clearly Mina bolted on her own. But who knows? Even if she did leave on her own two feet, where did she go? Would she be safe when she returned to her place?

"Thank you."

"Of course. Now talk me through this one more time. The last time you saw Leyla was when?"

"Last night at the Poolside Lounge."

"That place is pretty sordid. Why would you go there?"

"Why would I not?"

Morrison shrugged and smiled. "Never mind. So you walk in..."

"I walk in. I get a drink. I walk over to the pool. I see Leyla and Mina."

"I'm hearing from the bartender that Leyla was hanging out with a whole crew of gangbangers, is that correct?"

This preppy woman sounded odd talking about crews of gangbangers. She tucked her hair neatly behind one ear.

"Not exactly. There was a group of us: Mina and her boyfriend André, who seemed to be in charge, plus Leyla, a college student named David, and another guy named Terry, who seemed like he was some kind of right-hand man for André. A couple of other guys were hanging around, too, but I'm not sure they were really gang members."

"What do you mean, you're not sure?"

"Well, from the stories I've done on this, I thought most of the organized gang activity in this region stems from MS-13 coming out of the DC suburbs. But those guys are Latino, so—"

"What stories are you referring to?"

"I'm a reporter for the Weekly Breeze."

She sat back and considered me with fresh eyes.

"None of the guys last night were Hispanic. That's why I wonder about the gang angle."

"Latino gangs don't seem to be the source of the violence on Ocean City's streets this summer. Most of the people involved in these altercations are African Americans and whites."

"But why do you think they're gang members?"

"Haven't you seen these clowns? They're all 'gangsta'," she said, using air quotes.

"Yeah, but 'gangsta' is a music and fashion trend. Have you seen the clowns on MTV? C'mon, we all dressed like idiots when were were teenagers."

"The people you were with last night: were they teenagers?"

"Point taken. Maybe those guys were gang members of some sort. I'm not trying to be obstructive, seriously. Just skeptical."

Morrison shrugged, nodded.

"There were some other guys hanging around, and they did all seem to be treating André as a kind of leader. Oh, and I guess I should tell you, André goes by the name Sniper Trigga." I snickered.

The detective glanced up sharply. "Interesting."

"David seemed more interested in talking about post-Soviet-era politics than, well, whatever a 'gangbanger' is interested in talking about."

"Post-Soviet-era politics?" Detective Morrison barked out a laugh.

"Apparently he's a history major at Howard University."

She rolled her eyes.

"We'll see about that," she said. "We'll haul that whole group of punks in soon enough."

"Detective Morrison, while I'm here, can I ask you about the body that was found in the Dough Roller dumpster early this morning?"

"Not my case, but I'll get you the press release."

"Thanks. Do you know who the investigating officer is on that one?"

"Lapin caught that case."

"Good coverage of the Firemen's Parade," Donald said later that afternoon at the office. "Good color. I especially liked your interview with the female firefighter there at the end."

A bubbly young volunteer firefighter from Prince George's County had spoken to me with enthusiasm about her work. "Fire!" she enthused in teen-speak. "I wanna, like, fight it."

"Thanks." I grinned at Donald. "Which photo's going to run with the story?"

"Either the one with the little kids waving American flags as the fire engines roll by or the one with the pug in turnout gear. I can't decide."

"That's a tough one," I conceded, but I knew enough not to get between a gay man and a pug.

I had rehashed with Donald the events of last night and this morning. I'd already written an article detailing the missing women but hoped like hell they'd be found before the paper went to press at the end of the week. We had the police scanner turned up so we both could hear it, but so far no news.

I also wrote a short news story about the body in the Dough Roller dumpster, using information I picked up in a press release.

"Do you know an OCPD officer named Lapin?"

"Peter Lapin, yeah, he was hired a couple of months ago."

"You have any kind of connection with him?"

"No, I only know him because he was the officer on that animal-cruelty case last month."

A Snow Hill man had been caught with a pit bull puppy mill on his farm. Conditions were grim, apparently. I couldn't stomach it; Donald had to cover that one. "As I recall, that was his first OCPD case."

I shuddered at the memory of the photos of the caged puppies. I never should have looked.

"Lapin's the officer on the Dough Roller case."

"Sorry, can't help you. We didn't go out for drinks and become besties after that Snow Hill mess."

I went online and read about Azerbaijan. Fun facts: it's the largest of the Caucasus nations, located between the Black Sea and the Caspian Sea. The region, named for the Caucasus Mountains, is east of Turkey and north of Iran. If that helps. I stared at Google Maps for a while, considering the patchwork of country names in that part of the world. They all seemed inscrutable and vaguely threatening.

Like all of its former Soviet state neighbors, Azerbaijan gained its independence in 1991, as David had said. The country was known for its oil and gas, sitting on the largest oil reserves outside of the Middle East. Because of this, all the big oil companies were trying to get their foot in the door. Shell, Exxon, BP: all those companies I love to hate as I gas up (whenever I borrow Tammy's car, that is) and hand over my hard-earned cash.

If Mina came from an Azeri oil family, she was extremely wealthy. Why the hell was she in Ocean City selling frozen custard?

9.

I TOOK A BREAK to microwave a Weight Watchers frozen entree for lunch. The sauce over the spaghetti was thin, and the tiny meatballs made a mockery of what I really wanted: a Belly Busters meatball sub with extra cheese. Slurping a can of Diet Dr. Pepper with a straw, I Googled the address for Uncle Abe's new building and found a business that appeared to be much more than a few greasy computers and an Internet connection.

At least on their website, Ocean Gateway International Student Services offered job placements, housing referrals, shuttle service to and from JFK in New York, and tourist trips for seasonal workers to DC, New York, and points farther away.

"Donald, do you know anything about a business called Ocean Gateway International Student Services?"

"Not specifically. Is it one of the organizations that helps the overseas kids who come in as summer workers?"

"Looks like it."

"Yeah, back in the eighties and nineties, kids sometimes paid a bunch of money to one of these services, and got dumped here in Ocean City. Maybe their job offer was legit, maybe not. Maybe they had housing waiting for them, but usually not—or it was overcrowded, or way out of town. Anyway, the US government cracked down on those outfits. You know my friend Trish?"

"She's does marketing for the Chamber of Commerce, right?"

"Yes. She came over as a Russian college student in 1982. She worked as a maid in OC but lived in a dive way out in the country past Salisbury with six or eight other girls."

"Seriously? I'm sure that's not what the work-exchange brochure said."

"Exactly. But hey, she got lucky. She married the hotel's night manager, and now they've got two kids in college."

"So they're mostly legit now, these companies?"

"As far as I know. Why, what's your latest conspiracy theory?" Donald's eyes twinkled. "Are you thinking that Leyla's and Mina's disappearance has something to do with that? Because, seriously, your fascination with the Russian Mafia is really cute, but the cops are probably right. It's much more likely to have something to do with Mina's boyfriend."

Donald was often exasperated at my tendency to see a nefarious plot around every corner.

"Okay, I hear you. That's not the whole reason I want to know, though." I told him about Uncle Abe's latest real estate acquisition and the business currently on the first floor.

"Lovely," Donald said acidly. "I suppose his first order of business will be to paint the building lime green."

"He prefers safety orange."

Donald and his partner, Wesley, have money and taste oozing from their pores. They live in a beachfront penthouse apartment in North Ocean City. They throw dinner parties where the table is set with mysterious extra forks and spoons. The interior of the Weekly Breeze office looks like an English manor house, having received Donald and Wesley's cast-off furnishings after their last home redecorating binge.

I stood up from my chintz-upholstered desk chair and stretched. "I'm going to check out this Internet cafe student center thing. Now I have a real excuse to walk in there. Maybe they can give me some information that will help Leyla. Or even Mina," I said grudgingly.

"Go get 'em, tiger," Donald said. "I'll call you if I hear anything on the scanner."

I rode the crowded bus almost nine miles down the entire length of Coastal Highway, the damp, air-conditioned air redolent with body odor and suntan oil. There was a bottleneck at the bus doors as a group of three teenage girls tried to wrestle with beach chairs, bags, and an umbrella while talking and giggling, each into their own cell phones.

On the sidewalk, I turned away from the beach and walked a couple of blocks in, finding the address Abe had given me.

It was a particularly ugly building, painted the color of overcooked peas. It appeared as though a big old three-story house had been "modernized" sometime in the 1960s to accommodate a business on the ground floor. The porch had been ripped off and a plate-glass facade added, with an aluminum-framed glass front door. A sun-faded sign hung across the length of the house: Ocean Gateway International Student Services. Smaller letters around the edges of the sign read "Internet Cafe, Travel Services, International Calling, Student Housing." The window glass was covered in posters showing Ocean City, New York City, Niagara Falls, and a couple of amusement parks in Virginia.

A bell tinkled as I pushed the door open and entered a wide, bright room. One side was lined with computer stations, two of them being used by young guys slouched down in plastic chairs. The other side of the room had a line of slightly over-sized phone booths. Two worn and mismatched but reasonably clean sofas faced each other across a square coffee table in the middle of the room. The table was littered with tourist pamphlets and teen fan magazines, dog-eared and brightly colored. The titles were in Cyrillic. A through-the-wall air conditioner wheezed and struggled to keep the room sort of cool, and an oscillating fan whirred in one corner.

At the back of the room was a massive sixties-era metal desk, and behind the desk sat the most beautiful man I had ever seen.

Kim Kash

10.

ELLO," he said with an easy smile. "How can I help you?"

The man's shoulder-length, dark hair was a bit wavy and scruffy, his skin a luminous shade of brown, and he had a smoking-hot five o'clock shadow. His Clash T-shirt showed off a lean, flat stomach. The Clash killed hair metal, or tried to. As if. So I hated that band—but this guy? I'd listen to Phish for this guy. I smoothed down my faded red cotton sundress, took a deep, nervous inhale, and smiled.

You can father my children. No, no, I didn't say that. What I said was, "Hi. I'm Jamie August, reporter for the Weekly Breeze. I'm here because I'm doing a story on student workers in Ocean City and I have some questions."

"Sure. Have a seat." He pointed to a Perry Mason-style wooden chair facing his desk. "I'm Sam Nasser."

We shook hands. His was strong, warm, dry.

"I was going to have some coffee. Can I pour you a cup?"

His voice sounded rich, self-assured, and American but somehow more... polite? He rose and disappeared through a door covered with a beaded curtain with a waterfall painted on it. He returned a moment later with two steaming mugs.

"Coffee on a hot day is somehow refreshing. Don't you think?" he asked, handing me a mug.

"My grandmother always used to drink hot coffee in the afternoon in Baltimore, even in the summertime. And she never had AC."

"See what I mean? Strange." He took a sip.

My phone rang faintly from the bottom of my bag. I pulled it out as the last few bars of my ringtone version of Bon Jovi's "Dead or Alive" faded out. It was Tammy. She could wait.

Sam snickered. "That's pretty funny."

"What?"

"Your ringtone."

"It's Bon Jovi." I stared daggers at him and his Clash shirt.

"So," he said briskly. "How can I help?"

"Do you own this business?"

"Yes. Why?"

"I don't know anything about overseas work programs and I was wondering about the kind of business that goes on here. Am I talking to the right guy?"

He offered a game smile and nodded. "Yep. There are over three thousand foreign student workers here in Ocean City this summer. Ocean Gateway arranges transportation from overseas and links students with work opportunities here in town, and, frankly, we also make sure the students who come here aren't taken advantage of."

"Taken advantage of?"

"I make sure their working and living conditions are up to standard, that they don't end up in some kind of compromising position they wouldn't know how to deal with. Unfair wages, unreasonable accommodations, illegal working conditions, stuff like that."

"Do you see a lot of that kind of thing?" I asked, scribbling away as though a story was in the offing. Who knows? Maybe it would end up being a Weekly Breeze piece.

"No, but these kids are like any other college students—not necessarily savvy about their rights as workers. They also come from places where it's not always okay to speak up. So I do what I can to make sure their rights are protected and their work is legitimate."

"You have a pretty stable business, then?"

"Me? Yes, why?" He looked at me oddly.

"Oh, no, I mean a stable industry," I backpedaled. "Companies that arrange international student work."

"Sure, I suppose. I've been in business a few years. Unless American kids decide to start scooping ice cream and selling carnival tickets again, like they used to, I don't think my company is in any danger of going under."

I switched tactics. "Where are you from?"

"From Maryland."

"The Eastern Shore?"

"No, the DC area."

"Whereabouts?"

"Why does this matter?"

"Sorry, it doesn't." I stopped writing, taken aback, and took a sip of coffee.

He paused, thought for a moment. "I'm touchy about questions like that."

"Questions about where you're from?"

"Yeah. I mean, I'm American, we're all American. Why do people always look at me and want to know more?"

"Wow. I didn't have any particular reason. I'm also from Maryland and I thought, who knows, maybe we were neighbors as kids or something."

He laughed. "Okay, I'm from Rockville. For me it's a much more loaded question. I'm a first-generation American, from Lithuanian and Lebanese parents."

"So, what's the problem?" I was honestly puzzled.

"The problem is some people take me for a Muslim terrorist. Or an illegal Mexican immigrant. I find myself having to establish my American credentials more often than I would like. It's annoying."

"I've never thought about that before. Am I allowed to ask how you ended up in Ocean City?"

"You are allowed." He laughed. "My family came here every summer when I was a kid, and I've always loved the beach. After college, I went into the Peace Corps for a couple of years, in Armenia, and when I got out I decided to come here and start a business working with the kids who come here from other countries. Despite all that negativity we just talked about, I love helping kids get a taste of

69

life here in the United States. It's a huge milestone in their lives. These days I work almost exclusively with students from eastern Europe—countries that used to be a part of the Soviet Union."

"Do you get people from all economic levels?"

"Not really," he said. "It's expensive to get here, so these are comfortable, middle-class kids. Maybe not by our standards, but they are college students, and their life is easy compared to the many kids whose families are still reeling from generations of deprivation, even starvation, both before and after the Soviet era."

Sam gazed around the office, threadbare but shipshape, with quiet dignity.

"I guess I'm lucky that I have absolutely no frame of reference for what you're talking about," I said. He nodded in acknowledgement. "What about the other end of the spectrum, though? Do you ever get any really rich kids who want to come to Ocean City for summer work programs?"

"No, not really," he said. "At least, not that I know of. Why?"

"Okay. I've gotten involved in a weird situation," I said, deciding to trust him. I was satisfied that I had enough information to give Abe the thumbs-up on Sam's business. Furthermore, I instinctively trusted Sam. Furthermore still, I wanted to stay there, talking with him, breathing the same air as him. I was smitten.

11.

I TOOK ANOTHER SIP of coffee, now cool.

"I have a couple of friends from Azerbaijan," I continued. "They were here working for the summer, and they've disappeared."

"Disappeared?"

"Yes. They're roommates, and they work together on the boardwalk. I saw them when I was out last night at the Poolside Lounge. One of them stayed out all night with her boyfriend. This morning, she showed up for work, but the other girl didn't. We went together to the apartment they share and found it totally trashed. It appeared as though the missing girl had been there and had been taken."

"That's terrible. I haven't heard anything about this. What are their names?"

I told him.

"Oh no. Leyla and Mina are my students. I should get in touch with the police. I need to call their parents!"

"The police already know. Kohr Brothers didn't get in touch with you?"

"No, nobody did! Why didn't you tell me about this in the first place? Why are we sitting around chitchatting?"

"I figured they couldn't be your students or you'd already be all over this. I'm sorry. Of course I would have told you sooner if I had known."

Sam ran a hand through his hair, picked up his desk phone, and dialed. I watched his troubled expression turn to one of frustration as he hung up. "No answer at Kohr Brothers. Okay, tell me what you know."

"Mina—the one who showed up for work this morning—was freaking out. She said something like, 'they got the wrong girl.' I asked her what she meant, but she wouldn't say anything else. When we were at the apartment, I pressed her to tell me what she knew, and finally she said she would show me something instead. She went into the other room and then bailed."

"What do you mean, she bailed?"

"I was waiting for her to come back into the kitchen with whatever it was she was going to show me, but she never did. A couple of minutes went by, and I went to see what she was doing, but she was gone."

"Huh," Sam said, leaning back in his chair. "What do the police say?"

"Well, at the Poolside Lounge they were hanging out with some tough-looking guys. The cops seem to think this is somehow gang-related."

"But you don't think so?"

"That apartment was torn apart. Somebody was searching for something."

"Like what?"

"I have no idea."

Sam pondered this. Started to speak, then stopped. "Do not quote me in your 'informational story' about student workers—the one you're coincidentally writing right around the time two of them disappear." He paused and gazed at me pointedly. "Don't quote me on this or on anything. Are we clear?"

"Yes."

He narrowed his eyes and considered me. "Eastern European women are very attractive."

I felt my skin flush, hating that I was having such an obvious reaction. "Yes," I said evenly. "Mina and Leyla are both beautiful. Different but both beautiful."

"Sometimes, girls arrive here and find that they are very... successful socially. Maybe Mina got a little taste of that and it went to her head, made her think she didn't need to bother with the day job— or answering your questions either."

"Maybe that's it," I said, unconvinced. "Maybe she took off with her new boyfriend. But that doesn't explain what happened to Leyla."

"No, it doesn't. Now if you'll excuse me, I need to call Leyla's and Mina's parents. Thank you for bringing me this news. And next time, seriously, tell me why you want to speak with me. No wonder nobody trusts reporters. ..."

Quite sure there would be no next time, I reached across the desk to shake his hand. "You won't find yourself quoted in the Weekly Breeze. You have my word. And even if you don't appreciate it, consider how your eastern European students might feel about the free press we enjoy in the United States."

He smiled wryly. "You really think we have a free press in this country?"

"We do in Ocean City. I assure you, Rupert Murdoch has no interest in the *Weekly Breeze.*"

12.

I LEFT THE OCEAN GATEWAY International Student Services office and walked over to the boardwalk to get that Kohr Brothers cone I missed this morning. Surely they were open by now.

It was late afternoon, the air heavy and hot, the ocean radiating with a hot, metallic shimmer. No surprise—the boardwalk was packed.

I felt my phone vibrate in my purse, and answered as I stepped down onto the sand to get out of the crowd.

"Another body, another dumpster," Donald said with no preamble. "St. Louis Avenue. I'm texting you the address."

"When?"

"I heard it on the scanner not two minutes ago. Police are on their way."

"I'll be there. I'm less than five minutes away."

I made quick time through the neighborhood and arrived as the police were setting up a barricade around the shady back corner of a rooming house parking lot. We were right around the corner from Leyla and Mina's place. My stomach was tied up in knots.

I joined a few other onlookers and watched as two plainclothes detectives pushed open the lid of the dented green dumpster. I snapped a few photos with my phone. A squad car was parked to block our view, and several officers had been posted to keep the small crowd away from the scene—but they couldn't mask the smell that wafted out.

I winced and reached around in my purse for a pack of gum. I popped two pieces of Trident in my mouth, hoping the mint flavor would help my nose cope with the stench of decomposing flesh on a summer night.

The two guys peered into the dumpster, both recoiling from the smell. One of them snapped on a pair of gloves, reached in, and pulled out what appeared to be a chef's knife.

I snapped a photo of the detective with the knife. The light was starting to fade from the evening sky, and my phone's flash went off. The detective holding the knife instantly scanned the crowd, glared at me, and hollered for the duty officers to disperse the crowd.

I cut around the corner and found myself staring at Mina and Leyla's Talbot Street building.

I called Donald.

"The body is still in the dumpster, and from the smell of it, there's no rush to get it out."

I told him about the knife—and the missing piece from Leyla's Wusthof set.

"This sounds grim, Jamie. But there's no use sticking around there. It may be hours before the body is moved, and they're not going to let you see it when it is."

"Gross! I wouldn't want to." I worked hard on my hard-boiled investigative reporter shtick, but c'mon.

"I agree. We're not going to know anything more until at least tomorrow."

"We don't even have the identity yet of the Dough Roller guy from this morning."

"Correct: we do not. They still haven't released any information."

"Well, I got the photo anyway: police detective brandishing murder weapon."

"Presumably. Oh, Jamie, this is all so distasteful. I'm going to have to redo this week's whole front page. I think the Baptist Church bake-off will have to get bumped to page five."

It's not that the smell of a dead body made me hungry, of course. I simply wanted to replace the bad sensory experience with a good one. I retraced my steps to the boardwalk. The frozen custard stand was open for business, with a long line of customers. I got in line. I'd get my Kohr Brothers fix today after all. Those Thrasher's fries this morning were great, but when you've got an urge for Kohr Brothers, really, nothing else will do.

A sallow, midthirties guy with the beginnings of a comb-over was working solo behind the counter.

"Hey, are you the manager?" I said when I reached the front of the line.

"Yep. Brad."

"Do you have any news about Leyla or Mina?"

"Who are you?"

"I'm a friend of theirs. I came by this morning for a cone."

"What do you know about what happened to them?" he asked, eyeing me cautiously.

I gave him the basics of my encounter with Mina, omitting the fact that she gave me the slip.

"Cops told me about you," he said. "You're lucky those gangbangers didn't get you too."

"You think that's what happened?"

"What else? You hang with a tough crowd, you're likely to get hurt. You know what I'm saying?"

I changed the subject quickly, as it seemed like Brad was about to elaborate further on the dangers of hanging with a tough crowd. I already knew about that: I'm from Baltimore.

"Did Leyla or Mina have any other friends? Other coworkers or people in the nearby shops?"

"How should I know? When they're out here taking orders like they're supposed to, I'm back in the office getting my own job done."

"Okay. Hey, Sam at Ocean Gateway was pretty flipped out about the missing girls."

Brad scratched his head with a latex gloved finger. "Good. He should be. Yuri came by this morning, but you can't really tell what that guy's thinking."

"Who's Yuri?"

"From the agency. You know, it would have been nice if Mina had bothered to call me before she took off."

The guy behind me in line said, "Hurry up and give the guy your number so I can get my cone."

I quickly gave my order to the furiously blushing Brad.

I slipped into the crowd of people drifting down the boardwalk toward the Ferris wheel, like a leaf in a slow stream. I felt a growing unease as I worked my way through the vanilla cone.

Who's Yuri?

Above all the normal, cheerful boardwalk squealing, a bloodcurdling scream rang out. A knot of people rushed toward the Haunted House, which was next to a huge video and Skee-Ball arcade. Then a second scream filled the air.

The crowd stampeded in the direction of the screams, and a mustachioed man in a John Deere work shirt drove my cone into my chest with a flailing elbow. I fought my way to the front of the Haunted House. People were pointing and snapping pictures of something on the second-story balcony of the 1960s-era ride.

As I got closer, I could see it: a limp arm dangled through the crooked wooden balcony rails. I dropped what was left of my cone got and snapped a few shots. Three sets of crime scene photos in one day. Maybe I should find a job in Detroit or Mexico City.

I heard sirens approaching, and then the crowd pressed close again as an emergency crew fought their way through with a stretcher.

The officers and paramedics rushed into the Haunted House, past the creepy, wooden-slatted ticket booth and through a discreet emergency exit door. They appeared on the balcony a moment later. The medics set up the stretcher across the tracks used to move the coffin-shaped cars across the balcony during the ride.

The last time I went on this ride was with Tammy, after several mai tais. We laughed so hard at the zombie (or was it a skeleton?) getting flushed down the toilet that Tammy threw up.

The arm disappeared from view, and a few moments later, the medics lifted the body onto the stretcher. I saw a shock of blond hair for a second, and then the view was obscured.

I shivered in the hot evening air. A moment later the paramedics emerged and the police fanned out to push the crowd back for the stretcher. I snapped more photos, flash on, earning some glares from the medics. Thank goodness I didn't know anybody on this crew.

My last boyfriend was a firefighter. He fled Ocean City after declaring his love for me and then admitting he was on the payroll of some very bad guys who were out to kill me. I wasn't sure whether that firehouse connection would help me or hurt me with these paramedics.

I was cautiously hopeful that my luck with men would improve soon. At the moment I had a strictly casual, once-in-a-while hookup thing going with a surfer named Trevor who worked in retail.

My reverie was broken when the crowd stepped back as police personnel unrolled crime-scene tape across the entire front facade of the Haunted House. Says something about me: when my brain goes into energy-saver mode, it starts thinking about sex.

"Aw, man," a pimply boy next to me with a mesh-back baseball cap said. "They gotta close the whole ride?"

A policeman snapped at him, "No problem, kid, give us a few minutes to remove the victim from the tracks and then it'll be right back in business." He turned away from the kid and continued to unroll the yellow tape. The kid's friends exploded in the kind of viciously derisive laughter heard only among middle schoolers.

"What does that guy know?" he whined. "We didn't miss nothin'. We've been looking at that body all day!"

13.

I GRABBED THE KID'S ARM.

"Hey!" I said. "You said you've been looking at that body all day? What do you mean?"

He shook his arm free and faced me in defiance. "I meant what I said. It's been there all day. Who are you?" He was posturing for the sake of his friends; I could see the nervousness in his eyes.

"I'm sorry for grabbing your arm," I said. "I'm only trying to find out what happened. I'm a reporter. Did you really see the body?"

"Sure, we all saw it," the kid said, and the others nodded in agreement. His attitude did an about-face, as he was suddenly a source of important information.

"Hot blond chick. Clean shot through the forehead, execution style," said another boy wearing a shirt that said "I (splat) Zombies." He put his finger up to Mesh-back Cap Guy's head and pulled the trigger with his thumb. "Bam! Just like in Call of Duty."

"The Haunted House is old school, but we love it," Mesh-back said.

"For sure. It's so old even my mom rode it when she was a kid," a girl piped up, grinning, her braces gleaming in the sodium lights and neon, flickering on in the gathering dusk.

"Yeah. Me and my cousins here ride it a bunch whenever we come down the ocean." Mesh-back said it Baltimore style: downey ocean. "They're always adding something new. We thought that blond lady was, you know, the latest feature."

"Totally," Zombie Splatter said. "It's a sick place for a corpse. It was right there on the edge, by the corner of the deck. It seemed like we were gonna run right over it, but the track turns away at the last minute."

"Yeah, they should totally add another feature there, you know, because now they know how good that spot is," Braces Girl said.

As the sky grew dark I waded through the crowd to Coastal Highway and rode the bus north to the Breeze office, which was locked when I arrived. I typed my notes about the body on the Haunted House tracks and the one in the apartment dumpster, and uploaded all my photos. I called Donald at home to tell him about the Haunted House body.

"Third time's a charm," he said. "I hope OCPD's public information officer is working overtime. Hopefully tomorrow they'll put out at least the basics on all three of today's dead bodies."

"The Haunted House one sure sounds like Leyla."

"We can't run any details based on the hearsay of a bunch of preteen cousins."

"Of course."

"What is this town coming to?" Donald moaned. "The Weekly Breeze used to cover beauty pageants and classic car shows. Now it's nothing but police blotter from front to back."

"It's not quite that bad, Donald. Don't forget, I'm attending the sixty-fourth annual American Legion Independence Day dinner dance tomorrow night."

"God Bless America," he said with relief.

I called the police station and asked for Detective Morrison.

"Jamie, how are you holding up?" she said, briskly but sounding genuine.

"I'm doing okay, thanks. I'm calling as a reporter for the Weekly Breeze because I was down at the boardwalk and saw the commotion at the Haunted House."

"Yes..."

"I'm wondering if you can tell me if the body they found is Leyla."

"We're still investigating," she said. "You'll have to talk to the duty officer in charge."

"Sure, but I wanted to talk to you because you know about Leyla's situation."

"What makes you think it's Leyla?"

I told Morrison about the conversation I'd had with the kids on the boardwalk.

"Ah, crap," she said. "So much for keeping the details out of public circulation."

"Um, yeah. Everybody who rode the Haunted House all day today rode right past that body," I said.

"I tell ya, these gangland shootings have finally made it down Route Fifty to Ocean City. I guess even out here we can't get away from the DC and Baltimore gangbangers."

"So you've got something that indicates this is gang-related?"

"Jamie, I can't give you the particulars of the case, you know that."

I sighed. "Okay, but I've got something else for you. I was also there when they opened up that dumpster on St. Louis Avenue."

"You're touring all the sights today."

"I saw the knife they pulled out."

"Jamie, that may be critical evidence in that case and is absolutely not for public release."

"I thought you might say that."

"You better believe it."

"I get it, I get it. But I think I know something about the knife."

I told her what Mina said about the knife missing from Leyla's butcher block.

"That would link the two cases," she said.

"Well, sure. When I got to that dumpster I figured the body inside must be Leyla. It's right around the corner from her place. But now I think that's not true, because I think Leyla was the one on the Haunted House balcony."

Morrison sighed. "I can't comment on this, really."

"Please, Detective Morrison. Off the record: was Mina in the apartment dumpster? This is Jamie the friend, not Jamie the reporter. If you know, please tell me."

93

"The body was male."

I started to breathe again. Mina was a royal pain in the ass—but I didn't want her dead in a dumpster.

"Thank you."

"Officers are continuing to be vigilant out there on the roads. We are doing absolutely everything we can," Detective Morrison said with efficient optimism. "She'll turn up."

Hopefully not in the same dramatic fashion that Leyla did, I thought. And not in a dumpster.

14.

AN HOUR LATER, Tammy and her boy-friend, Dustin, sat in her living room and drank Coors Light with me. Tammy put out a bowl of Doritos because she's hospitable like that. They even muted the television.

When the eleven o'clock news came on, we turned the sound back on and watched the coverage. Candy Holloway from the local news station stood in front of the Haunted House, her shel-lacked hair deconstructing before our eyes. The police tape flickered around in the sea breeze. The camera panned up to the railing where the body had been found, then continued on to the balcony of the apartment house next door and the stores and boardwalk attractions around the Haunted House. All were empty—too empty for a summer night.

The newscast's also-ran woman reporter, whose nose was a little too big and her suit not as well-fitted as Candy Holloway's, stood in the parking lot behind the apartment building on St. Louis Avenue and reported on the bodies that had been found dumped there and behind the Dough Roller. No identities were released, no details other than that citizens were being urged to report any strange smells emanating from trash receptacles.

"Stinky dumpsters in July? That's going to short-circuit the phone lines," Dustin said.

The coverage turned to a handsome, earnest male reporter, standing in front of the Poolside Lounge. The line of wannabe gangstas and gangsta hos stretched down the block in their baggy pants, fake bling, and hooker dresses. The reporter looked awkward in his suit as he stood on the sidewalk and outlined the story of the missing Russian workers.

"They're Azerbaijani!" I said.

"What's the difference?" Dustin asked innocently.

Tammy, a librarian in Ocean City's branch, was on him instantly.

"What's the difference?" She got up and grabbed an atlas off a bookshelf.

"Oh boy, here we go," Dustin said, unable to suppress a little grin.

Tammy thumped the Doritos on the floor and opened the large, heavy reference book across the coffee table. She traced a pink fingernail across the page. "This," she said, stabbing the page, "is Azerbaijan. And this up here," she said, stabbing a point farther north and east on the map, "is Russia."

"Okay. Got it," Dustin said.

She paused and read for a few minutes while Dustin and I watched Candy Holloway's hair turn into a rat's nest as she continued her earnest reportage.

Tammy looked up, research done. "The most important thing about Azerbaijan, the thing that makes it so important, do you know what it is?"

"Mail-order brides?" Dustin guessed.

Tammy shrugged, conceding. "Okay, the other thing that makes it so important?"

"I give up."

"Oil," Tammy said. "Azerbaijan has oil. And everybody wants a piece of it. Western oil companies, the Russians, the Iranians—all of them are bending over backward to be the ones to bring all that oil to market."

"But Russia has its own oil too, right?" I asked.

"Sure, they have some, but it's lower quality than the stuff in Azerbaijan. Plus, it's way the hell in Siberia."

"How do you know so much stuff, Tammy?" Dustin laughed. "It's ridiculous."

"I'm a librarian. It's my job."

The news coverage changed to a press conference from earlier in the day, where the police chief talked about police efforts in response to the upswing in gang activity in Ocean City. Increased foot and bike patrols of the boardwalk and downtown areas, higher police presence all over the city: the whole department was working overtime to ensure that the city remained safe and pleasant over the Fourth of July holiday and throughout the summer.

"Blah blah blah," I said.

The TV blared with man-on-the-street interviews of families who had decided to pack up and go home early, concerned about violence over the holiday weekend.

A woman standing behind a display counter full of sunglasses said she was worried her sales would fall off during this weekend, the peak tourist time of the year.

"Hey, don't we know her?" Tammy said, pointing at the TV.

"Oh! That's the lady from the Quiet Storm. She tried to sell me a seventy-dollar sundress."

"That's right. It was Roxy, though, and it was really cute."

"So is the dress I bought that day at Daffodils for eight bucks."

"I guess, but the Roxy one didn't have any glitter on it."

"See? I got such a better deal."

The newscast cut to archival footage from earlier in the season, showing dudes walking on the boardwalk in baggy pants with their boxers hanging out. More guys in baggy pants in handcuffs against the hood of a car.

The news anchor reported that the shore town of Wildwood, New Jersey, recently banned saggy pants.

"Hey, what do you guys think of that?" I asked. "Do you think banning saggy-ass jeans will make a difference in the crime level in the city?"

"I think it's stupid," Tammy said.

"People will always wear stupid stuff and think they're hot shit," Dustin said. "I mean, what if all the gangstas started hiking their jeans up to their armpits? Like, gangsta old men?"

"Right?" Tammy said. "See, then they'd have to change the ordinance to say you can't wear your pants too high!"

"Yeah, and then all the old men would start getting arrested," I said.

"I think they ought to arrest people for wearing socks with sandals," Dustin said.

"There's a real crime," Tammy nodded.

I popped another beer, threw a leg over the brown plaid armchair flanking the sofa, and ate another handful of chips.

"Hey Jamie, how's Operation Bikini going? You're looking pretty good," Tammy said.

I stopped crunching. "Um, fine," I said, my mouth full. I took a gulp of beer. "I'm wearing my bikini this weekend, no matter what. This week might not be so great for my fitness overhaul. So I might go up to Rehoboth and wear it there."

"Dude," Dustin said to me. "You would look totally amazing in any bikini right now, compared to some of the chicks I see out on the boat." He shook his head in despair.

Dustin worked for a charter fishing company down at the inlet, taking tourists out on deep-sea fishing trips.

"Aw, thanks Dustin."

Tammy gave Dustin a peck on the cheek. "You are a nice man."

Dustin grabbed Tammy and pulled her onto his lap. "I am not a nice man." He barked out an evil laugh.

I took that as my cue, shoving another handful of Doritos into my mouth, gathering up my giant purse, and blowing them a kiss on my way out the door.

.

15.

FOUND MYSELF in the living room lacing up my Reeboks early the next morning, before the devil in me could talk my auto-pilot brain out of a run. The morning news was on, and my eyes fully opened and focused when Candy Holloway and her helmet of hair appeared in front of the Haunted House. Her live report confirmed rumors that the body found shot and dumped on the tracks at the popular Ocean City boardwalk ride was Azerbaijani student worker Leyla Dovzhenko. No further information was available about the Dumpster Deaths, as Candy dubbed them.

In my heart I'd already known the body at the Haunted House was Leyla's. Still, my eyes were wet with tears as I willed myself out the door and down the creaky wooden stairs.

Out on the street heading north, the sun was starting to break through the clouds, and the temperature was rising to July's normal wet heat.

I hit my stride, and soon I had reached the halfway point, turning south on the boardwalk and feeling the relatively cool sea breeze on my damp skin.

The Kohr Brothers stand was open, with another young girl behind the counter along with Brad, the manager.

"Hey, Brad," I greeted him. He gazed at me blankly.

"Jamie, I'm the one who held up the line last night."

"Oh, right, sorry about that," he said. It didn't seem like Brad had gotten much sleep.

"I guess you've heard the news about Leyla. I'm sorry," I said awkwardly. He nodded.

He took my order, and as he was dispensing the soft custard into the cone, I asked about Mina.

"I haven't seen her, but you just missed Yuri."

A chill passed through me.

"I did? When was he here? Do you still see him around?" I searched up and down the boardwalk, though of course I wouldn't have known Yuri if he had stepped up and introduced himself.

"Nah, that was maybe forty-five minutes ago."

"What does Yuri look like?"

"I thought you knew those guys," Brad said, handing me the cone.

"I know Sam, the owner."

"Oh. Well, Sam hires some weird people. Guy is intense, and his English is not so good. Wears a tracksuit, Adidas or something. Who wears a tracksuit in July?"

"Huh. Okay, well, thanks again, Brad. Here's my card, in case you hear anything." I pulled a slightly smeared business card out of my smartphone armband. Would Nancy Drew ever leave home without a calling card card? No, she would not. "I hope she turns up soon."

Brad put the card into the register drawer.

I licked my cone. "Where are you, Mina?" I said to no one as I turned toward home.

Out of the shower and smelling halfway decent again, I decided to suck it up and stop in at OGISS before going to the Weekly Breeze office. I didn't think I was on Sam's list of favorite people, but I wanted to tell him about this Yuri guy.

I had a fashion crisis. The sparkly underwear choice was easy, but the rest of the outfit was vexing. Finally I pulled out my favorite denim miniskirt and a snug-fitting red-and-white gingham button-down shirt. I put a shimmery coat of pale lip gloss on, hopefully to better enhance my tan, and gave my hair an extra toss and spray. If Sam was going to throw me out on my ass, I wanted to look good for it.

Twenty minutes later at OGISS, Sam glanced up from the group of students at his desk. His face registered surprise, disapproval, and did I detect a faint glimmer of interest? Certainly I felt a crackle of energy when our eyes met. I'm good at inventing crackles of energy, though, I shamefully admit. He was muscly and tan in his pale blue Surfrider Foundation T-shirt.

"Jamie. What a surprise."

"Hi, Sam. There's something I need to talk to you about."

"I'm a little backed up here, but have a seat, and I'll be with you."

His eyes may have drifted over to my legs for a split second as I sat on one of the couches. Possibly. I picked up a Russian newspaper and flipped through it, scanning the ads and photos.

I also listened to Sam's voice as he spoke in rapid, clipped, and utterly mysterious syllables to the group at his desk. I had no clue what they were talking about, but clearly they were unhappy.

One customer finished a call in one of the international phone stalls and banged the booth door carelessly as he left it. The aluminum frame on the front door screeched when he walked out. Sam glared in frustration.

Eventually his conversation with the students closed. Sam stood from his desk and nodded curtly at them. As they filed out the door, Sam rubbed his eyes. He looked rumpled and tired.

I gave him a sympathetic smile.

"Everybody wants to quit their jobs, end their contracts, leave here. They're freaking out. I need a break."

"Oh man, that sucks. I guess I can sort of see why, though."

"I am sorry about Leyla, if you guys were friends," Sam said. "I heard the news this morning. I just hope Mina wasn't one of those other bodies—"

I shook my head no. "They're not releasing anything yet, but neither is her."

"That, at least, is good news."

"Listen, I wanted to tell you that a guy named Yuri came by the Kohr Brothers stand this morning asking if they've heard from Mina. He says he's from Ocean Gateway."

"Yuri?"

I nodded.

"There's no Yuri here."

"So who's Yuri?" We stared at each other. A shiver went down my spine that was not entirely due to Sam's hotness.

16.

’M STARVED. Have lunch with me," he said.

I smiled at him in surprise. "Okay." It was eleven thirty, and I was still full from the Kohr Brothers cone, but I wasn't about to turn down this lunch invitation, even if he did seem ambivalent about me at best.

He flipped the door sign to CLOSED, locked up, and we walked to Fat Daddy's pizza and sub shop.

"Their garden vegetable pizza is great," he said, suddenly casual and friendly, like he had put aside all tension from yesterday's meeting and today's gruesome discussion of corpses. "Want to share one?"

"Sure. I always get either that one or The Works," I said, indicating the one with sausage and pepperoni plus every vegetable you can think of. "Fat Daddy's makes a great pizza, but honestly, they should stop it with the barbecue chicken pizza, the roast beef pizza. It's not right."

"It is strange," Sam agreed. "Actually, the best pizza I have ever eaten in my life was at the Vatican."

"The Vatican? Like, in Italy? What, did you share a pie with the pope?"

"Nope. I got a slice at the cafeteria at the Vatican's museum. It was really simple: this perfect, light, crisp crust, topped with fresh mozzarella, a couple slices of tomato, a few olives and some olive oil. It was more like what we would put on bruschetta. Not heavy at all."

"No sauce?"

"No sauce."

"Huh. So, you've been to Italy. I would love to go to Italy."

"Go, then. You should travel as much as you can," he said earnestly, abandoning all pretense of cool. "I spent my junior year of college in London and got to travel around Europe while I was there."

"Wow. The farthest away from home I've ever been is Las Vegas."

He stifled a grin. "Las Vegas! Well, I guess that is a strange and foreign land in a way. But never even to Canada? Never to Mexico?"

"Nope. I'm from Baltimore, and summer vacation always meant Ocean City for my family. Once we went to the Outer Banks in North Carolina, but my sister and I complained the whole time that there was nothing to do. We all loved coming here, so I guess my parents figured, why mess with it?"

"But what about your ancestors, where are they from?"

"There's some Polish, some Italian, and some German in the family tree somewhere, but both sides of my family have been in Baltimore for at least a hundred years, so it's all a little blurry."

"It must be really comfortable to have your roots so deeply planted," Sam said.

"I honestly never thought about it."

The pizza arrived and conversation ceased as we dove in.

After we finished off the last slice, Sam said, "I'm sorry if I was hard on you yesterday."

"It happens," I said, smiling. "I've heard worse."

"I've really enjoyed talking to you today."

"Me too," I said, feeling shy and tongue-tied.

"Would it be okay if I invite you to dinner? I would like to cook for you."

I laughed with nervous pleasure. "I would love that."

"Okay. I'll call you soon."

We smiled at each other awkwardly and parted ways on the sidewalk outside of Fat Daddy's, not sure whether to shake hands or hug. In the end we did neither; I gave him a little wave and walked away.

Out on Coastal Highway, I caught the next northbound bus to work. An elderly man clutching a folding aluminum beach lounge chair with raw, sharp edges nearly stabbed me to death with every lane change. OC's a dangerous place.

17.

THE AFTERNOON IN THE OFFICE went by quickly, with calls to be made and background to be compiled about tonight's American Legion Independence Day dinner dance. I also put together the outline for a story about the city's two fireworks displays (one uptown and bayside, one downtown over the ocean near the inlet). That one would be completed at the last minute before press time, on the night of the Fourth itself.

Around four o'clock, the Breeze office line rang. I picked up.

"Yo, is this Jamie August?" I vaguely recognized the voice.

"Who is this?"

"It's Terry Montgomery, from the club."

"Terry?"

"Yeah, you know, from the other night at the Poolside Lounge, with that girl Leyla."

"Right, I remember you. You were talking to her—you and that guy from Howard University."

"Yeah, that's right. I'm calling you from the police station. They got me cuz they think I killed Leyla."

"You're at the police station now?" I sat up straight. Donald turned to face me, interested.

"Yeah."

"Have they arrested you?"

"Yeah. They say I was mad at her cuz I couldn't git wit her, cuz of that Tito Jackson college kid. They sayin' I iced her cuz she disrespected me."

"Tito Jackson? I thought his name was David."

"Man, whatever."

"By the time I left, you were already talking with that tall woman over by the bar."

"Yeah, see, you saw how it was. That girl Leyla, she wasn't dissin' me, you know what I'm sayin'? We just didn't have no kinda connection. So I hooked up with that other girl."

"Can't you get her to tell the cops this?"

"Nah, I don't really know who she is. I mean, we spent some time and all, but it was one of those one-time deals, you know what I'm sayin'?"

I knew what he was saying.

"Yo, but I heard you was a reporter, and that's how I found you."

"But why are you calling me, Terry? You need a lawyer!"

"I don't know no lawyers around here. But you do, right? I need a good one, fast."

Oh no. He didn't understand that mostly I wrote about sand castle-building competitions and church fundraisers.

"But don't you have any family? Shouldn't you be calling them?"

"Nah. ..."

"What about André? Why can't he help you?"

"Yeah, he might not want to be helping me right now."

"What do you mean?"

"Last night, he and Z had a big fight, like they always do, but this time she walked out."

"Who's Z?"

"You know, the other Russian girl."

"There are three girls?"

"Nah, man, I mean Mina."

"Why'd you call her Z?"

"I don't know. That's what André calls her."

"Okay. So Mina was with you guys yesterday—after she bailed out on me?"

"Yeah, she was. I heard about that. That girl is off the hook. See, you know what I'm talking about. So she and André had this big fight after dinner last night in the hotel suite. She threw a lamp at him, and then she ran off."

"That's not cool."

"Yeah, that's what I said late last night when we was all chillin' in the suite. But André, he didn't like me talking about his woman like that. He said she was upset after she saw the news about Leyla on TV and got emotional and whatnot. Then he got real worried about her—I guess once he stopped being mad, he got worried. He told me to get the fuck out there and find her before somebody grabbed her like they grabbed Leyla."

"Ooh."

"So I been on the street since about four this morning trying to find her. André got a Sniper Trigga thing up in New York tonight. I figured somebody would call me when it was time to roll out, and everything would be cool. But nobody ever called, so I guess they left without me. Cops picked me up while I was waiting in line for a crab cake sandwich at the Crabcake Factory."

"That's rough—they didn't even wait for you to get your sandwich?"

"Nah, man, cops be hard down here."

I heard the sarcasm in his voice and grinned a little.

"Listen, though, Imma tell you somethin' straight up. I got to get out of here. I don't have time to wait for no court-appointed bullshit. If Z is walking around out there somewhere, I got to find her and keep that crazy bitch safe. If something happens to her while my ass is sitting inside here, André will kill me. I might as well be dead, for real."

"The police are trying to find her too. You know something the cops don't know, someplace she might have gone? It might help if you offer to assist the police. They could keep you safe from André."

Donald had rolled his desk chair over and was now sitting on the other side of my desk, staring. I tried to wave him off, but he stayed put, straining to hear both sides of the conversation.

"I don't know where she could be, but I tell you this: if the police get her, she in just as much danger."

"What are you saying, Terry?"

"You know what I'm saying." He paused a beat.

"How do you know?"

Terry paused. "Me and Leyla were tight. I mean, not tight tight, that's not—"

"Right, go on."

"We was chillin' with the crew a lot of nights, though, and she told me some things, like the Russian Mafia got a connection here in the Five-O."

"How would she know that?"

"Because she was here to watch over Z."

"Wait, what? You're saying she was Z's bodyguard?"

"Yeah, only Z didn't know it. Z thought she was some random exchange student. She was always using Leyla, acting like her friend sometimes but mostly disrespecting her, treating her bad and making her do all the work at the ice cream place. But Leyla took it."

"Why did Leyla tell you this?"

"One of my jobs is running security for André's girl, you know, whoever that may be. A rapper's girlfriend needs protection, for real, that's one of the things I do in the Sniper Trigga organization."

"André is really a rap star?"

"Girl, would you please educate yourself? He been on the Billboard Top Ten for over a year."

"Okay, okay. So it probably became obvious pretty quickly that both you and Leyla were doing the same job."

"Right."

"But Leyla never told you why she was guarding Mina."

"Nope. That was a need-to-know that I didn't need to know, you know?"

I stopped to parse that.

"Girl was tough," Terry continued. "She could drop any nigga in the crew with her bare hands. And she did knife practice in the hallway up in the suite when Z was out with André."

"I cannot picture that at all. She seemed so sweet."

"Leyla could kill a man. I'm telling you this right now: she did not go down without a fight."

This was blowing my mind.

"But what does any of this have to do with the Russian mob? And who's Mina, or Z, or whatever the hell?"

"I don't know. If I get out of here, maybe I find out. So you got a lawyer?"

"I'll try, but I can't promise anything."

"That's all I'm asking," he said. "This is jacked up."

18.

I DISCONNECTED AND GAPED at Donald, who was gripping a pen and a legal pad, ready to scribble notes.

"Spill it."

I replayed the entire conversation for Donald, who took notes with an astonished expression plastered across his face.

When I finished, he put down the pen and pad. "You can't recommend a lawyer. You need to keep your distance."

"But it could take days for the court to appoint a lawyer for Terry."

"This is true, Jamie, but you have to stay neutral. You're the reporter."

"Yes, I know I'm the reporter."

"You forget the neutral part sometimes. A lot of times. You need to be careful."

I shot him an exasperated look. "Fine."

"I know you're trying to do the right thing," he said, softening. "I'm not saying you're wrong for wanting to help. But in this case, you're already tangled up in this story to the point that if I had anybody else I could trust, I'd take you off of it—"

"No way! This is my story!"

"—but I don't have anyone else who could do the job right. You're the one, so calm down."

I calmed down.

"And that's why you have to tread very, very carefully," he continued. "Report the story. Do not steer it."

"Okay. I understand."

I sighed, feeling awful for Terry. If I couldn't get him a good lawyer—and Donald was right, of course I couldn't—I wanted to do something, to go out and comb the streets for Mina. I wanted to question every Haunted House employee and figure out how Leyla's body got up there. Clearly it had been dumped out of one the ride's coffin-cars, but how could that have happened with no witnesses? And who were the other two corpses?

19.

NOBODY UNDER THE AGE of sixty-five would be at tonight's American Legion dinner dance, so why was I having an epic clothing crisis? Well, there was the wait staff. So there you go.

Thinking of today's lunch with Sam and my—dare I say it?—upcoming date with him, gave me a case of the butterflies. Nevertheless, it was important not to close off other options. I stared into my closet.

Last winter I won a freezing bikini contest. It was an emergency: I jumped onstage to escape from a psycho killer, but I guess that's what all the girls say. Anyway, one of my prizes was a shopping spree at the chic South Moon Under clothing store. From that windfall I had a beautiful Thai silk wrap dress in deep blue and purple. I pulled that out and paired it with strappy black sandals. Such an elegant outfit, but the dress came down almost to my knees!

Then the Maryland shore girl side of me hollered in favor of a skintight red minidress and stilettos.

The classy wrap dress won out, mostly because I didn't want to walk around—and potentially even dance—in those stilettos. Thanks to that shopping spree last winter, it appeared as though two women shared my closet. Sometimes I thought two women shared my brain.

I walked to the American Legion, sharing the sidewalk with crowds of vacationers and breathing the heavy salt air and traffic fumes of the bottlenecked Coastal Highway. The air was so thick with humidity that the streetlights glowed with orange halos.

Inside the Legion hall, my eyes adjusted to the dim lighting, and I snagged a plastic cup of chardonnay from the bar. I scanned the room and spotted a couple I met last winter when that arsonist was out to get me. He burned out their vacation rental apartment. It was a bonding experience.

"Hey, Merv. Hey, Dot, how are you?" I said, giving each of them hugs and pecks on the cheek.

"Jamie, how are ya, hon?" Merv said.

"Oh, Jamie, you look so beautiful tonight. She looks really snazzy, doesn't she, Merv?"

"Oh, yeah, she does."

"Doesn't she?"

"Definitely, yeah, Jamie, you look great." Dot and Merv clucked and nodded.

I beamed, of course. "So, are you guys down in Ocean City permanently now?"

"For the summer, you know," Merv said.

"Yeah, we're not down here full-time yet."

"Still got the kids and all."

"Yeah, Chucky's goin' in the seventh grade next year so we're thinking of maybe makin' the move outta Baltimore."

"Checking out schools down here in Worcester County."

He pronounced it correctly: Werster.

"Ashley's doing really good, really likes her Brownie troop," Dot said, "but I don't know, maybe they got that here."

"Dot, I'm sure they got Brownies down here."

"Well, I know they got Brownies, but what if Ashley don't like these Brownies as much? I mean, her and Tiffany and Sharnell are really good friends—"

This could go on for hours.

"So, where are you staying for the summer?"

"Sunrise Paradise," Dot said.

"Of course," Merv said.

"Where else we gonna go?" Dot said, eyes widening at the very thought.

"That's the only place for us," Merv nodded.

"The kids love it," Dot said.

"We love it," Merv said.

"What's not to love?" Dot beamed.

Sunrise Paradise was one of Uncle Abe's rental apartment buildings. It's the place that got torched last winter, cutting short the Slomkowski family vacation and nearly killing us all. But Abe had done well with the insurance settlement. He repainted the outside an eye-popping turquoise, and revamped the apartments' interiors, upgrading from Naugahyde and plaid decor to stridently beachy themes.

"We got our same apartment back, and now it's got a nice new coat of paint on the kitchen cabinets and a whole new bathroom," Merv said.

"Oh yeah, Ashley loves that new bathroom vanity. It's pink and shaped like a shell," Dot said.

"I am so glad you guys are happy and you're able to stay all summer, gosh," I stammered.

"Yeah, I got a new job at the school cafeteria so I'm off summers, and Merv got some summer work down here at Gold Coast Mall."

Merv worked in Baltimore as a security guard at one of the city's sketchiest shopping malls. So I was feeling pretty good about my safety level next time I needed to pop into Gold Coast for some wind chimes or a charm bracelet.

"How's that going, Merv?" I asked. "You seeing any of the gang trouble that everybody is freaking out about?"

Merv rumbled with laughter, his belly bouncing up and down and his beer sloshing over the edge of his cup. Dot's bell-like laugh rang out.

"Oh, hon!" she squealed.

"We're from Baltimore!" Merv chuckled.

"I guess that's a no," I said.

We said our good-byes, and I made my way to a seat. I joined a table with a gaggle of real-estate agents, plus Jerry Mulvaney, owner of Mulvaney Chevrolet in Salisbury, and his wife.

"Well if it ain't the prettiest ace reporter on the DelMarVa Peninsula," Jerry said, wrapping me in a hug. I squeaked as he squeezed me tight, then un-tangled myself for a much daintier hug from the missus.

We sat down to a standard chicken dinner, but hey, this is Maryland's Eastern Shore: chicken country! Though it was standard, bland fare, by God it was all-American.

After dinner, I spotted Uncle Abe across the room and worked my way to him.

"Did you see the Slomkowskis?" I asked. "They're sitting over at the corner table."

"I'll be damned! I gotta go say hello to those guys. They're my best tenants. Wish I could fill Sunrise Paradise with families like that."

"I'll bet," I said. "They sure do love that place. Not too many can say that."

Abe gave me the evil eye, then took off to glad-hand Merv and Dot.

I made the rounds of the hall with my reporter's notebook and pen, collecting happy quotes and making sure I noted everyone's professional titles correctly.

"As the East Coast's Number One Family Re-sort—make sure those are all in caps—Ocean City is the premiere place to celebrate Independence Day," City Council member Betty Farrell said. She delicately pat-patted her matronly gray hairdo.

"Why?"

"The city has—what?"

"Why is Ocean City the best place to celebrate the fourth?"

"Honey, where are you from? What kind of question is that?" Betty pulled her round frame up as tall as she could and stared at me, shocked.

"I'm from here, Betty. I love OC! But what if I had never been here before? Tell me why I should spend Independence Day here."

"Oh, I see what you mean. Well now. Where else are you going to find ten miles of white-sand beach, guarded during the day and groomed every night, all free and open to the public? Hmm? Not in Delaware. Where else can you find a beautiful Atlantic coastline on one side and a sheltered bay for boating and kayaking on the other—within blocks of each other? I ask you."

"Thanks, Betty—"

"Ocean City is the white marlin capital of the world, did you know that? No better fishing anywhere. And is there any place in the world that kids would rather go than Ocean City? There is not."

"Yep." No stopping Betty now.

"And where else can you find one city putting on not one but two major fireworks displays?

And"—she grabbed my arm—"is there anything more powerfully beautiful, more poetic, than a Fourth of July fireworks display over the moonlit Atlantic Ocean? This is America, honey. Right here." She let go of my arm and fanned her face delicately.

My reporting mission was accomplished.

The deejay started up the dancing portion of the evening with "Celebration" by Kool and the Gang, of course. Jerry Mulvaney spun me around the floor, his lead so strong that it didn't matter when I couldn't follow his fancy footwork. He delivered me to the bar afterward and handed me another plastic glass of chardonnay.

As I stood catching my breath, the dark-haired young bartender with pale, luminous skin, smiled at someone behind me. She held out a generous glass of red wine, and I felt a hand on my shoulder for a moment, gently easing me over.

The bartender said something in Russian as she reached out with the plastic tumbler. At least, I think it was Russian. It wasn't Spanish or Italian, I knew that much.

I turned to catch the man behind me scowl at the bartender's words. The man looked to be in his late forties. He carried some extra weight, but he wore a neat, dark suit, and his light hair was freshly trimmed. I realized I'd seen this guy before. He was the police detective who found the knife in the dumpster.

The detective caught my eye and did a quick double take himself. His eyes were a chilly, deep blue. Could he have recognized my face from last night's crowd?

He took the glass, nodded curtly to the bartender, and turned away. The detective spoke Russian? I didn't know whether to catalog that trait as really smart in an OC police officer or oddly suspicious. Or both. I watched him move easily into a crowd of other clean-shaven law-enforcement types. He slapped one guy on the back and laughed easily at something another one said.

I turned back to the bar and did a quick e-mail check to see if there was any news about Mina. Nothing. As I was sliding my phone back into my purse, it chimed with a new text message. I checked the screen, then grinned and took a big swig of wine.

"Your place, 11:00?"

My surfer friend with benefits was at my service. I leaned against the bar and tried to think about Trevor but found only images of Sam going through my head.

"Sorry, not tonight," I texted back.

I wrapped up and got out of there by ten p.m., and was asleep at home by eleven.

20.

MINA WAS STARTING to lose it. Her $500 Dubai haircut was squashed under an "I Heart OC" ball cap, and she had traded her Jimmy Choos for a pair of fake Keds sneakers. She clung tightly to the $8,300 Valentino handbag, happy in the knowledge that at least that was real.

She peered out from a dark doorway at the back of Trimper's Rides, a sprawling complex of indoor and outdoor rides and arcade games that anchored Ocean City's boardwalk.

So far she felt like she had done pretty well: yesterday morning she had gotten away from Jamie, that annoying woman on the ice cream diet. Last night she had made a spectacular exit from André's penthouse suite. She replayed the scene again in her mind, proud of herself for standing up for her principles, though she had already forgotten why she had started that fight. Something important. He didn't appreciate her enough—that was it. Yes. Fuck him.

She could see how this would play out in the movie about her: Misunderstood by everyone who once loved her, Mina had to go into hiding, be a survivor. She was strong. So beautiful and so strong.

She was also short on cash. So she had shoplifted the cap and the sneakers from a boardwalk shop, which was kind of a thrill, actually.

She blended in with the late-night crowd at the carnival-like southern end of the boardwalk, trying to resist the temptation to give in and return to André's hotel suite. She could easily have made up to him and ordered a lobster dinner from room service. She was getting hungry and her resolve was weakening.

Then she thought she saw a familiar face on the boardwalk. A man she'd noticed several times, scanning the crowd, looking for someone. Was he looking for her?

In a state of panic, she'd slipped into a small storage room at the back of the arcade. As the hour grew late and the crowds wandered back to their hotels and condos, employees buttoned up Trimper's for the night.

At first she was frightened by the prospect of being locked inside the dark arcade all night, trapped behind the heavy metal doors.

Then she realized that she had stumbled into the perfect hideout. It was securely locked. Nobody was in there but her. And she had at her pilfering fingertips an endless supply of chips, pretzels, candy, and soda from the snack bars. The emergency exit signs provided enough glow for her to loot the various concession stands.

Now, sleep-deprived but hopped up on sugar and caffeine, she reached into her purse, pulled out a bottle of Angel perfume, and spritzed herself generously. She offered a quick prayer of thanks to French fashion designer Thierry Mugler for creating a fragrance so powerful, so sexy, that it could carry her through any hardship—even a morning without a scented bubble bath.

She ventured out into the summer morning from her secret hideout. She mixed in with a big crowd of teenagers and walked past Kohr Brothers. And there was Jamie August again, in her stupid running shorts. Fucking hell.

As she watched the reporter chatting with the pasty, ridiculous Kohr Brothers manager, an idea began to form in her mind. She narrowed her eyes and considered it. It wasn't ideal, but it was the best thing her sleep-deprived, candy-fueled brain could come up with.

She paused in a shop doorway, pretending to admire some hand-carved, nautical-themed wooden plaques. She read the personalized samples: "The Hershel Family," "A bad day at the beach is better than a good day at work," "It's five o'clock somewhere." She puzzled over the last one. Of course it's always five o'clock somewhere in the world. Was this some kind of American religious slogan?

When Jamie walked past, cone in hand, Mina casually turned and followed.

21.

ACK HOME AT THE KITTY LOU, I un-
laced my sneakers, dissatisfied after another
morning run along my usual path. I felt
sweaty and also sticky from the post-run soft-serve
that had dripped down my chin. I decided that,
starting tomorrow, I would take a different route.
No more Kohr Brothers. There were too many bad
associations with that place. Plus, I was ready for a
different daily junk food fix. Maybe some Dolle's
salt water taffy.

There was a knock at the door. I peeked through
the peephole, then yanked the door open and

pulled Mina through, slamming it closed behind her.

Before I knew what I was doing, I threw my arms around her. Simultaneously, I began berating her like I was her mother. "Mina, where have you been? I thought you were dead! Everyone has been searching for you! Are you okay? What happened? How did you know where I live?" I pulled away and glared at her, needing an answer to that last one first.

"I follow you from Kohr Brothers. Easy."

"Of course," I said, feeling like an idiot.

"I need help," she said, making herself comfortable on my couch.

"Right. This is where we left off, isn't it? You need help. I ask you to tell me what's going on. You vanish."

Mina dropped her eyes, then fished in her purse for a tube of lipstick. She applied a fresh, flawless coat of glossy magenta.

"Yes. I tell you now."

No sorry, no acknowledgement of anything. What a spoiled bitch.

I sat on the other end of the sofa, crossed my arms over my chest. Realized I smelled awful. Then I took another sniff and nearly gagged. Mina smelled like air freshener in a whorehouse.

"I'm waiting," I said, unable to put words to the olfactory onslaught.

Mina sighed. "Okay. My name is not Mina Smith. I am Zamina Allyev." She searched my face for some kind of instant recognition.

I snickered. "Smith? That's what you're going around saying your last name is?"

"Is common family name, no? Is problem?"

I rolled my eyes and told her to continue.

"Also, I am not university student here for summer job."

"Yeah, that much is pretty obvious."

"It is?"

"Mina—Zamina—hey, that's why André calls you Z."

Her eyes widened in surprise. "How you know?"

I dismissed her question with a wave. "That Kohr Brothers gig is probably the first time you ever had to hold down a job in your life."

"How you know these things?"

I laughed at her. "You were painting your nails while Leyla did all the work. Leyla opened the stand in the morning while you slept in at André's hotel suite. You didn't know how to make change. You were rude to customers. Honey, you're clueless."

"Oh," she said, nervously pushing her cuticles back.

"So tell me something I don't already know."

"I am hiding in Ocean City." She fell silent.

"From what?" This was like pulling teeth.

"I cannot tell you."

I stood up, grabbed my cell phone off the table, planted myself in front of the front door, and started dialing. "Then you'll tell it to the cops." I felt a stab of worry as I hit the connect button, remembering Terry's veiled reference about a Russian Mafia presence in the department.

"No! Stop! I tell you! No police!"

I shut off the phone. "This is the last chance you get. Talk."

She carefully wiped a tear from her made-up face. Sighed dramatically. I put a hand on my hip and tapped a running shoe on the floor.

"Okay. I tell you. My father is businessman in Azerbaijan. Well, we live in Dubai now, but we are from Azerbaijan."

I gestured with my hand as if to say, get on with it. Mina looked wounded.

"He has valuable property. Very valuable. He tries to keep me locked up to be safe but I say no, I escape. Many times. He try to keep me, but I always can get away. Always I can pay someone, I can ask

142

someone nicely, yes? I am good at this. The last time, when he sent someone to bring me home from Paris—"

"You ran away to Paris?"

"For Fashion Week."

I stared at her.

"He sent head of security for me. I come home again. My father says if I won't stay home in stupid, boring safe house, then I must go to a place no one will find me. And I must work. Otherwise, he will cut me up."

"Cut you off."

"Yes."

"So you picked Ocean City?"

"No, how would I know about Ocean City? I know Milan. I know Barcelona."

"Got it. You're a real jet-setter."

"Jet-setter? What is this?"

"Forget it. How'd you end up here?"

"My father has business partner. His niece worked in Ocean City last summer. She liked, said was good program. She worked at CVS Pharmacy."

"That's a weird place for a job at the beach."

"No, is good. Is AC and there is discount on nail polish."

There was that.

"So I had a choice: boring safe house or Ocean City work-away program. I say okay, I will come here and work until—well, until is safe. While I am here, I have no credit cards, no ATM cards, no store credit, no car, no housekeeper, no one to do my laundry, nothing, nothing!"

"Sounds rough, baby."

She glowered at me. "If I can do, then when it is safe, I can stop and he will give me a lot of money." She stared at me, wide-eyed. "A lot of money. If I get fired or something stupid like that, I am cut up."

"Cut off. But what are you talking about? Safe from what?"

"He has this thing he will sell to some people. Others want him to sell to them instead. I am at risk."

"Why?"

"Those other people, they might kidnap me. Then my father sell to them instead."

"Sounds kind of extreme. What kind of property are we talking about?"

"Very valuable."

"Yes, you said that already. What is this property?"

She faltered, worrying the straps of her purse. Then she looked me in the eye.

"Is oil rights. In Caspian Sea."

22.

THE PIECES FELL INTO PLACE.

"So you think whoever grabbed and killed Leyla meant to kidnap you."

Mina nodded miserably. "She was wrong girl."

Mina didn't seem to be aware that ensuring her safety had been Leyla's primary job, as well as Terry's. I wondered who else in Mina's life might secretly be trying to keep her safe, and thought it best not to raise that question with a girl determined to give her security detail the slip.

Instead I told her about the mysterious Yuri, who had turned up at Kohr Brothers asking for her.

"You see? Is not American gang problem like police always say. Is Russian."

"But aren't you from Azerbaijan? What does Russia have to do with this?

"Russians want oil rights. My father sells to Shell instead."

"And they would send someone to kidnap you?"

"Of course. Is good for negotiation."

True.

"And where have you been all this time?"

"I was with André, but then I leave him and sleep on boardwalk."

"Come on. You did not sleep on the boardwalk. The cops would never allow that. Plus, the entire police department is out searching for you. They would have spotted you in a hot minute."

"Well, near to boardwalk. Is not important. Important thing was to leave André because he is not the one for me."

"Do you know how to reach him?"

"I will not talk to him again."

"I think you're going to have to," I snapped. "You know Terry?"

Mina nodded. "He is Sniper Trigga roadie."

"Yeah, something like that. He's been arrested for Leyla's murder."

"Is not possible. He and another girl were with André and me that night."

"So you can give him an alibi! And you can get André to hire a lawyer for him. They're probably trying to use him to get to André, because they think he's responsible for other recent gang activity."

"But André and his friends are not gang. André is great rap artist. Sniper Trigga."

"I know, but the detective handling Leyla's case doesn't believe that."

"You see why I not go to police? The police do not believe."

"Yeah, but if you tell her where to find André, maybe they'd let Terry go."

"But André did not kill Leyla."

"Mina, I know that."

"Please call me Zamina. Is my real name."

"Okay, okay. Zamina. Don't you see? They can't say Terry killed Leyla if you can prove he was somewhere else. André is throwing his friend Terry under the bus here."

"André threw Terry under a bus?"

I shook my head. "Sorry. André is letting his friend go to jail by not coming forward."

"Is too bad about Terry," Zamina said. "He seems like good person."

"Okay then. We need to help him."

"Is not possible."

"What do you mean, it's not possible?"

"I leave André. He is not the one for me."

I was ready to strangle her.

"Zamina, I don't give a rat's ass about your love life. I want to clear Terry of a crime he didn't commit."

"No. Not possible. André is very heartbreak. Not happy with me. I cannot talk to him."

I couldn't decide whether this girl was more cruel or more stupid.

"So what do you want with me, Zamina?"

"I need a place to stay." She surveyed my apartment with interest.

"You need... oh no. No no. Not a chance," I said, horrified at the thought of housing this creature under my roof.

"I need."

"Too bad. Can't help you. No, let me be clear. I can help you. But I won't."

"Why not?"

"Because you won't lift a finger to help anyone else. Because you think of nothing, not one single thing, except yourself. Because you would let an innocent person go to jail rather than speak to your ex-boyfriend. Because, because you are a selfish and mean person, and I will not have you in my home!" By the end of that rant, I was standing over her and shouting.

Zamina shrank away from me, into the corner of the sofa. She was crying again, but this seemed different. These didn't look like crocodile tears.

I stomped into the kitchen and poured myself a glass of water, belatedly rehydrating after my run.

A moment later, Zamina appeared in the kitchen doorway. She had patched up her makeup awfully fast.

"If I help Terry, will you help me?"

I leaned against the counter and surveyed her cooly.

"You'll tell the police where to find André?"

"I cannot do."

"Get out," I said.

"No no! Please! I cannot do because I do not know where André is. He was supposed to leave this morning. Before the fight, he want me to go with him."

"You don't know where he was going?"

"New York. Is all I know."

"Well, then how are you going to help Terry?"

"I tell police I was with André. I say that Terry was with us."

I considered this. It was a start.

"I will not go to police station, though. Not possible. This detective for Leyla, you trust?"

"I think so."

Zamina paused. "Okay, if you trust a little, then I trust a little. She come here, I tell her."

"You drive a hard bargain. I'll call Detective Morrison."

"I do this, then I stay with you."

"No, Zamina. You can't stay here. It's not safe for you, and not only because I would probably kill you." She flushed. "If you followed me home, lord knows anybody can find me."

"I see. Yes, you are right. Where can I go?"

I narrowed my eyes and stared at her for a minute.

"I have an idea."

23.

I T TOOK SOME CONVINCING to get Morrison to drop whatever she was doing and come to my apartment. But she did, and when she saw Zamina at my dining table, her face broke into a relieved smile.

"Are you—"

"My name is Zamina Allyev. You know my name Mina Smith."

"I am relieved to see you. Please, tell me what happened."

Morrison and I joined Zamina at the table.

Zamina related the story of having a "disagreement" with her boyfriend and leaving him, but being afraid of returning to her apartment and instead hiding out "in the area of the boardwalk." Morrison asked exactly where she'd gone, but Zamina's English dipped to indecipherable levels for this explanation.

"Okay, never mind," Morrison finally said. "Now why are we meeting here and not down at the station?"

"I do not trust police."

"But I am police."

"She trust you a little," Zamina said, pointing at me, "so I trust you a little."

"Hey thanks," Morrison said wryly.

"But I am from Azerbaijan, former Soviet Russia. We not trust police."

"Things are a little different here." Morrison chuckled. "Why should you be afraid of going to the police? Is there something else I should know about?"

I hoped Zamina would tell Morrison about the oil deal, but she didn't breathe a word. I remained silent on that subject, but I told Morrison about the Kohr Brothers manager's odd visit by a guy in a tracksuit named Yuri.

"And you say Yuri's not with the Ocean Gateway agency?"

"No, they've never heard of him."

"This is why I need to stay vanished," Zamina said.

"We've got police alerted in three states. We're expending a lot of resources on a search—for you. Surely you understand I have to call that off."

"But I need."

I fought the urge to slap Zamina. Instead I said, "If this Yuri has an in with the OCPD—"

Morrison shook her head and started to interrupt.

"I'm not saying he does, not at all. But if word gets out somehow that the search for her has been called off, then she could be in real danger from the same people who got to Leyla. And maybe from the same people who killed whoever was in the dumpster on St. Louis. And maybe the Dough Roller dumpster too. There are a lot of bodies piling up!"

Morrison was quiet for a moment, thinking. She seemed to come to a decision. "Jamie, you're going to see the press release about this soon enough, so I may as well tell you now: Leyla's fingerprints were all over the knife they found with the body on St. Louis Avenue."

"Oh shit," I said.

"Is not possible," Zamina said.

"We believe Leyla Dovzhenko was the perpetrator of the St. Louis Avenue stabbing."

"Who was the victim?"

"Still unidentified."

"What about the Dough Roller body?"

"Not a stabbing. That victim, also still unidentified, was beaten to death. So we can't point to Dovzhenko for that one."

Or maybe they could. I kept my mouth shut about what Terry told me of Leyla's array of hidden talents.

"I am afraid," Zamina said.

Morrison agreed to wait one day before sharing the information that Zamina had reappeared in Ocean City. Little did she know, that was enough for our purposes.

As promised, Zamina made a sworn statement that Terry was with André and his crew during the hours when Leyla had been murdered.

"Are you going to release him?" I asked.

"This helps his case, believe me. But I can hardly release him based on one person's testimony. He's still our prime suspect."

"What about everybody else she was hanging out with that night? What about that guy David?"

"David Wilson, the Howard University student? We pulled him in right away, but we had to let him go."

"Why?"

"Turns out that Councilman McGill and David's father serve together on the governor's economic development committee."

"Which means what?"

Morrison looked Jamie in the eye. "Which means we let David go."

"I guess Terry's father doesn't serve on committees with any city council members."

Zamina gave me an "I told you so" look.

Morrison left around eleven a.m., and a few minutes later I cranked the stereo in Tammy's '96 Chevy Cavalier as Zamina and I eased into Coastal Highway traffic. Foghat's "Slow Ride" blasted from the classic rock station. Fitting. Finally we made it to the drawbridge, and had to wait some more as the Duckaneer tourist boat from bayside restaurant M.R. Ducks sailed into the inlet. Finally the metal bridge grates lowered into place and the traffic began rumbling across it again.

"How is Baltimore?" Zamina asked a few miles later. "Is good shopping?"

I considered this. "I guess it's like anywhere else these days. A long time ago we used to have our own department store chain, Hochschild Kohn, but that's gone, and so is Woodward & Lothrop in Washington. Now we've got Macy's."

"Is Gucci?"

"Uh..."

"Juicy?"

"What?"

"What about Valentino? Is Valentino?"

"Zamina, I am a reporter for a newspaper they give away for free. I have no idea if you can find Valentino in Baltimore."

"Oh." Zamina pouted and stared at the corn-fields unfolding to the horizon.

"But, see, this is why you're going to love the plan I cooked up for you."

"Mmm? What is plan?"

"You'll see."

I had it all worked out with my sister, Lindsey. We were headed to Maude's, my sister's vintage boutique in Baltimore's campiest neighborhood. But I wasn't about to tell Zamina that I had gotten her a job selling used clothing.

Driving in from the south, the view of Baltimore is dramatic. Zamina had been dozing, but now her eyes were wide. She left fingerprints all over the passenger's side window as she exclaimed over the tall downtown buildings punctuating the skyline and the Ravens and Orioles stadiums, throwing their shadows on the red-brick neighborhoods.

I cut through the city, turning onto Thirty-Sixth Street and passing Cafe Hon, one of Baltimore's most kitschy diners. It was so popular that it seemed almost a parody of itself, and I couldn't afford the place—no blue-plate specials within my reach there. Zamina gaped at the two-story pink flamingo hanging off of the building's fire escape.

"What is this place?"

"You're gonna love it, hon. It's going to be a new cultural experience for you, I guarantee it."

A fat man in a floral housedress tripped down the sidewalk after a toy poodle on a leash, his cigarette hand trailing dramatically behind him.

Zamina pointed silently in abject horror, her manicured fingernail tapping against the window glass.

"Welcome to Hampden," I said.

24.

FOUND A PARKING SPOT in front of Maude's Vintage Boutique, a block down from Café Hon. We got out and stretched, the hot afternoon tempered a little by the leafy maple trees, though even they were a little droopy and faded in the heat. In front of a yarn store, one tree's trunk was swaddled in a knit cozy, like a teapot.

I popped the trunk and told Zamina to grab her suitcase.

"This place is small."

"Honey, if you wanted skyscrapers you should have stuck with André and gone to New York."

She shook her head. "No, I mean, is good. It is... charming? Is the word?"

"Yes, that's exactly the word! One of Baltimore's nicknames is Charm City."

"I stay here?"

"Sure. My sister lives right around the corner. This is her shop."

"Your sister is Maude?"

"No, her name is Lindsey."

"Who is Maude?"

"Uh, I don't know. It's one of those old-school names that is so frumpy that it's back in style now."

"Frumpy?"

It's complicated trying to explain this stuff to a nonnative English speaker. What's frumpy?

"Frumpy. Means old-fashioned, out of style, up-tight, stuffy. You know?"

"Oh. Why give a shop this, uh, frumpy name?"

"You'll see."

A bell tinkled on the door as we entered the shop. Lindsey came out from around the back counter, looking ravishing. She's three years older and thirty pounds heavier than me. She's voluptuous, luscious, like a 1950s pinup girl.

Today her wavy, dark hair fell loose to her shoulders, and she wore a wine-colored off-the-shoulder crushed-velvet tea dress, platform pumps, and cat-eye glasses. A delicate tattooed tendril of cherry blossoms swirled over her shoulder and down her left arm.

I tugged my sweaty Raven's T-shirt down over the waist of my running shorts and shuffled my sneakers on the timeworn Oriental carpet.

"You're looking... sporty," Lindsey said with a wry smile, pulling me in for a hug. She smelled like coffee and musky perfume.

Suddenly I was acutely aware that I had not bathed today.

"You like?" Lindsey said, twirling her dress. A customer toward the back of the store eyed Lindsey's dress and pawed through a rack in vain. "I bought every stitch from an estate sale in Roland Park."

"Wow. Really great." I turned and put a hand on Zamina's shoulder. "Lindsey, this is Zamina, the girl I was telling you about. She needs a place to stay for a little while and is happy to earn her keep."

Zamina whipped the ball cap off her head and pulled herself up to her full height. She stood so that her giant Valentino purse accentuated her curvy bust, which was currently plastered in a tank top with "Party Girl" spelled out in rhinestones.

Zamina tore her eyes away from Lindsey to give me a puzzled glance. Then she smiled sweetly and extended a hand to Lindsey.

"I am happy to meet you," she said, as formally and properly as she could.

"Zamina, what a beautiful name," Lindsey said. "It's a pleasure. I can use some extra help here, especially with the new inventory I've gotten in."

"I will work here?"

Confused, Zamina looked at Lindsey and then at me.

"You didn't think you were going to freeload off my sister, did you?" I took a step back from her.

Lindsey crossed her arms across her ample bosom, creating an even more impressive display of cleavage. She eyed the two of us.

Zamina got it together quickly. "No, no, I do not think this. I am honored to work in your beautiful shop. I know fashion, I will make good work."

"You okay with this, Lindsey?" I asked. I was feeling a little squeamish about dumping this train wreck of a girl on my sister, though I couldn't imagine how Russian mobsters or anybody else would find her here, three hours away from the beach in a funky vintage clothing store. Detective Morrison was the only person in OC who knew.

Unless the OC cops had a leak. I couldn't think about that.

"Yes, this will work out," Lindsey said briskly, sizing up Zamina. "These clothes are going to be amazing on you. We'll put together a few outfits to start with. Can't have you greeting customers in that getup." She pulled Zamina deeper into the shop.

"Is Chanel?" Zamina asked as she plucked a tweedy pink suit from a rack. Lindsey's face broke into a delighted smile.

"Indeed. That's a classic. It's from their 1985 spring collection," she said, and their patter continued, Zamina's halting English mingling pleasantly with Lindsey's throaty Baltimore twang.

25.

HE SENSIBLE THING would have been to turn the car around and drive straight back to Ocean City. I had to be back there in time for the fireworks, but I couldn't come to Baltimore without seeing my parents. Besides, I probably could write about the Ocean City fireworks display based solely on the photographer's pictures. What's to say, except that there was a big crowd and the shows were spectacular as always? But that's not me, I realized. I'd have to make it a quick visit.

I cut through the city to the old Dundalk neighborhood and found a parking spot a few houses down from my folks' place. The August home was in the middle of a long row of two-story, brick townhouses. Some were tarted up with siding or Formstone. Ours was plain red brick. Always had been, since before I was born.

I walked up the concrete steps to the deep, nearly square front porch, and saw that Mom had sewn new cushions for the old metal glider furniture. The faded green aluminum awning sheltered the porch from the day's heat.

I opened the door with my key and shouted hello to my mom. She hurried into the living room seconds later.

"Jamie! What're you doing here, hon? Did your father forget to tell me you were coming up? Everything okay? It's so good to see you." Mom squeezed me in a tight hug that smelled of peach-scented soap and extra-strength dryer sheets.

"I'm just stopping in to say hello. Everything's fine," I said.

Mom took a step back and gave me the patented mother's once-over. "Jamie, you're looking so athletic! Smell kind of athletic, too," she said with a cheerful wave of her hand in front of her nose. Her hand fanned her chin-length feathered hair. "Did you go for a run in Patterson Park or something?"

"Oh, uh, sorry about that. Maybe I'll take a quick shower." I decided right then that I need to switch from running to swimming. Less smelly.

"Sure, hon. You go on up, and I'll call your father. He's gonna be so happy to see you. I'll tell him to come on home and pick up some crab cakes from Faidley's. We were gonna go down the corner for some sandwiches before the fireworks, but this is a special occasion!" She gave me another squeeze.

"Mom, I can't stay long, really. I have to get back down to OC."

"There's always time for a crab cake." I had no argument with that. "Take a shower," she said, pulling a face, then went back through the dining room and into the kitchen. I gazed around the living room, noticing the new La-Z-Boy recliner in the corner, in prime TV viewing position. Over the years, Mom and Dad kept the modest old row house—handed down from my grandma—in good shape. I took my running shoes off and left them by the front door, then padded up the stairs—hardwood with a beige deep-pile runner—and into the house's single bathroom.

When Lindsey and I were teenagers, the battles were epic for bathroom time. For a good five years or so, my dad gave up and peed in the back alley, joining the stragglers coming home from Ernie's Bar and Grill on the corner and the occasional junkie.

Wrapped in a towel after my shower, smelling like mom's peach shower gel, I sat on the bed in what had once been my room but was now the sewing room and guest room. I pulled out my cell phone and called Donald, updating him on the Zamina situation and assuring him I'd be back to the beach in time to cover the inlet fireworks as planned.

I padded across the hall to Mom and Dad's room and raided their closets. I found a pair of flat-front khaki shorts on Mom's side. They were a little loose so they rode low on my hips, but I was okay with that these days. In my dad's closet I scored a well-worn short-sleeved button-down shirt in a faded blue plaid. I knotted the shirt at the waist.

I couldn't bring myself to put my dirty undies back on, so I went commando. I grabbed my sweaty running clothes from the bathroom floor and carried them downstairs.

"Much better, sweetie," Mom said. "Hey, those shorts look better on you than they do on me. You should keep them. Now give me your other clothes, and I'll go down and run them through the wash. Your dad's on his way home with the crab cakes. You go down the corner and pick up a case of Coors."

She handed me a twenty and took my dirty laundry. Aren't moms great?

26.

FIFTEEN MINUTES LATER, she and I were out on the front porch enjoying cold beers and a fresh can of cocktail peanuts. I gave her an extremely edited version of the story about Zamina and Leyla, telling her only that Leyla may have gotten involved in some gang activity, though the police didn't know for sure, and that Zamina was scared and wanted to get out of Ocean City. No need to mention Russian assassins or anything like that.

Soon my dad rolled up in his work truck. "Rick's Roofing. We've Got You Covered," it said in black script lettering on the side. Mom and I watched as he did a fat U-turn at the end of the block, and came back to park across the street. He nosed in behind Mom's maroon 1984 Monte Carlo. The truck's heavy diesel engine rumbled and echoed off of the canyon of row houses.

I gave Dad a cheery wave as he got out of the truck, both hands full of brown paper bags from Faidley's, the stand that has been dispensing to-die-for crab cakes in the city's Lexington Market since 1886.

Good God, I loved Maryland.

Dad's belly was a little more padded than the last time I saw him, but his smile was still bright and his tan was still dark from years up on roofs all over Baltimore, city and county. He wore his knit work shirt untucked, and cargo shorts that hit right at the knee, with athletic socks slouched down around his work boots. He'd sported that same look every summer since I was a teenager. I caught Mom checking out his legs and stifled a grin.

"Jamie Girl!" Dad said, clumping up the steps and squashing me in a hug as Mom took the Faidley's bags in the house. "How are you doing?"

"I'm doing great, Dad. Thanks for coming home early."

"Benefits of owning your own business," he said cheerfully.

We sat next to each other on the glider sofa, the springs squeaking heavily. He took off his ball cap and ran a hand through his hair, which was cut a little long and feathery, '70s rocker style. Which was about right, since he'd been a '70s rocker. Still was. Dad played guitar in an old-dudes band that headlined for benefits down at the fire hall once in a while.

"I started running," I said, boasting shamelessly.

"I can tell, hon. Still not smoking?"

"Nope. It's been a year now."

"Good girl."

He brought me up to speed on the neighborhood happenings: the Jacksons on the corner moved out, and some yuppie couple moved in. Ripped out the kitchen, and he heard they're installing granite and a Sub-Zero fridge. The house across the street was still a rental. Dad was worried there might be some business going on in there that shouldn't be.

"A crack house or something? No way, not on this block," I said.

"Nah, I mean, it's not abandoned, but it's a little rough, and we've got some traffic rolling up there late at night."

"What are you gonna do?"

"I don't know," he said, taking a swig of the cold beer Mom had handed him and gazing at the ragged house across the way. "Keep an eye on it for now."

I told Dad about the rise in visible gang activity in Ocean City, and he talked in nostalgic tones about the bygone era of organized mobsters back in the '50s and '60s. "I mean, crime is crime, but those guys had some style. Not like now."

"So a man should wear his gold on his pinky finger and not on his front teeth?"

"Yeah, exactly!" Dad said with a laugh. "Exactly."

I leaned back and finished my beer, relaxed and happy to be home.

Soon after, Mom laid out our Faidley's feast on the dining room table: crab cakes, fried oysters, fries, macaroni salad, cole slaw, the whole deal.

It felt easy and comfortable to be back home in Dundalk. Full of Faidley's food, I wanted nothing more than to pop another beer and hang out on the porch. But I had to do my job, so I bid my folks farewell for now.

"Come back soon, hon," Mom said.

"Yeah, Jamie, you better head back this way soon," Dad called out as I hit the sidewalk. "You're wearing my favorite shirt."

I was on Route 50 on the outskirts of Salisbury when my cell phone rang.

"Jamie, it's Donald. Are you back from Baltimore?"

"I'm about forty-five minutes out."

"There's been a shooting on the boardwalk."

27.

PUT DONALD ON SPEAKER, and he relayed what he had so far on the shooting. On the boardwalk at Second Street, a fight broke out among two big groups of guys—a mostly black group, and an all-white group. A bunch of paintings on display at Ocean Gallery had been damaged as the crowd surged away from the fighting and into the frames that were always stacked six-deep around the outside of the shop.

Police had already been dispatched to the scene when shots rang out. The panicked crowd trampled three senior citizens (taken to Atlantic General Hospital, now in stable condition). When police officers finally got the crowd to disperse, one person was left. He was lying on the boards with a bullet through his thigh.

I approached Ocean City at dusk, the sun glinting in my rearview mirror. Traffic heading west—away from the beach—was heavy. I crossed the inlet bridge into the downtown area, which seemed deserted except for the stream of cars on the way out. Police barricades had been set up to direct traffic away from the old town and inlet.

I parked. It was after eight p.m. on the Fourth of July, but almost all the shops were shuttered. Police tape fluttered in the breeze, cordoning off several of the boardwalk's busiest blocks. The Ferris wheel stood silent and still.

More police tape was strung across the boardwalk at Second Street, where the legendary Ocean Gallery was still brightly lit. The art emporium's facade was eye-popping, with hand-painted signs ("Art That Rocks," "It's Astounding!") and acrylic seascapes hung like shingles from boardwalk to roofline.

I saw two uniformed police offers, three young women, a couple of other people, and—wait. Was that Sam? The old-fashioned street lights shone down on a head of dark, bobbed hair. I walked toward the group, and as they turned to me, I could see it was him.

"We'll be putting out a press release in the morning," Morrison said as I approached.

"I know about the gunshot victim," I said anyway. "Gang violence?"

"Victim had several priors. Witnesses saw two distinct groups of young men fighting. Eyewitnesses say it was two gangs. All of this will be in the PIO's bulletin," she said to me, then turned to address the group. "Okay, we're done here. Go home, get some sleep," Morrison said to the haggard girls—eyewitnesses, I guessed.

"Why are you here?" I asked Sam.

"Those are my students," he said, indicating a couple of exhausted-looking girls. "They work at Ocean Gallery. They saw the shooting. So you're covering this for the paper?"

I nodded wanly. "I'm covering all the bodies piling up around town."

"Your personal interest in those two girls from Azerbaijan is tied awfully close to what you're writing." He crossed his arms. "Isn't there some kind of rule against that in journalism?"

"Yes," I said. "Welcome to small-town reporting. My editor already said he'd pull me off the story if only he had someone else to put on it."

"High standards over there at the Weekly Breeze." He smiled wanly and shook his head.

"Hey, fuck you," I barked. "I take my job seriously, and I do it well. And the Weekly Breeze does a damn good job of covering the news here, especially considering the resources we have to work with. Seems to me you've got a problem with news reporters, period."

The summer workers who had begun to leave had turned back and were now staring at Sam and me.

"I have no problem with reporters. I simply like to know when I'm talking to one."

"You're talking to one."

"I'm sorry. It's late. You're right." He gazed at me earnestly and put a hand on my shoulder.

I felt my expression soften, and I shrugged. His touch was like a sedative.

The students drifted off down the boardwalk, murmuring quietly in—what? Russian? I was beginning to notice and recognize its cadence.

"Let me walk you home."

I wanted to punch him. I also wanted to walk home with him. I didn't bother to tell Sam that Tammy's car was parked a block away. We walked right past the car, and all the way back to my apartment.

28.

"COME IN FOR A BEER?" I asked when we reached my door.

Sam looked into my eyes, and my stomach flip-flopped. "Sure."

We entered the apartment, and I was relieved that the place was reasonably clean. There was a laundry drying rack set up in the corner of the living room, but most of my X-rated undies were hanging behind running shorts and T-shirts. Most of them.

He sat on the sofa, and I went out to the kitchen and grabbed two Coors Lights from the fridge.

"This has been one of the longest days of my life," I said, plopping down next to Sam on the sofa and popping the top of my beer. "Cheers!"

We clinked beer cans, and I sighed with satisfaction after a big gulp.

I wanted to tell Sam about Zamina's reappearance, but every person who knew her whereabouts was one more vulnerable link in the chain. Instead, I told him about Lindsey: how glamorous she is, and how I've always been the dorky little sister in her shadow—and still was.

"I can't picture you being in anyone's shadow," Sam said, turning to face me.

Maybe it was a non sequitur, but I couldn't wait any longer. I put my beer on the coffee table and kissed him.

Sam laughed, taken by surprise, then responded with slow confidence, his fingers trailing through my hair and cupping the back of my head. My arms encircled his shoulders. I breathed in his smell: clean, warm, a little salty.

"I wanted to do that the first time I laid eyes on you," I said a moment later, pulling away to gaze at him, smoothing a lock of his hair behind his ear.

"Oh yeah?" It sounded like he thought I was joking.

"Yes," I said and kissed him again, running both hands through that sexy, blunt-cut hair. "But I have to tell you, I have kissed a guy with long hair before."

"So I'm not the first?"

"Nope. My tenth-grade boyfriend Ricky had a mullet."

"I'm so sorry."

We began making out in earnest, and his hands strayed across my body and inside my shirt. He found only bare skin.

He kissed me deeply and began planting kisses down my neck. "Why did you really come into my office that day?" he breathed into the hollow of my throat, hands resting on the buttons of my shirt.

"Hmm?"

"That first day I met you. Why were you there?" He undid one button.

I pulled away. "How many times are we going to talk about this? I told you, I was doing an article on summer workers."

"Nope," he murmured, leaning in and planting a trail of kisses down the V of my shirt. "I still don't believe you. You wanted to know about me, about my business in particular. You wanted to know if Ocean Gateway was a successful company. Why?"

I cradled his head to my chest, feeling his breath and his lips, staring saucer-eyed at the ceiling. My brain wasn't firing on enough cylinders to come up with a clever answer.

"My Uncle Abe is buying your building, and he wanted me to check out your business."

There. I said it.

Sam sat bolt upright. "Abe Vello?"

"Yes."

"He's your uncle?"

"Guilty as charged," I said with a sheepish grin. "He made an offer on your building, and your landlord accepted it. I'm surprised you don't already know this."

"No, I didn't know."

"Well, Abe won't bother you," I said, trying to wave the whole thing off.

"Your uncle is one of the worst slumlords in Ocean City."

"Well, not really, I mean, he can be kind of disorganized—"

"I tell my students never to rent from Abe Vello. And you work for him?"

"Not really—"

"Just the occasional undercover job?" he said, standing up and pulling his shirt back into place.

"Sam, no, it's not like that. Please let me explain."

"You should have explained sooner. Damn it, you've always got some hidden agenda."

"Hey, I haven't done you any harm!"

"You weren't honest with me."

I gritted my teeth and took a breath. "You're right. I wasn't. I'm sorry."

Sam stormed across the room to the front door. Our eyes locked, then he walked out the door and was gone.

Time for a cold, cold shower.

29.

I N A FIT OF PURITANICAL penance, I got up early the next morning (not that I'd slept much) and went on a ten-mile run. I was trying to sweat out the guilt. That didn't work, but at least I felt good about running that far. It was a new personal record.

I was in the *Weekly Breeze* office by nine a.m., reviewing the flurry of new OCPD press releases when something on the police scanner's never-ending white noise caught my attention.

"Apartment break-in reported, 504 Talbot Street, first floor. Unit 901 responding."

"Donald, that's Zamina's place!" I said, and he tore his eyes away from his screen with a start.

"Get down there," he barked.

"I need your car," I said, and he threw me his keys.

"Buy a car, Jamie," he growled.

"Give me a raise," I retorted.

"Go! Go!" He shooed me out the door.

Beggars can't be choosers, but Donald's Acura coupe was a big step up from Tammy's Chevy Cavalier. I turned the key and immediately was bombarded with Stevie Wonder and Paul McCartney's "Ebony and Ivory." I ejected the disc from the car's CD player—Greatest Hits from the '80s—and flipped around the radio stations until I found one playing Led Zeppelin's "Kashmir". I remembered listening to *Physical Graffiti* on the stereo at home when I was a kid. My parents owned the CD, which was a signal even then that they weren't all square.

I fought traffic the whole way to Zamina's neighborhood at the other end of Ocean City, and parked half a block down from her building. Two police cruisers were parked in front.

The apartment door was ajar, and I came up the walk and knocked gently.

An officer I didn't recognize opened the door. Late twenties, bright red hair.

"Yes? Can I help you?"

"I'm Jamie August from the *Weekly Breeze*—"

"This is an active crime-scene investigation, ma'am. I'm going to ask you to leave—"

"But I know the person who rents this apartment."

The officer glanced back into the living room and waved his partner over to the door.

The partner was the Russian-speaking cop from the American Legion party, the one who had discovered the knife in the dumpster on St. Louis Avenue.

"Pete, this lady's a reporter, but she says she knows the resident of this unit."

His eyes bore into me—or maybe it only seemed that way, they were such a startling, dark shade of blue. He gave no indication that he recognized me. "Do you have a way to get in touch with the resident, miss?" he said.

"No," I said, hoping I wasn't flushing the way I sometimes do when I lie. "But maybe your colleague Detective Morrison will be able to help. This was also the apartment where Leyla Dovzhenko lived."

The red-haired officer consulted some notes. "Lease was held by someone named Abdullajamida or something Allyev. Foreign phone number. You know this guy?"

Meanwhile, the blue-eyed officer—his name had come back to me: Peter Lapin—was starting to close the door. "Thank you miss, now please—"

"Wait, hold on, Leyla Dovzhenko?" the red-haired cop interrupted. "Isn't that the homicide victim from the Haunted House?"

"Yes," I said, pushing the door open again. Lapin let it go. "She was friends with the girl who rented the apartment. She slept on the couch."

"We were aware," Lapin said.

"You knew that, Pete? I didn't," the red-haired cop said. "I'll get Morrison over here." He stepped away and used his radio to contact headquarters.

Lapin's glare could have sliced me open. He turned on his heel and walked away from the open door. I stepped in and gaped at the damage to the apartment: floorboards had been pulled up, couch cushions ripped open. It seemed whoever had broken in the first time had returned to finish the job.

"Holy crap, didn't the neighbors complain? It's like a truck ran through this place."

"The other three apartments are vacant," the red-haired officer said. "Half of Ocean City has cleared out. Landlord called this thing in himself. He came into town when all his tenants started bailing out, found the door open when he showed up to inspect the empty units in the building. That's why I have the rental agreement right here."

Lapin had been in the kitchen, but now pushed open the swinging door, exasperated. "You may as well write the newspaper story yourself." To me he said, "That leaseholder information is part of this ongoing investigation and is not to be printed, do you understand?"

"I do understand," I said. The red-haired cop looked sheepish. "I won't print it. Relax."

Lapin glared at both of us, then turned and went back into the kitchen, letting the door swing closed behind him.

A few minutes later, Morrison came striding into the apartment, hair wet, polo shirt and khakis freshly creased.

"How did you know about this break-in, Jamie?" she barked without preamble.

"Police scanner."

"Oh." She rolled her eyes and smiled ruefully.

"I recognized the address. This is the second time the place has been tossed in a week."

"Yes. Do you have any information you'd like to share with me?"

The swinging door to the kitchen was propped open. Lapin had his back to us, and his movements paused.

"Possibly," I said, stepping outside, glancing over my shoulder. Morrison followed, looking puzzled and concerned. I walked to the end of the building, beyond Zamina's apartment, and leaned against the wall. Morrison joined me.

"Have you seen the name on the lease?"

"I saw it, and I assume it's Zamina's father. That's not uncommon."

"Yes, but do you know who Zamina's father is? One Google search and the whole thing will make sense."

Morrison started getting annoyed. "This isn't some kind of a game. Talk to me."

I lowered my voice. As Morrison listened, wide-eyed, I told her all about the oil deal, like Zamina should have done yesterday. I also revealed to her, as I should have done before, that Leyla was a highly trained security operative, likely hired by Zamina's oil tycoon father to protect his daughter, the kidnap target.

When I told her Leyla and Terry had both been working, albeit for different employers, to protect Zamina, Morrison closed her eyes and groaned.

30.

Y OU NEED TO GET her back here," Morrison said when I revealed Zamina's whereabouts. "I can't protect that girl if she's not here."

Zamina's plan was to stay under the radar in Baltimore until her father's oil deal went down. I wondered if a blond, Russian bombshell wearing vintage Prada in Hampden could technically be considered "under the radar."

"Unless you lock her up, you can't protect her here," I said. "And maybe not even then, if what Leyla told Terry about a Russian Mafia connection inside OCPD is true." I paused, and gazed pointedly back at the apartment door. "Why bring her back to the place where you know people are gunning for her? Russian hit men or East Coast gangstas—either way, she wasn't safe here."

Morrison turned and leaned her back against the wall next to me. We both gazed out at the street, which was a jumble of old clapboard houses chopped up into apartments. Porch rails were draped with beach towels and bathing suits. Wind chimes tinkled in the light breeze.

"You shouldn't have gotten involved in this, Jamie. And you should have told me what Terry said to you about Leyla."

"Would you have believed me?"

"Doesn't matter. You should have told me anyway." She sighed. "It's not your job to protect that girl from whatever she's gotten herself into. It's my job."

"I'm sorry. I get that, seriously. But she doesn't trust the police, and maybe I don't trust them either—not all of them, anyway. How did Lapin end up on this call in the first place, and not you? Why was he pissed off when I showed up and had his partner call you? Who is the victim in the St. Louis Avenue stabbing? If Leyla was the killer, why did she toss the bloody murder weapon in on top of the body with her prints all over it?"

"I am working this case with every resource I've got."

"I believe you. But would you bet your life that there's nothing crooked going on here? Because Zamina wouldn't bet hers. And that's why she left Ocean City."

"You should have kept me informed, Jamie. By withholding information, and by removing that girl from the jurisdiction where I can protect her, you have interfered with this investigation. I could arrest you for this." I could tell Morrison was saying that only to prove a point—but it felt like a slap in the face.

It was the second time in as many days that I'd had to apologize for things I'd done to try and help others. I could forget the whole thing with Sam, of course. My credibility was shot with him.

But I couldn't help but feel that I had done the right thing for Zamina, even if Detective Morrison didn't think so. How could she think that the OCPD had the manpower to protect Zamina on the busiest night of the summer—especially in light of last night's boardwalk shooting? The girl was much safer thanks to me. I felt misunderstood and ill-used.

I bit my tongue to keep myself from saying more. I wanted to lash out at the detective, but I knew she could throw me in jail if she wanted to. I felt my resentment building.

"Okay, Jamie. I'm going to call Zamina on her cell, and tell her about this break-in. She can stay in Baltimore for the time being, but you keep me informed if she goes anywhere else, or even thinks about going anywhere else, or gives you any further information at all. Because somehow I can't see her telling me on her own. Will you do that?"

"Yes. But please, please don't tell anyone else where she is," I said as humbly as I could. "Nobody else knows, not even her agency." She nodded and strode back inside the ruined apartment.

Back in the comfort of Donald's car, I took a few deep breaths and forced my heart rate down. I cranked the AC but left the car in park as I dialed Zamina from my cell phone. She picked up on the first ring.

"Why are police calling me?"

"Did you speak to Detective Morrison? That was quick."

"I pick up. I hear it is police. I hang up."

"Zamina! When the cops call, you need to talk."

"No. They only mess things."

I didn't feel like arguing very hard on that point.

"The police were calling you because your apartment was broken into again last night. The place is completely trashed. Couch cushions torn open, floorboards pulled up, holes in the walls."

"Is okay."

"It's okay?"

"Yes, they not find."

"Not find what?"

"Not find anything," she said defiantly. "Is nothing there."

I knew I wasn't getting the whole story from her; I wondered if anyone ever did.

"How's it going in Hampden?" I said, giving up.

"I love Hampden," she said, giggling. "Is fun and crazy here."

"I'm glad you're having fun. Be really careful, okay?"

"Don't worry. I am with many strong men who dress just like me. Is fine."

"Good. Be sure to keep a low profile."

"What is low profile?"

"Don't do anything to draw attention to yourself."

"Oh. I try, but is not possible."

Zamina's favorite expression. "What do you mean, is not possible?"

"This weekend is big parade in Hampden, for Day of Independence. I will be on Maude's Vintage Boutique parade float with my new friends."

I planted my forehead in my palm. "Are you crazy? You can't be in a parade! You're supposed to be hiding out!"

"My father told me to have American summer. This is the most American. I do."

"Seriously, no!"

"Customers are in shop now. I must go help. Bye, Jamie!"

The line went dead as my jaw went slack. Hopeless. The girl was hopeless.

Because I was such a good girl, I duly went back inside the apartment and let Detective Morrison know that I had just spoken to Zamina and relayed the news about her apartment.

"What is wrong with that girl?" Morrison said. "She hung up on me!"

"She doesn't trust you."

"What did I ever do to her?"

"You're the police."

"That girl needs to be locked up for her own good."

I opened my arms, palms out. "There ya go."

31.

BACK AT THE *WEEKLY BREEZE* office, I worked alone through the afternoon, filing a police blotter story on Zamina's apartment break-in, and writing a piece on an upcoming beach cleanup and barbecue at Assateague State Park on the undeveloped coastline south of Ocean City.

Next up was a summary of a city council budget subcommittee meeting. My head felt heavy. The air was warm. The office was silent. I stared at my notes, unseeing. My mind flashed back to last night, over and over again.

Finally I gave up trying to work. I allowed myself to wallow in self-pity. I couldn't stop thinking

about Sam, even though I knew the whole thing
was a lost cause and he could sometimes be kind of
a jerk, besides. My heart physically ached. I told
myself it was better this way. He was prickly, overly
sensitive, and way too serious. The wrong guy, for
sure. Better that things ended before they really
began.

I jumped up, grabbing my keys, and walked out
the front door, locking up behind me. I walked
down the sidewalk and into the surf shop two
doors down.

"Hey, Jamie, 'sup?" Trevor said, putting aside a
surf mag, his shaggy blond hair bright against his
deep summer tan. Trevor made ringing up Billa-
bong T-shirts seem somehow edgy and sporty.

"Hey, Trevor."

"I missed you the other night." He smiled suggestively.

"Yeah, me too, but you would not believe how
busy it's been this week."

"Don't worry about it. So what's the latest news,
Scoop?"

"Oh, you know, the usual. Unsolved murders.
Gang violence. Russian mobsters roaming the
streets."

"Epic."

I leaned on the counter and grinned. He leaned across and playfully bit my ear.

I squeaked and laughed. A teenage girl came in, chatting on her cell phone and oblivious to us. We chatted aimlessly. Trevor said he caught some decent waves on his early morning surf. I told him about a new bar over by Northside Park.

A mom came through the door with three boys who looked to be between six and thirteen. Trevor nodded to the mom and said, "Hey, dudes" to the kids. "'Sup?"

The mom gave Trevor a tired smile, then addressed her kids: "Boys. We have fifteen minutes and then we have to go meet Daddy and your cousins at Fish Tales."

The kids dashed into the aisles, exclaiming over a display of airbrushed longboards, while the mom turned to a sale rack of sundresses. A moment later some more customers came in, and Trevor had to check on the availability of a rash guard in size XXL.

I told him I'd see him again soon.

"Hope so, babe," he said and flashed me a sexy smile.

Out on the sidewalk, I paused to watch dark clouds sweep across the afternoon sky. It smelled like rain. I felt a little better after my visit with Trevor. A little.

"I am very heartbreak," I murmured aloud, imitating Zamina's heavy accent.

Back in the Weekly Breeze office, I saw that I'd missed a call on my cell phone. From Sam.

My heart pounded. I paced as I dialed my voice mail.

"Jamie, they showed up at Ocean Gateway. ..." Sam's voice was shaking, and he was talking twice as fast as normal. "It was Yuri. Big, mean-looking guy. Adidas tracksuit, comb-over. He walked right into my office, along with two other muscle-headed Russian guys. He said he knows I'm your friend, and he knows you're hiding Mina."

I could hear even on the tinny voice-mail recording that Sam was breathing heavily.

"He said if I didn't tell him where Mina was, he'd kill me, kill my family, and then come after you. He was smoking, and he grabbed me and burned my chest with the cigarette."

He paused, and I could hear him struggling to get his voice under control.

"Yuri was getting ready to stick his cigarette in my eye because I couldn't tell them anything"—I cringed in horror—"but then a busload of summer workers came into the office. They were returning from a New York City trip. There were about thirty of them. Yuri backed off and said, 'We will see you again,' and then the three of them left.

"So. Um, I'm going to call the police now. Be careful. Maybe they're coming for you next." The voice mail ended.

I looked up as three bulked up, smelly men in tracksuits swooped into the office.

32.

ONE GUY CLOSED and locked the door, then watched impassively as the other two pinned my arms to my chair's armrests, and each stepped on one of my feet. The dirty soles of their shoes ground into the bare skin on the tops of my feet, and my forearms felt like they would split open. I cried out in fear and pain.

The third guy stepped up and slapped me, hard. My head jerked to the side, and my ear began to ring.

"No more noise," he said, bringing his face close to mine. I could smell his greasy lunch and the cigarette he must have had afterward.

"Yuri?" I asked, tears streaming down my face.
He nodded and arranged his face into a brief, polite
smile.

"Where is Zamina Allyev?"

I realized I was in no position to bargain. "Baltimore," I said immediately.

Yuri glanced at the goon holding my left hand.
This guy was much smaller than Yuri and had a
nose that was weirdly too thin. He instantly pivoted his right elbow to pin my shoulder and then
bent my pinky finger sideways with a wet snap.

I screamed in agony. Yuri slapped me again.

"Baltimore is big city. Tell me where."

Between desperate gulps of air, I cried out,
"Hampden. She's working at Maude's Vintage Boutique."

The guy on the right brought his elbow up
against my shoulder. It seemed I was about to get a
matched set of broken fingers. Then the front window exploded into a thousand shards, and the nose
of Donald's Acura crashed into the office.

Several bystanders screamed, and Donald laid
on the horn.

The three goons jumped away, probably realizing they had to beat it before dozens of rubberneckers could ID them. "Thank you for your cooperation," Yuri said, and the three men stepped through the broken window and were gone.

Donald jumped out of his car, its nose crumpled and steaming, and ran over to me. "Jamie! Who the hell were those men? Are you okay? Oh, your finger!" He gaped at my pinky, bent sideways like a boomerang, and fainted. Fortunately he fell away from the glass shards and landed with a heavy thud on the carpet.

I got control of my breathing, then picked up the desk phone. Rather than use my left hand, I placed the receiver on the desk and dialed with my right. I knew the number by heart, and some detached part of my brain was impressed that I was able to remember it even now.

With my right hand I held the receiver to my ear and waited. Trevor bounded in from next door. "Babe! What happened?" He stared at Donald on the floor, and then at my hand, which I was holding away from my body in distaste.

"Hey, Trevor," I said, trying to make my voice stop shaking. "Would you mind calling 911?"

"Uh, yeah, of course. That's not, like, who you're already calling?"

"No, I'm calling someone else," I said. "Please call for me, okay?"

"Yeah, okay." Trevor backed out, staring at me in horror.

The phone rang six times, then voice mail kicked in.

Lindsey's voice crooned, "It's Maude's Vintage Boutique, thanks for calling. Devastated to have missed your call, but we hope you'll try again." There was no beep, no way to leave a message. Lindsey was way too old-school cool for voice mail. And she refused to carry a cell phone.

Next I called Lindsey's home phone number and let it ring ten times. No luck. She and Zamina were probably out on a Friday night bar crawl, turning heads and breaking hearts.

Next I called Zamina. Straight to voice mail. At least she had voice mail, though I questioned whether she ever actually checked her messages. "They're coming for you," I said, my voice pitched way too loud and high, and my breath becoming more ragged. "They know where you are. They broke my finger, and I told them. So, yeah. It hurts like a bitch. I would've told them anything. You've got to get out of Baltimore right now. For real."

The phone slipped from my hand and hit the floor a split second before I did.

I came to in an ambulance, one medic leaning over and saying something to me while the other hung a bag of clear liquid on an IV pole.

"Hey, there you are," the first medic said with a smile. He had gray hair, a mustache, and friendly hazel eyes. "How are you feeling?"

"It hurts, it hurts." The full force of pain from my finger seemed to stab all the way up my arm and into my heart.

"I'll bet," he said. "Sarah here's going to take care of that."

The other medic was young, maybe twenty, and wore neon-pink lip gloss. She opened up a kit and put it on the bench seat next to her. With a firm, expert touch she cleaned the inside of my right arm with an alcohol swab, examined my veins, then said, "This is gonna hurt for a second, then you're going to feel a whole lot better."

"Hey wait, wait, I gotta call Detective Morrison," I said, trying to sit up.

Both medics eased me back down. "Whoa, try not to move, please."

My agitation grew. "No, seriously. You gotta get Detective Morrison. Can you radio or something?"

The two paramedics exchanged glances. "We'll reach him."

"Her."

"Who?"

"Detective Morrison is a woman." I was crying again.

"Yes, okay, I promise you, we will alert Detective Morrison to the situation."

"Thank you," I said and lay back.

Sarah expertly pierced the inside of my elbow with the needle, and quickly inserted the IV and taped it into place.

Almost immediately the pain ebbed away and I hardly noticed or cared as they straightened my crazy-pointing pinky finger into a splint. Soon the ambulance arrived at Atlantic General Hospital. I hadn't even realized it had been moving.

33.

ONCE IN THE HOSPITAL, the great care I had gotten in the ambulance worked against me. It was a Friday evening in July at the nearest hospital to Ocean City, and I was in stable condition. You can believe I waited for hours before an ER doctor could see me. I wasn't about to die, like the other poor schmucks arriving there from car accidents, overdoses, and heart attacks.

I spent a fair amount of time worrying about where I was going to get the money to pay for this hospital visit. I did have basic health insurance since I got hired on full-time at the *Weekly Breeze*, but I had never actually put it to the test. Finally I decided I may as well not even think about such scary things, since there was absolutely nothing I could do about them.

Fortunately, one of the medics had tucked my cell phone into my purse, and put my purse next to me on the stretcher, which was parked in some sort of anteroom.

I fished out my phone. No messages.

I called Zamina again but still got no answer.

Then I called Sam. "They got me too," I said.

"Oh no. What happened? Where are you?"

"I'm cool, just waiting at the hospital. I'm high on something really good from the ambulance, but my pinky finger is broken thanks to Yuri."

"Those bastards!"

"Yeah. They got what they wanted. I told them exactly where to find Zamina."

"You knew where she was?"

"Yes."

"Jesus, Jamie, why didn't you tell me?"

"Don't start with me." I hung up. Nobody else was going to give me shit today.

The phone immediately rang again. I let it go to voice mail, tears streaming down my face. I felt completely unglued.

Twenty minutes later, gentle fingers stroked my cheek. I woke up to find Sam gazing down at me. "I'm so sorry," he said "You didn't tell me where

Zamina was because you were trying to keep her safe. I should have understood that."

I sniffled and smiled a little.

"And I'm sorry about last night at your apartment. I regret what I said to you. I was being unfair."

"You were?" I grinned.

"What you said was true: you never meant me any harm."

"Nope," I said. I felt him kiss me as I zoned out, beaming, eyes closed.

I woke up when they wheeled me into the ER. A nurse gave me a fresh round of excellent pain meds, and then a doctor reset and put a cast on my pinky finger.

By midnight I was patched up and ready to go. Sam was nowhere to be seen, but Tammy was waiting in the lobby. I must have called her during a lucid moment. The waiting room was now even more crowded.

"Hey baby, you poor thing," Tammy said. "Come on. I'm taking you back to my place."

I was too woozy to protest. Tammy expertly worked the side streets to avoid the lights on Coastal Highway, and soon I was tucked in and drifting off to sleep on her lumpy plaid sofa.

34.

A T SEVEN THIRTY A.M. my phone rang, jarring me out of a profoundly deep sleep. I attempted to reach into my purse with my left hand but was quickly reminded of my cast. I awkwardly shifted, then rooted around in my bag with my other hand until I found the phone.

"Hello?"

"Good morning, Jamie, Detective Morrison here."

"Ah, thank God it's you."

"I don't hear that nearly often enough."

I sat up and attempted to brush my hair off my face but ended up clocking my forehead head with the damn cast.

"Ouch!"

"What's that?"

"Nothing, sorry. Okay. So, listen, we gotta get to Baltimore. Yuri and his awful friends are probably on their way to Baltimore for Zamina, if they're not already there."

"Hey, whoa, whoa, what's this 'we' business?" she protested. "We are going to stay right here in Ocean City, and that's an order. I'm on my way in to the station now. I know you're probably feeling a little rough, so can I come to you? I need the whole story."

"I'm staying at a friend's house."

"Give me the address."

I did.

"I'm on my way." She hung up.

Tammy wandered into the living room, her blond rocker hair sticking out with charming bed-head abandon. She wore pink short-shorts and a black spaghetti-strap tank top.

"Cops are on their way," I said. "Sorry."

"Wouldn't be the first time," she said.

"Really?"

"Kidding. Well, I guess this means I gotta go get some doughnuts."

She smoothed her hair down a little, grabbed her purse, applied some sparkly lipstick, slid into a pair of wedge-heeled flip-flops, and walked out the door.

Twenty minutes later, I was reasonably washed up and waiting on the sofa when Tammy returned with a dozen assorted from the Fractured Prune. Detective Morrison trailed behind her.

"That's not such a big cast," Morrison said. "You got lucky."

"You should have seen my finger. It was sticking straight up at a right angle from the back of my hand."

The two of us sat down at the dining room table while Tammy went into the kitchen to make a pot of coffee.

I described yesterday's run-in with the Russian goons. She'd heard about Yuri's visit to Sam as well. She let me know that Donald hadn't required medical treatment, though she couldn't say the same for his car.

"He may have saved your life," she asked.

"I know! Those guys were working me over, and he crashed right in."

"It was a dramatic entrance," Morrison said.

"Donald has flair. And he gets the job done."

Morrison laughed.

"Listen," I said, gesturing with a half-eaten margarita-flavored doughnut. "I can't reach Zamina or my sister. I blabbed to the Russians—"

"You had no choice."

"Still, we have to do something. Those guys may have already tortured and killed Zamina. Not to mention my own sister." I frantically stuffed the last of the doughnut in my mouth.

"I know you're concerned, Jamie, but we are working with the Baltimore City Police."

"We are?"

"I am. Of course."

"Oh good. So have they got Lindsey and Zamina somewhere safe?"

"Well, no, not yet."

"What does that mean?"

"It seems your sister's shop is closed and no one came or went from her residence last night."

"What if they already got her?"

"Unlikely. My Baltimore colleagues have been keeping an eye on both locations ever since you told me Zamina was there."

"Really?"

"You thought I'd let that girl run loose in Baltimore?"

"Wow, that's great! I'm so relieved. Unless, of course, there are Russian mob connections in the Baltimore force."

"You watch too much TV."

"So, then, where is Zamina? Where's my sister?"

"Well, we only know they haven't been at Lindsey's home or the shop since yesterday around noon."

"So they could be tied up and getting tortured in some warehouse down by the waterfront?" I yelped, in full panic mode.

"No. Think about it," Morrison said. "Yuri and his man came after you late yesterday afternoon. By that time, Zamina and your sister had already gone... well, wherever they went."

"This is not making me feel a whole lot better."

"I promise you, Jamie, there are a lot of good people working on this."

"And what if there's one bad one?"

"What's making you say that? Do you have any indication we've got somebody rotten on the force?"

"Did you know Peter Lapin speaks Russian?"

Morrison stopped and stared at me. "Seriously? That's what you've got?"

"Well, did you?"

"No, I didn't know that. I speak Spanish. Does that make me MS-13?" Morrison stood up, her chair scraping against the linoleum floor. "We do the best we can with the resources we have. Please contact me if you learn anything new, and do not leave Ocean City. Are we communicating here? Am I clear?"

"My sister is missing. What do you want me to do?"

"I want you to stay here. Don't make me take you in, Jamie. I will throw you in lockup if I think you're going to go stumbling around Baltimore and potentially get yourself killed."

I stood up and faced her across the table. I was hopping mad, and I could feel the blood throbbing in my head and jaw, which was swollen from Yuri's explosive smack.

Tammy marched in from the kitchen and plunked a trio of coffee mugs down on the table. She smiled at us with strident good cheer.

"Coffee?"

35.

JAMIE, LET'S GO to the beach," Tammy said gamely, sipping from a mug that read *Librarians Do It Between the Covers.* "You promised you'd wear that leopard-print bikini, and I think today's the day."

"I don't want to go to the beach," I sputtered. "How can I lie around on the beach, today of all days?"

"What else are you gonna do? Plus, if there are any stray Russian mobsters running around, you're probably better off not hanging around at your home or office."

"Listen to your friend," Morrison said, gulping her coffee, grabbing a banana cream pie doughnut, and letting herself out of the apartment.

We made a quick run to my apartment so I could change into my fringed leopard print bikini—Russian thugs be damned. Over it I wore a neon-pink fishnet-weave cover-up. I examined myself skeptically in the mirror. I could pull off the bikini. But with the cover-up, I looked like a New Jersey mermaid caught in a psychedelic drift net. I felt hesitant about walking into the living room.

"Classy," Tammy said.

"Hey, you were the one who insisted I get this whole outfit."

"I did not insist."

"I tried it on as a joke, and you said it looked great."

"It does look great."

"Then don't be snide."

"I mean, it looks trashy, but great. Seriously!"

I squinted and stared hard at her.

"The neon with the leopard print is kind of a mixed metaphor," she amended.

"I hate you."

"It's especially terrific with that cast," she added.

"Bitch."

"Come on, let's go."

The crowd was enormous on this hot, sunny day. Even though a flood of tourists left Ocean City earlier in the week, the crowds were clearly on the upswing again. I wondered how many of the people on the beach were day-trippers who had gotten up and on the road early for the three-hour drive from D.C. or Baltimore.

Tammy and I squeezed into a spot on the sand near the Haunted House, which was back in action with the coffin-shaped train cars rolling across the rooftop balcony every few minutes, packed with squealing, laughing vacationers. The Ferris wheel turned and glinted in the sun. The scents of cotton candy and popcorn drifted through the air, mixed with the endless, intoxicating smell of the sea.

Tammy spread a big Mexican blanket, and the moment for my bikini debut had arrived. I pulled my fishnet cover-up over my head, studiously ignoring the group of middle-aged men to our left. They all stared, and one dipped his Ray-Bans low on his nose and quietly whistled. A young teenage boy to our right plowed a foot into his sandcastle turret when I gave my chest a little shake to straighten out the fringes on the lower edge of the bikini top.

Good to know I still had it goin' on.

Tammy and I applied some Coppertone and stretched out to catch the morning rays. Tammy lay on her stomach and untied the top of her black bikini. Soon we were both sweating.

"I'm going for a dip," Tammy said, retying her suit and sitting up.

"Huh. You have fun with that," I said, eyeing my cast with distaste.

"Oh, hon, I'm sorry," she said.

I shrugged. "Go on."

She threaded her way through the patchwork of beach blankets, chairs, towels, umbrellas, and sand castles, and plunged into the waves.

I sat there, sweating.

I turned around to check out the boardwalk, and inspiration struck, along with a fresh pang of worry. Kohr Brothers! I wanted some ice cream—and I had to tell the manager about what Yuri and company did to both Sam and me. Hopefully they hadn't paid a repeat visit to the ice cream stand. I put on my cover-up, grabbed my purse, and slid my feet into Tammy's wedgie flip-flops.

Up on the boards in my leopard-print/fishnet ensemble, I got more than the usual number of once-overs and whistles. The busker who "played" the stand-up bass dropped his bow, but the tune played on thanks to the boom box hidden under his chair.

All those early morning runs had been worth the misery, I decided.

"Hey, Brad," I said when I reached the Kohr Brothers counter. "Still short-staffed?"

"Yeah, you want a job? We'd sell out in five minutes if you got up here wearing that." He was scratching his belly and ogling me, joking but maybe only halfway. Let's face it: the outfit was pretty over-the-top.

"Aw. Thanks, Brad. That's sweet of you."

Then he did a double take and said, "Yeah, but what happened to your hand? And is that a bruise on your cheek?"

"Right, I need to talk to you about that. And I need a large chocolate waffle cone with M&M's and chocolate jimmies."

"Don't you usually get a small vanilla?"

I scowled. "Just make the cone."

He shrugged.

As he put together my zillion-calorie treat, I told the story again about Yuri and his henchmen's visits yesterday to Sam and me.

"Yuri from the employment agency?" He turned sharply from the ice cream dispenser.

"You're thinking of the same guy, but Yuri is not from any employment agency," I said.

"Oh. Oh no."

"The guy is Mafia. Not your normal Jersey Mafia. Russian Mafia."

Brad handed me the gigantic cone with a profoundly distressed expression on his face.

"This is terrible," he said.

"Yeah. I hope they don't come back here to your stand again."

"No, I mean, I feel responsible for them coming after you."

"What do you mean?"

"See, they did come back here. They came here yesterday morning. I told them I honestly had no further information to give them about Zamina, but I gave them your business card, like you asked me to."

"Oooooooh, shit. I did ask you to pass along my card if you saw him again. That was before I knew he was a murderous thug, of course."

"I'm sorry."

"You couldn't have known."

"Still."

I shrugged, licked my cone, and crunched on some M&M's.

"Well. Uh. At least let me buy you a cone. This one's on the house."

"Really? Thanks, Brad!" See? Every cloud has a silver lining.

36.

I TURNED AWAY AND SAW Tammy coming toward me across the hot boards. She wore a long, ripped Metallica T-shirt over her bikini, and my cheap green plastic flip-flops.

"You stole my shoes," she said.

"They go better with my outfit."

"Yeah, I guess they do."

"Do you want to share this? I thought I wanted a large waffle cone, but I'm three bites in and already feel stuffed."

"You are becoming such a health nut." She grabbed the cone and took a big bite.

We sat on one of the boardwalk's big wooden benches and watched the crowd go by. After a moment, Tammy nudged me.

"See that balcony there, in the building next to the Haunted House?" She pointed to a two-story building with shops on the bottom level and apartments on top.

"Yeah."

"I'll bet you could climb over that balcony rail and get onto the Haunted House roof."

We stared at it. The cacophony of sounds around me vanished, and I felt a chill.

"You're right."

We continued to watch the balcony, but nobody came in or out of its sliding glass doors.

I finished off the cone. "Tammy, you are the smartest person I know."

"Flattery will get you everywhere."

"I hope so. I have a little job for you."

"Uh oh."

"It'll be easy." I laid out my plan and hardly had to twist Tammy's arm at all. I know she's my best friend, because she's the one I always break the law with.

We brushed the stray jimmies and cone crumbs off—tricky for me, because they were stuck in the fishnet weave of my cover-up. Then Tammy walked ahead and entered a door underneath the balcony we had our eye on. There was a small, weather-beaten sign hanging over the door that read only, "Hotel." The sign was shaped like an arrow and was hung askew so that it pointed to the door.

I waited for five minutes and then went through the same door. Inside was a long, dim passageway, painted in easy-scrub high-gloss white. Linoleum in a 1970s green-and-white pattern stretched down the length of the hall. I walked quickly, scrunching my toes to minimize the wedgie flip-flops' thwack thwack noise, and was relieved to find that the small lobby at the back of the building was empty. A set of double glass doors led out to a small parking lot. I realized that the boardwalk entrance Tammy and I had used was actually the hotel's back door.

I quickly ducked behind the counter and saw no computer at all. Yes! I flipped open the old-school ledger to the latest entries and used my phone to snap a picture of the last page, which was two-thirds of the way full.

I heard Tammy's voice at the top of the stairs that flanked the wall opposite the reception counter.

"Wow, Ana, thank you so much for showing me the room. My boyfriend is gonna flip when I tell

him it's available right now! He has loved the
boardwalk since he was a kid, and the place we're
renting now is so boring! It's so far north, it's practically in Delaware. This is right in the beating
heart of Ocean City!" Tammy was gushing, loudly,
so I could hear every word.

"Can be noisy," replied a heavily accented voice.

"Well, sure, but we can sleep when we go back
home to Philly. Do you get a lot of complaints
about noise?"

"Sometimes. People are stupid. There is Whack-
a-Mole downstairs. Of course is noisy."

Tammy laughed. "Seriously! And what about the
room that was being cleaned, the one on the end?"

"What about?"

"I mean, you can probably hear screams of torture in that one!"

"Torture? What are you talking about?" the voice
said sharply.

"You know, from the Haunted House!"

"Right. Yes. No. Probably. I must get back to
desk now."

37.

THE LOBBY FAINTLY ECHOED as they began descending the stairs. I slipped out the glass doors and walked around the row of buildings, back to the boardwalk.

I sat on a long, wooden bench. Tammy joined me a minute later. "Did you hear that?"

I felt sick. "Yes. They could have tortured Leyla for hours in there and nobody would have known the difference. That woman in the lobby knows something."

"I think you're right. Did you get the info from the guest register?"

"Yep. I figured a place like has probably been around for fifty years or more. Why bother to modernize? And I was right: they still use a paper guest-registration book. I got a picture."

"Good. Let's see."

A teenage couple sat on the other end of the bench, and the girl draped one tan leg across the guy's lap. They shared a large bucket of Thrasher's fries.

"Let's get back on the beach," I said, scanning the crowd for Russians in tracksuits, or anyone else who seemed to be watching us.

We tracked across the sand and found our blanket. We sat, and I stuck my phone inside my beach bag so that the screen was out of the sunlight and slightly more visible. Huddled over the bag, I peered at the picture.

"Okay, what's the room number of the apartment next to the Haunted House?" I asked.

"2D."

The entry was right there: 2D. Rented for the week by one Tony Jones. Cash payment up front for the week. Checked out last night.

"Tony Jones. Yeah, right," I said.

"Well, that wasn't so useful," Tammy said.

"No, it was worth it. They checked out yesterday, which tells us they've probably left Ocean City."

"They're in Baltimore."

I felt a cold stab of fear rip through my belly. Tammy must have seen me flinch. "I'm sorry, hon."

"I'm sure the police are doing everything they can in Baltimore," I said, not feeling it at all.

I flopped back on the blanket and closed my eyes. I felt the pure heat of the sun on my skin and let the sounds of the day wash over me. The murmur of voices around us, the footfalls of people walking across the sand, the squeals and laughter of kids in the surf, and all of it overlaid by the endless, soothing, rhythmic, never-ending tides. ...

"Jamie."

"What? What?" I bolted upright.

"Hey, hey, relax, hon," Tammy said, leaning back on her elbows on the blanket.

"Oh. I guess I fell asleep."

"You needed it. Sorry, I didn't mean to wake you. I realized something, though. Should have thought of this sooner. I wonder if there's anything left in that hotel room over there that the cops would find useful," Tammy said, turning to stare at the row of neat white balconies next to the Haunted House. "The cleaning lady was going to town in there. The fumes were outrageous, like she was using straight bleach."

"I don't know, but Morrison ought to check it out."

"Yeah, but she can't hear it from us. You're sup-posed to leave it to the cops."

"Definitely. So, it's gotta be anonymous. But what happens if we call in a tip and the cop we're talking to is dirty?"

"Are you still freaking out about that cop who speaks Russian? You really think that means he's a card-carrying Russian mobster?"

"Of course I don't think that. I just... don't trust that guy."

"Well, there's nothing we can do about him right now."

We packed up the beach bag and picked our way through the crowds to the carnival midway and played a round of water pistol bullseye to get change for a five. Then we walked all the way to the far end of the boardwalk, where an old pay phone still stood next to the Ocean City Life-Saving Station Museum.

"I'll do it," Tammy said. "They'll recognize your voice for sure. All the cops know you."

I nodded a rueful thanks as Tammy dropped coins into the phone and dialed.

"Cool! It still works!"

I turned my back and scanned the crowd while I listened to Tammy's end of the phone call.

"Hi, I'm calling with an anonymous tip about the murder at the Haunted House. ... No, I said anonymous. ... Uh-huh. Do you want to hear this or do you want me to hang up?"

I frantically gave her the universal slash-across-the-neck signal.

Tammy interrupted whatever they were saying on the other end of the line. "Check out Room 2D at the boardwalk hotel next to the Haunted House. Room 2D. They're cleaning it real hard."

She hung up and we lost ourselves in the crowd.

38.

ZAMINA HAD NEVER felt more alive. After yesterday's long day with Lindsey—three estate sales in the Washington, DC, area—they had gone for dinner and drinks in Georgetown, and at Zamina's insistence stayed at the Four Seasons.

When they checked in Zamina had directed the hotel clerk to call her father about the bill. The elegantly coiffed hotel clerk seemed unfazed as she passed the handset to Zamina, whose father had insisted on speaking to her directly. She was pleased at how panicked he sounded, though somewhat deflated that she was unable to share with him the vivid, painful experience of losing her roommate. He already seemed to know about it.

He had immediately booked them into a Royal Suite—
$15,000 per night got them a private entrance and bullet-
proof glass, among many other amenities. He wanted to
be sure they were safe—even though Zamina suspected it
wasn't her safety he was concerned about as much as the
safety of the certain something she had in her possession.
Her father would never disinherit her while she had this
for leverage, no matter what he might say. Regardless,
Zamina wiped her mental balance sheet clean for the
travesty of business class rather than first on the flight
from Dubai to Dulles.

It was all turning out to be such an exciting adventure.
Well, except for Leyla, Zamina reminded herself. She was
a sweet girl.

She put that thought out of her head for the moment,
because now the Hampden neighborhood's Independence
Day parade was about to begin.

Zamina carefully adjusted her shellacked chignon and
gave her strapless push-up bra a discreet lift. She sat up
straight on the top of the backseat of a bright-blue 1968
Camaro convertible, and arranged the wide skirt and
crinoline of her vintage red floral sundress. She wore
wrist-length white gloves. White pumps sat on the floor,
next to her huge, incongruous Valentino purse. The owner
of the Camaro, a suave elderly gent wearing a bowling
shirt that read Oliver, instructed Zamina not to step on
the upholstery with high-heeled shoes.

There is so much to learn about American culture, Zamina thought.

Lindsey sat next to her in a violet tea dress with an equally flouncy skirt. Her dark hair was parted on the side and styled into a dramatic, sleek wave. "Have you ever been in a parade before, Zamina?"

"No, never!" She beamed, radiant with excitement.

"You're fabulous, honey. You were made for a parade. We're about to start. Here's your flag. Flag in your left hand, parade wave with your right, like we practiced. Got it?"

Zamina shifted the flag to her left hand and nodded. She braced herself as the car started forward, then relaxed into the easy rhythm. Wave, wave, wave the flag with the left hand. Elbow, elbow, wrist-wrist-wrist with the right, and hold that megawatt smile. The petroleum jelly on her teeth kept Zamina's grin wide and bright.

In front of their Camaro was Fifi, a fifteen-foot-tall pink poodle that was propelled by a team of bicyclists. An Uncle Sam top hat had been fastened onto Fifi's head for the occasion. Behind them were three more antique cars with the rest of the Maude's Vintage Boutique salesclerks and entourage. Assistant managers Philomena and Danny were directly behind the Camaro in a '63 Cadillac convertible, resplendent in their own vintages dresses. Danny was reapplying crimson lipstick that he had pulled from a tiny, jeweled evening bag. Zamina had never seen a man with a five o'clock shadow work a backless evening gown with such panache.

"This is best day of my life," Zamina said, planting a kiss on Lindsey's cheek. "Is all because of you."

"Oh, honey, it's only a short, little parade! I'm happy you're here, though. You were a big help yesterday at those estate sales—I would have missed those Christian Louboutin pumps and clutch if it weren't for you."

"I know these things."

"You have an eye for fashion."

Their chatter continued through teeth bared in parade smiles, their American flags fluttering merrily.

Then Zamina saw Lindsey's smile falter. Zamina turned to see what Lindsey was looking at. A man leaned out an open window on the second story of a row house, above the heads of the crowd lining 34th Street. He raised a pistol with a silencer and took aim. Right at them.

Lindsey grabbed Zamina and jerked the two of them onto the floor of the Camaro as a shot ripped cleanly through the top of the back seat where Zamina had been sitting a split second before.

Zamina screamed. The driver must have panicked, as a moment later their car crashed into Fifi the Poodle, which began bobbing dramatically.

A second shot rang out, much louder. After a couple of seconds, Zamina inched her head up and watched the shooter fall out the window, clip the edge of the porch roof, and land on the sidewalk below.

"Run!" Lindsey said, pushing the passenger seat forward and wrenching the passenger door open. Zamina hauled herself through the door, keeping low, then reached back to grab her shoes and handbag. Lindsey had slumped back on the floor, and there was blood. Zamina screamed again.

"Go!" Lindsey gasped. Zamina wavered for an instant, then took off in a barefoot sprint with her shoes in one gloved hand and her handbag in the other. She wove through the crowds, down an alley, across a street, and into another alley. She ducked into a doorway, out of breath.

She slipped on the pumps, grateful she hadn't stepped on any glass in the alley. She listened for steps but heard none. Poking her head out for a view of the street at the far end of the alley, she saw a city bus go by.

Zamina hurried to the street—Keswick, according to the sign. She spotted a blue bus stop sign and a bench at the end of the block. She dashed over to the bench, lettered with the words, "Baltimore, The Greatest City in America." She frowned, thinking, I did not know this.

She glanced up and down the street. No buses. Anyone can see me out here, she thought, and retreated to the front porch of the house right behind the bus stop bench. The porch was heavily shaded by a dark-green awning.

A sweaty man in a tracksuit rounded the corner from Thirty-Fourth onto Keswick, scanning the street. Zamina ducked down below the level of the porch railing and watched between the heavy vertical posts. The man seemed furious and a bit panicked. He walked right past the porch, but he was clearly distracted by the cell phone conversation he was having.

"Dmitri is down," he said in Russian. Zamina's second language was Russian, but she struggled to understand his thick, unfamiliar accent. "Allyev must have new security on her." Zamina furrowed her brow. Her father had security on her?

"I am on Keswick. She's not here. ... Did you check that bookstore on Thirty-Fourth, in the house with the big porch? ..." He stopped a few paces from Zamina, listening intently, then blew out a frustrated sigh. "Slow down and explain. You interrupted a meditation group? ... Vlad, this was supposed to be get in get out, low profile. This is bad, very bad."

He continued down the block, then rounded the corner in the direction from which Zamina had come. She stepped down onto the sidewalk as a cab approached.

"Train station, hurry please."

39.

AMMY TRIED TO TALK me out of it, but I
went home to my apartment. Those Russians
were long gone from Ocean City. I was safe,
even if the City of Baltimore wasn't.

I peeled off the fishnet cover-up and felt the
tight hotness of sunburn. The full-length mirror
hanging behind my bedroom door revealed my entire torso, front and back, burned in a distinct fishnet pattern.

"Oh no!" I said aloud, turning to see the damage
from every angle. I hurled the cover-up into a corner. "I'll have to wear a muumuu for the rest of the
summer."

Completely distracted by visions of lurking Russian mobsters and permanent fishnet-patterned scarring, I turned on the shower and stepped in, dousing my nonwaterproof cast.

Feeling the water soak down to the skin of my pinky, I let out another wail of distress. I turned off the water, sank to the floor of the shower stall, and wept like a child. I wondered if I was having a delayed reaction to the drugs they'd given me in the hospital—I'm a weeper on pain meds, and that's a fact.

After a few moments of unadulterated self-pity, I faintly heard my phone ring.

"Pull your shit together, hon," I said to myself. I got on my feet and wrapped myself in a towel, wincing at the sunburn pain, and grabbed my phone in the bedroom.

A call from my mom had gone to voice mail. I called right back, and she answered in a panic.

"Lindsey's been shot!"

I sat down heavily on the bed.

"Danny was in the parade with her, and he called me on her phone. She's got me in there as her emergency contact, you know, and he said she was bleeding like crazy. She got hit right there on Thirty-Fourth Street in the Fourth of July Parade.

My God, what is Baltimore coming to?" Her voice cracked into a sob.

"No. No no no. Is she... ?"

"I hate this city!" she said in an anguished rasp.

"Okay, Mom, where is Lindsey now?"

"They're taking her to Shock Trauma."

Hearing that my sister was being taken to the R Adams Cowley Shock Trauma Center made me want to retch. It's the first facility in the world built specifically to treat severe traumatic injuries. Perfect for a city consistently on the short list for the US murder capital and heroin capital.

"Do you know anything else?"

"I don't know—" She lost it in another fit of crying.

"Mom. ... C'mon, Mom. Where's Dad?"

"He's coming home right now," she said, calming a little bit. "He's coming home to get me and then we're going to the hospital."

"Okay, that's good. Mom, Shock Trauma is the best place they could take her. Let's focus on how lucky that is. They could have taken her to Bon Secours." From my firefighter ex-boyfriend, I knew Baltimore medics call that place Bone Suckers.

My mom sniffled. "Let me tell you this. Whoever hurt my daughter is going to pay."

I didn't trust myself to speak.

"You father's here. I've gotta go." Her voice sounded stronger.

"I'll find you and Dad at the hospital as soon as I can get up there."

I managed to end the call before I really did retch. My parents would never, ever forgive me for dropping Zamina in Lindsey's lap and putting her in harm's way like I did. I felt the weight of this come crashing down on my shoulders.

Meanwhile, murky liquid was seeping from my cast. I put on a pair of worn-in jeans and an old, soft rugby shirt—easy on the sunburn. I laced up my sneakers and felt ready to figure out my next move: getting back to Baltimore.

I called Tammy but got no answer at home or on her cell. I sent her a text, but she never hears any of her phone's alerts because her purse is like a black hole, completely swallowing all noises. No luck reaching Donald, either, though I did leave him a message telling him I was going to Baltimore and why.

Next I tried Uncle Abe, who needed to hear the news about Lindsey getting shot, and also would maybe drive to Baltimore with me. But then I remembered he was several miles out to sea, on his annual chartered Fourth of July-weekend fishing trip. He had been going offshore fishing on Independence Day weekend every year for as long as I could remember.

My old friend Big Mary was at a family reunion in North Carolina, so I crossed her off the list. Big Mary's best friend Trina's car was almost always in the shop. Shit!

I didn't want to dial the next number, even after last night's emergency room reunion, but there was nobody else. He picked up on the first ring.

"Sam."

"Hey, how are you feeling? How's the hand?"

"I need a big favor."

"Are you crying? What's going on?"

"My sister has been shot, and she's in the hospital. I need a ride to Baltimore."

He gasped. "Of course. Right now?" I heard some rustling around. "I'm on my way."

40.

STARED AT MY DRESSER blankly. How long would I be in Baltimore? Who knew? I threw together a few shorts, a miniskirt, T-shirts and undies, dumping them into a black and orange DelMarVa Shorebirds duffel bag. I dropped in my toothbrush and makeup kit, and tried to put my hair in a ponytail. It came out messy and lopsided because my left hand wasn't working so well.

Twelve minutes later there was a knock on the door. I peeked to make sure it was Sam, then let him in.

He enveloped me in a hug without speaking. It hurt my sunburn, but I didn't care. It felt great to be next to him. We stood together, breathing. I could feel the tension drain from my body.

"Ready?" he asked when I finally pulled away.

I nodded. He wiped a stray tear off my cheek and smoothed a strand of hair behind my ear. "You are beautiful," he said.

"Please don't make me cry again," I said, fresh tears welling up along with a smile. Our eyes met and he gave me one small, gentle kiss.

"Come on," he said. "Let's go." He carried the duffel out, and I locked up the apartment.

Sam drove a black Subaru station wagon, at least ten years old but clean and in great shape. It had a roof rack, and when he opened the hatchback I saw a milk crate with a snorkel and fins.

When we got out on the straight, flat expanse of Route 50, I told him what I knew.

"Lindsey got shot while she was riding in the Hampden Fourth of July parade, and she was taken to Shock Trauma."

"What's her condition?"

"I have no idea."

"Where was she shot?"

"I don't know."

"And where is Zamina?"

"Who knows? I can't reach her. I left her a message last night after"—I waved my plastered left hand around, and a drop of liquid oozed out and rolled down my fingertip. "Knowing her, she probably never checks her messages."

Sam sighed. A few miles later, he asked, "Do you have other siblings?"

"Nope, it's just me and Lindsey. If she's... If she doesn't... If she..."

"Stop," he said gently. "We'll be there soon."

Three hours later, we pulled into the parking lot at Shock Trauma.

We came through the double glass doors, and the triage nurse saw my hand and said, "Oh. You got it wet." She crossed her arms in disapproval.

"Uh, yeah, I did, but that's not why we're here," I said, resting my cast on the counter. It was starting to give off a sour smell.

"You're gonna have to get that recast," she said. "And you're gonna wait a while," she said, glancing at the teeming Saturday night waiting room.

"Right, I get it, but right now I need to see my sister, who's here because she got shot."

"Oh, okay then," she said, like that was somehow much better.

I gave her Lindsey's name, and she directed us into the large, bustling emergency department. I heard Lindsey's deep, throaty laugh before I saw her. My knees nearly buckled in relief.

There was Lindsey in a hospital bed, left arm in a sling. She was surrounded by all of the Maude's Vintage Boutique staff, still in their parade formal wear, plus my mom and dad, plus at least half a dozen elaborate floral arrangements. She had a jade-green silk scarf draped around her shoulders. Leave it to my sister to accessorize even a hospital gown.

I rushed to her side, and we executed an awkward hug, me avoiding her sling and she avoiding my cast.

"What happened to you?" Lindsey said, wrinkling her nose at my cast, which was smelling more rotten by the minute.

I quickly turned to hug my mom and dad, who also exclaimed over the dingy, water-stained plaster. "Don't worry, I'm fine." I shrugged. "I'll give you the boring details later. Lindsey, what about you?"

"Hey man, it's Baltimore," Lindsey said with a casual toss of her head. "People get shot." We exchanged supersecret sister glances. "The bullet only grazed me. I got really lucky—it didn't hit the bone. It just sliced open my upper arm. The amount of blood that came out was really scary, but it's a superficial wound."

"I'm so relieved," I said, crying all over again.

"It wrecked my tattoo, though," she said. "I also broke my wrist when I dove down onto the floor of the car."

She hadn't said anything about Zamina, and I wasn't about to ask, with Mom and Dad and the whole world listening in.

Then I remembered Sam. He was hanging back a discreet distance from the crowd around Lindsey's bed. I brought him over for introductions.

My family and the Maude's staff—probably Lindsey would also call them family—all said their hello's and shook Sam's hand.

"Thank you for bringing our daughter here," my dad said.

"It was nothing, sir," Sam said. "I was glad to help."

Mom was giving Sam a critical once-over, and she smiled when he called my dad sir.

Several hours later, the boutique staff had gone home and Lindsey was wheeled into the casting room to have her wrapped wrist put in a hard cast. I walked with her and was surprised and happy to find that I knew the ortho tech.

"Ronnie Jameson, is that you?" I said, knowing full well that the guy in front of me with the blue scrubs, wire-rimmed glasses, and tight afro was none other than my tenth-grade lab partner.

"Jamie August?" he said, his face breaking into a grin. "Damn, girl! How are you?"

"Oh, I'm fine. My sister got shot, though," I said, like it was the most bad-ass thing ever.

"Would you stop?" Lindsey said, but she was smiling sweetly. "It's just a flesh wound."

"You got lucky," he said, turning his attention to her and consulting a clipboard with her patient information. "So your wrist is broken?" He gingerly loosened the buckle on her sling.

"Yes."

"No worries. We'll get you in a cast, and you'll be out of here in no time."

"Thank you," she said, putting on a brave face but clearly exhausted.

"And what about you, Jamie? What happened to you?" Teddy said, eyeing my hand. "You got that thing wet, didn't you?"

I nodded guiltily.

"I can tell. Smells awful." I blushed. "Don't worry about it. I'll hook you up with a new cast too."

And so it was that at 11:45 that night, we two August sisters left the hospital with fresh white plaster casts.

41.

MOM AND DAD TOOK us girls home to Dundalk. Several hours before, Sam had left for the long drive back to Ocean City. I had walked with him out to his car and we shared a nice kiss in the soft summer night. I promised to call him as soon as I knew when I'd be back.

I hoped I could convince Dad to drive me back to the beach tomorrow, but I figured they were so freaked out by what happened to Lindsey that they would really want both of us back home for a few days. If that was the case, I'd stay. Donald would have to deal with it.

Lindsey claimed the guest bed in Mom's sewing room, and I blew up an air mattress on the floor next to her. Then I called Donald. When he heard about Lindsey, he was really shaken. Donald loves Lindsey. Every time she visits me, I think he's going to switch back to his home team and marry her. He insisted on speaking with her.

After lengthy assurances that she really was going to be fine, and descriptions of her parade dress and that of every other Maude's employee, Lindsey made kissy noises into the phone and handed it back to me.

Back to business: Donald told me that OCPD had closed the case on the St. Louis Avenue body, determining that Leyla Dovzhenko had stabbed the still-unidentified victim to death. No one had come forward to identify the victim, and no match came up for his fingerprints. The victim had traces of Leyla's DNA in scratches on his face and neck, and also under his own fingernails, indicating a struggle between the two of them.

"Perhaps it was self-defense," I said.

"It was a single, efficient stab wound up between the ribs and into the heart."

"Just because she knew what she was doing doesn't mean it wasn't self-defense."

"There's nobody left to tell the tale."

"Yes there is. Leyla's shooter."

"The incidents are related, then?"

"Of course."

"How do you see it? Not that this is going in the paper."

"Two guys come in the door looking for Zamina. They find a blond girl from Azerbaijan, think they've found their girl."

"So they're after Zamina, not Leyla."

"Why would they want Leyla?"

"I don't know."

"No. Zamina's the kidnap target. I think that's who the two men came for. Leyla fights with one of them, manages somehow to stab him with her favorite kitchen knife. The other takes her out of there at gunpoint, drives her over to the hotel next to the Haunted House, tortures her until he realizes he's got the wrong girl, shoots her, dumps her on the tracks."

"What hotel is this?"

"There's a hotel with only a few rooms up on the second floor over Trimper's Rides. You ever notice those balconies up there?"

"I don't know. We don't get down to the boardwalk much."

"Anyway, that's my theory."

"Why do you think the guy realized finally that he had the wrong girl?"

"Because he killed her. Otherwise he wouldn't have. Zamina is no good to him dead."

"How does the gunman get Leyla to the hotel by himself? Scrappy girl like that, she's not going to go easy."

"Duct tape?"

"The police said nothing about tape on Leyla's body."

"Maybe he makes her drive?"

"Maybe. I don't know, doesn't sound right. Seems like if she had all those skills Terry said she had, she'd know how to drive into a tree and walk away from it."

"Well, I don't know." The extreme, extended adrenaline rush from the day was over. "I gotta go, Donald. I'll call you tomorrow. Send you the sidebar for the Jolly Rogers water park story."

"Thanks, Jamie. Give Lindsey my love."

We turned out the lights, and I listened to my parents' footsteps in the hall. The bathroom door opened and closed. The strip of light seeping under the bedroom door from the hallway finally went out, and a few minutes later the house grew still. A car with a bad muffler rumbled down the empty street, and then all was quiet. I was so tired I felt paralyzed—but my brain was still whirling.

"You awake?" I whispered.

"Yes."

"Did you see the person who shot you?"

"Not really. I know it was a white man, dark hair. I think the gun had some kind of silencer thing on it—like the barrel was longer than it should have been. You know what I mean?"

"Uh, sort of. I mean, from watching movies."

"Right."

"He was aiming at Zamina, wasn't he?"

"I'm pretty sure."

"She got away?"

"I don't know. I pushed her down, then told her to get out of the car and run. That's the last I saw of her."

"You think they got her?"

"I don't know. She's a clever girl."

At three thirty a.m. my cell phone rang, waking me from a restless half sleep. The display indicated a blocked call.

"Hello?"

"Am I speaking to Jamie August?" asked a deep, cultured voice with a heavy accent.

I sat up, and I saw the flash of Lindsey's eyes in the dark.

"Who is this?"

"My name is Abdulmajid Allyev. I am Zamina Allyev's father."

"Really?" Was this the next ploy in the Russian mob's attempts to find the girl? "How do I know you're Zamina's father?"

"Beg your pardon? I am calling you from Dubai to express our family's—"

"I doubt it."

There was a brief pause. "Ah. Zamina tells me you are an extremely intelligent girl. My daughter is lucky to know you."

"Sure. So how are you gonna prove you're not one of the same Russian shrivel-dicks who broke my finger and shot my sister?" I hissed into the phone, hoping Mom and Dad were still asleep in the next room. Lindsey was sitting up, wide-eyed, clutching her bed sheet.

"I am calling because of this violence, simply to express my most sincere—"

"For all I know you're one of Yuri's muscle heads, calling from a pay phone down the block. Save your breath, asshole. If you're still searching for Zamina, that means she got away from you, and that's good news to me. I have no idea where she is."

"I can see how you are strong enough to stand up to my difficult daughter," he said, chuckling.

"How can I prove to you that I am Majid Allyev? Hmmm, an interesting situation." He thought for a moment. "Zamina has told you about our family, I believe?"

"Yes," I said warily.

"And you know why she is in your country right now." It was a statement, not a question. He paused.

"Go on."

"So you know something of our... business holdings, yes? Zamina tells me you are a reporter. So I will hang up. You will figure out how to locate me, and ring back at my Dubai office. Please do call me back so that I may thank you and your sister properly and make you an offer."

He ended the call.

I stared at the phone, as if the breaking wave on my screensaver could reveal some clue.

"The hell was that?" Lindsey whispered.

"Guy says he's Zamina's dad, wants to make us an offer."

"Do you believe him?"

"I don't know. Maybe, yeah."

"So, what, he hung up?"

I told Lindsey about his challenge to find him and call him back in Dubai.

"Not bad," Lindsey said. "It would prove he's not calling from around the corner."

"Not necessarily. With Internet telephony and call forwarding, it's impossible to know for sure where anyone is calling from."

"Internet telephony?"

"Your Bakelite rotary phone is probably not equipped for this, honey. Don't worry your pretty little head," I said.

"I try not to," she replied, laying back and placing her casted arm delicately over her forehead.

42.

PULLED OUT MY LAPTOP and within ten minutes had located the Dubai offices of a holding company that included the various business interests of one Dr. Abdulmajid Allyev in Azerbaijan, Southeast Asia, and Dubai.

I dialed a long string of numbers on my mobile phone, and a silky voice answered, "AKS, Salaam Aleikum."

"What? Um, yes. ... Uh, do you speak English?"

Lindsey sat up again, a little grin on her face.

"Of course," she murmured. "Good afternoon. How may I direct your call?"

"I'd like to speak with, uh, Abdulmajid Allyev." I stumbled slightly over the pronunciation.

"Who shall I say is calling?"

"Jamie August."

"One moment please."

A moment later, the same distinguished gentleman's voice came on the line. "Twelve minutes. A little slow for an investigative reporter, Miss August." Allyev chuckled.

"It took a few minutes to connect your name to the holding company, through the oil and gas conglomerate and the privately held real-estate trust."

"That is the idea, yes," he said. "Now, on behalf of my family, may I please offer you my most sincere and humble apologies for the pain and suffering that Zamina has put you through, and also your sister?"

"Thank you," I said, at a loss for how else to respond. "He says he's sorry," I said to Lindsey. Then back to Allyev: "If you know Lindsey got shot, then that means you spoke to Zamina after the parade. She's okay?"

"Yes. She called me from the train station in Baltimore. I bought her a ticket to New York."

"What a relief," I said, and to Lindsey: "She took a train to New York."

"André," Lindsey said. I nodded in agreement.

"She has a friend there and says she is safe for the moment," Allyev said. "What can I do? I cannot keep her secure here. She will not remain long behind locked doors."

"I guess I can't blame her," I said.

"Happily, she has agreed to return home to us in Dubai."

"Really? That's good news, I guess. I don't really understand, though. Aren't you from Azerbaijan?"

"We are, but we have recently relocated to the United Arab Emirates. Considering my pending business transaction, I thought it safer to leave Azerbaijan. Plus, my wife and daughter prefer the shopping here," he said, and I detected a note of exasperation in his voice.

"Well, I'm happy to hear that Zamina has agreed to return home," I said, bringing Lindsey up to speed.

"We have a comfortable and secure home here. As a small thanks for everything you have done on Zamina's behalf, my wife and I would like to invite you and your sister to be our guests while you rest and recuperate from your terrible injuries. In fact, my wife insists. She is quite upset about the hardships we've caused for you. Zamina needs protection right now, but so do you and your sister."

"Oh well, that's very kind..." I was not following what he was saying.

"We have a comfortable penthouse near the Burj Khalifa, quite close to the best shopping—"

"Wait, hold on, what? Your guests where?"

"In Dubai, of course."

"But—" I sputtered. "You want us to come to Dubai?" Lindsey clapped a hand over her mouth to stifle a squeal of delight. She climbed down onto the air mattress and squeezed next to me so that she could hear both sides of the conversation.

"Dr. Allyev, we can't afford—"

Lindsey elbowed me in the ribs with her cast, then winced with pain and tucked in next to me again.

"My dear girl, you and your sister will be our guests. Do not concern yourself with the cost. Please. That is true also for your medical expenses. I have already arranged for a substantial donation to Atlantic General Hospital and also to Maryland Shock Trauma—a dramatic name for a hospital, by the way. All fees for the August family have been waived, and you will have free care for the next year. These injuries will heal quickly, Inshallah, God willing, but if you need more visits, you will be covered."

Lindsey and I stared at each other in wonder. We both would have been paying off those bills for years.

"Wait," I said to him. "How did you know I was treated at Atlantic General?"

"Zamina told me the Russians broke your finger. It was easy enough to determine where you had gone for care."

"We're supposed to have patient confidentiality in this country," I fumed halfheartedly.

Allyev gave a good-natured chuckle. "These things are flexible when a sizable donation is at stake."

I gaped.

I heard voices in the background.

"Forgive me, Miss August, I need to attend a meeting. I realize I have called you in the middle of the night—but it is early afternoon here in Dubai. I wanted to give you a few hours to prepare for your journey. So please, will you and your sister be our guests? You will fly to New York, where Zamina will meet you for the connecting flight to Dubai."

"I'm not sure," I said. Lindsey pinched me hard on the leg. I gave her a kick.

"The Emirates Air flight leaves from Dulles at sixteen hundred. I have taken the liberty of booking first-class seats for you and your sister, as well as for Zamina. I'll send a car to your family's home in Dundalk at eleven hundred. I hope you will accept the hospitality of the Allyev family."

And he hung up.

"Holy shit on a stick, we're going to Dubai!" Lindsey whispered frantically.

43.

"YOU SERIOUSLY THINK we should go?" I said, shifting to face her.

"You think an opportunity like this is going to come up again some other time? How many invitations have you gotten to stay in an oil tycoon's penthouse?"

"Isn't it really hot in Dubai?" I protested.

"They have a ski slope in one of the shopping malls," Lindsey said. "I think they've figured out the air conditioning thing."

"I don't know. ... "

"You're out of your mind, Jamie. I'm going," Lindsey said, hopping back into bed.

I lay back on the air mattress and closed my eyes. I didn't think it would be possible for me to sleep, but exhaustion soon overcame my jangled nerves, and I woke to the smell of pancakes and coffee drifting upstairs. I could hear Mom, Dad, and Lindsey talking in the kitchen.

I opened my laptop and found the numbers for both Atlantic General and Shock Trauma. Quick calls to their billing departments confirmed that all of my bills had been paid by AKS International. "This is the best insurance plan I've ever seen," the Atlantic General billing clerk said. "You're covered for anything and everything. I've never heard of this AKS outfit before. Where'd you get this kind of coverage?"

"Thanks, hon," I said, Baltimore-style, and hung up quickly.

Down in the kitchen, the family was sitting around a platter of blueberry pancakes. I poured a cup from Mister Coffee and pulled out a chair to join them at the Formica table.

"I already told 'em everything, Jamie," Lindsey said.

"You told them—"

"All about Zamina, your finger, the whole thing. Otherwise, how could I explain our all-expenses-paid trip to Dubai to stay with her in a billionaire family penthouse?"

"I didn't say I was going!"

"You're going."

"This is crazy," Dad said. "Who are these people, and how do you know they're not going to get you over there and take you hostage?"

"Dad!" Lindsey huffed in exasperation.

"I checked with the hospitals, and Dr. Allyev really did pay for all of our medical expenses."

"My goodness," Mom said. "That is generous. And so quickly! He had to pull some strings to do that."

"Also, I researched him in the recent press, and he really is in negotiation with Shell to sell a bunch of oil rights in the Caspian Sea."

"Yes, but you know someone is trying to kill their daughter, and you're going to get on a plane and fly off to the Middle East with her? You've both already been injured!" My mother, always the sensible one. "Don't you think that's a good enough reason to stay away?"

I slid some pancakes onto the plate that had been set for me, and added butter and maple syrup.

"I know, Mom. Maybe it's not such a good idea. What should we do?"

"I'm going," Lindsey said, stuffing a big bite of pancakes into her mouth and checking her delicate, vintage ladies dress watch.

"No you're not," Dad said, his face taut and stubborn. "I forbid my girls to go anywhere near that place."

Lindsey gaped. A bite of pancake stopped midway to my mouth. I leveled a cool glance at my father. "You forbid us?" I said. "Is that so?"

Mom gave Dad a death glare.

"You can't trust any of those people," he sputtered.

"Those people? What does that mean?" I demanded.

A brittle silence fell over the table. I put down my fork.

"It's ten thirty," I said. "The driver will be here in half an hour. I have to get ready."

I stood up from the table, having taken not a single bite of mom's homemade blueberry pancakes.

"Now, Jamie, don't be like that, hon," Mom said. "Your father is just worried about you."

"Seriously, Jamie, it's not safe over there," Dad said.

I turned back from the kitchen door with an incredulous laugh. "Dubai is not safe? Dad! You live in Baltimore. Get real." I shook my head and left the room.

A black Lincoln Town Car pulled up to the curb as I wrapped up a convoluted voice message for Detective Morrison. I figured she already knew about the shooting—else her Baltimore contacts aren't worth shit—but I wondered how she would feel about me flying off to pal around with Zamina and her family. Well, at least whatever happened would be well and truly out of her jurisdiction.

Dad had left the house—or been banished from it by Mom, I don't know. We hugged her somberly, and she stood at the door and watched us climb in the car. The plush sedan glided down the block and around the corner, whisking Lindsey and me from our working-class Dundalk family home to Dulles International Airport.

44.

I T WAS A TIGHT CONNECTION. They began calling for first class boarding as we arrived at the crowded international departure gate. We pushed through the crowd and found Zamina concentrating intently on her phone, texting. She wore fashionably ripped designer jeans and a gold silk shirt with a plunging draped neckline. Her feet looked natural and comfortable in six-inch python-skin platform stilettos.

"Zamina!" Lindsey leaned in and hugged her with her good arm.

"My friends." She offered a distracted smile and gingerly squeezed Lindsey around her good shoulder, then gave me a hug and a kiss. "I thought almost you not make it. They begin boarding. Is time for Champagne."

As we walked down the gangway, Zamina continued her furious texting. We stepped on board and turned left. Two flight attendants wearing pillbox hats artfully draped with scarves escorted us to our first-class seats. A third attendant, this one a tall, perfectly groomed Indian man, presented a tray with three Champagne flutes before I had even leaned back in the buttery leather seat.

We raised our glasses.

"To my friends who save my life, I want to welcome you to my home and my family, and I hope you enjoy my adopted country of Dubai." She smiled, but her face seemed strained.

We touched glasses and sipped. So smooth! I could probably drink a whole lot of these and not get a hangover.

"Are you okay, Zamina?" I asked.

"Me? Of course. Yes." Then she shook her head. "It is only André. I am together with him again, you know?"

"Yes, I figured."

"We are again argue, argue. Love is difficult."

"Maybe this little break from him is exactly what you need," Lindsey said.

"Maybe. Or maybe my father will not let me go back to him."

Lindsey and I stared at Zamina in surprise.

"You're pretty good at slipping away from him, from what you've told me," I said.

"Yes, but I am daughter of Muslim family. Not practicing so much, but still. I am with African-American rap star. Maybe this time my father will find a way to 'keep me safe'."

"But actual Russian Mafia hit men really are out to get you. We know this," I said, pointing to Lindsey's cast with my casted hand. "Your parents have had good reason for wanting to keep you safe."

"Yes, yes, I know," she said, like it was the same tiresome thing as always. "But now, with André, I am afraid they will try to keep me home and marry me off quickly."

"Oh," Lindsey said, subdued.

"That's pretty bad. Can they do that?" I asked.

"They would not do this, really, but would try to talk me in. Might be a bad scene, yes?" Zamina said, trying out the expression. "So in America I fight with my boyfriend and maybe get killed by Russian mob. In Dubai I have good security, but I get pressure to marry nice, rich man. What should I do? This is what I ask in my head. Is giving me wrinkles."

Lindsey gave a silly, fake gasp. "No! No wrinkles! We'll have to have a spa day. That's it! No more heavy thoughts. We'll drag your ass with us back to the US, I swear it."

Zamina laughed.

"You know what I'm most excited about?" Lindsey leaned across the aisle toward Zamina. "Shopping with you in Dubai."

"You will not believe!" She said with a hoarse squeal.

Wow, where'd our Champagne go? The wine steward was refilling our flutes almost as if I had sent him an ESP message.

Zamina glanced at her phone and her enormous diamond watch. I touched her wrist. "That's no knockoff, is it?"

She jerked her arm away, mortally offended, then her face lit up. "Ha! At Kohr Brothers that day, I told you it was replica. No. Is real Piaget. Even with stopwatch function." She took a small sip from her freshly refilled glass and stood. "Excuse me. I must use toilet."

Lindsey leaned over to me. "That's a Miss Protocle XL."

"So I've been told."

"That watch starts at thirty grand."

I choked, and Champagne shot out my nose. "That is ridiculous!"

"Don't be judgy," Lindsey said. "Let's figure out what to eat for dinner."

I snorted. We put our heads together and considered appetizers, entrees, and desserts. I let Lindsey handle the wine pairings, with the help of the ever-vigilant wine steward. I'm no wine snob; stick a glass in front of me, and I'll drink it.

Lindsey and the elegant Indian steward finished their conversation, and he picked up Zamina's full Champagne flute and began to carry it away.

"I think our friend will want that," I said.

He turned back with a puzzled expression. "But Ms. Allyev deplaned. Did she not tell you?"

I unbuckled my seat belt and jumped up. "She got off the plane? Damn that girl! I've got to go find her."

"Madam, we pushed back from the gate more than ten minutes ago. We are in the queue for takeoff."

"We are? I didn't even feel the plane move!"

"I'm terribly sorry, madam. She said there was a sudden emergency and that she would not be able to fly. Please sit down and fasten your seat belt."

"I guess she chose André and Russian hit men," I said to Lindsey.

She laughed ruefully.

"What should we do?" I fumed.

"What can we do?" Lindsey shrugged and finished her Champagne. "Enjoy a few days in Dubai."

The smell of fresh coffee woke me from a long, deep, dreamless sleep. I sat up and hit a series of buttons to return my perfectly flat, comfortable bed to its cushy lounge chair configuration. A freshly coiffed flight attendant handed me a cup of coffee and a breakfast menu.

I glanced across the aisle at Lindsey, and did a double-take. At some point while I was sleeping, she had changed into a fitted, floor-length, 1960s-era lounge dress in a deep-green and black pattern, with bat-wing sleeves that concealed her cast. She wore a black scarf over her hair and a pair of Jackie Kennedy-style dark glasses.

She turned to me and smiled, took a sip of coffee. She looked like she owned the place. "Rise and shine," she said. "We'll be landing soon."

"You changed your clothes. What the heck are you wearing?"

"Isn't this thing great? I love the whole arabesque style. So exotic and mysterious." She laughed, partly at herself. "I don't know if I tied the scarf right, though. I was planning on asking Za-mina."

I rolled my eyes and finished my coffee. In the restroom, I brushed my teeth and did what I could with my bed head. I smoothed out my V-neck T-shirt, put on a coat of sparkly lip gloss, and took inventory. My hair needed a wash, my face was greasy, and my Levi's were so baggy they had butt sag. Lately I'd been pretty satisfied with my appearance. Next to a high-maintenance diva like Zamina, I actually felt good about my look: simple but sporty. Next to fun, sexy Lindsey, I always felt like a schlump.

Outside the arrivals area, we found a driver holding a sign with our names printed on it, among many other drivers with similar signs. He insisted on taking our bags, examining my Shorebirds duffel with interest.

"Welcome to Dubai. I'm sorry Miss Zamina was not able to accompany you. A terrible thing about the accident."

Lindsey and I glanced at each other quickly. "Yes, terrible," Lindsey said tentatively.

"It is fortunate that Mr. André was not badly injured."

"A big relief," I said. Lindsey and I buckled into the back of a sleek black Mercedes. We exchanged wildly puzzled glances, and then she cracked a mischievous grin.

Soon we were motoring down the widest highway I had ever seen—sometimes eight lanes across.

"This is an S class," Lindsey murmured discreetly, running her hand across the leather seat.

"I don't even know what that means," I murmured equally discreetly.

Lindsey lowered her movie star shades and gave me a wry look. "Mercedes's flagship sedan. They start at around a hundred grand."

"That's more than Mom and Dad's house is worth." It was a smooth, quiet ride. Lindsey leaned back and sighed with pleasure.

Soon the Mercedes pulled into a circular drive and approached a glass tower building. I craned my neck but couldn't even see the top of it. It was definitely taller than any highrise apartment building in North Ocean City. We stopped under a wide awning in front of a gleaming set of glass doors.

The heat of the day was shocking. It felt like we stepped out of the air conditioned car directly into a clothes dryer. I instantly started to sweat, and my gas station sunglasses were no match for the fierce glare.

A doorman with dark, Indian skin opened the glass door and we hurried through. Inside, the lobby was all white with an enormous marble table in the center and a museum-sized urn full of white calla lilies.

The doorman brought our luggage inside and took it—where? The Baltimore girl in me didn't like losing sight of my bag. Meanwhile, another man in a neat, dark suit approached us.

"You are the August sisters?" he said in a cultured Indian accent. We nodded. "Welcome! Please, one moment." He stepped away and made a quick, quiet phone call. A moment later a spotless chrome elevator door opened and out stepped a white guy who looked like a bodybuilder in a bespoke suit. Lindsey removed her sunglasses and gingerly bit on one earpiece as she watched him approach.

"You must be Jamie and Lindsey August," he said with a restrained smile in an accent I couldn't identify. He sounded English, maybe, but not quite.

We stepped forward and made our introductions.

"I'm Mark Boshoff, head of the Allyevs' security detail. Welcome to Dubai, ladies. Please come up."

We got in the elevator, which was as large as my Ocean City kitchen, and Mark used a key to activate the button for the penthouse. My ears popped as the elevator shot upward.

By the time we slowed to a stop and the doors opened, I was feeling a little queasy. Then we stepped from the elevator directly into a foyer that had a glass wall with a view of the whole city. I grabbed onto the elevator doorway, dizzy with vertigo.

Most other skyscrapers stopped below the level where we were standing. Only a few pointed upward even higher than this. The sky was a brilliant, cloudless blue. Beyond the city, the sea spread out to the hazy horizon.

45.

I S THIS SAFE?" I stepped into the foyer, edg-
ing far away from the windows.

"Oh," Lindsey said, putting her hand to her
heart like she was about to say the Pledge of Alle-
giance.

"Gita, the August girls are here," Mark called.

Our bags were sitting on the floor in the foyer.
He picked them up and continued into the apartment and down a hallway.

A dark-skinned woman who seemed about my
mom's age came through a swinging door from
what must have been the kitchen. Her glossy black
hair was pulled carefully back into a bun at the base

of her neck, and her brown eyes gleamed with a friendly light.

"Welcome, ladies," she said, approaching us and bowing her head slightly. "I am Gita. How was your flight?"

"It was fine, no problems," Lindsey said. It was freakin' first class, I wanted to shout. Of course there were no problems. I simply smiled.

"We've all heard about Zamina's friend's car accident."

"It was all so sudden. Please tell us what you know," I said quickly.

"Well, as you're aware,, Zamina got a text from André's colleague after you boarded the plane. Amazing mobile phone coverage you must have in the US!"

Was that a twinkle in Gita's eye? I smiled and offered a noncommittal, affirmative "Mmm."

"Apparently a bus crashed into André's limousine."

"Terrible."

"André was rushed to the hospital unconscious."

"So of course Zamina had to go to him," Lindsey riffed.

"Of course. You'll be relieved to know that André regained consciousness soon after Zamina arrived at the hospital and will make a full recovery."

"I am so happy to hear it," I said. What was going on here? Did they believe this stupid story?

"We're all sorry to miss out on Zamina's charming company, but we're delighted to have you here."

Zamina's charming company? Now I knew Gita was papering over this latest vanishing act. Much classier than I could have managed.

"What a beautiful dress," Gita said to Lindsey, clearly moving us along to safer conversational territory.

"Thank you. When I found it, the labels had been cut out, but I think it's a Halston from the late '70s."

"Mrs. Allyev would know, certainly. She hoped to be here when you arrived, but she was delayed. I'm sure she'd like to see it."

"Sure," Lindsey said gamely.

"I will let you get settled, and after you've had a chance to clean up, you will have some coffee." I didn't really want any coffee, but it didn't sound like a question.

Gita led us down a long, wide hallway, lit by big brass lamps on heavy, elaborately carved tables.

"These are your rooms," she said when we reached the end, indicating doors on either side of the hall. "The one on the left is for Jamie, and on

291

the right is Lindsey's." She opened each door in turn and said, "Please make yourselves comfortable and let me know if you need anything. There are supplies in the bathrooms, and Madame put a few things in the closet for each of you since of course you did not have much time to prepare for your visit."

"She did?" I said, taken aback. "How did she know our sizes?"

"Zamina told her." Gita smiled merrily.

"How does Zamina know?" I retorted.

"Oh, Zamina would know," Lindsey said. "She sized up my customers the second they walked in the shop."

"Zamina is very good with fashion," Gita said. "She learned from her mother."

My room was decorated in serene shell-pink and white. The king-sized bed was made up in snow-white linens. A wooden writing desk faced another floor-to-ceiling window, this one with a view stretching past the city into a vast, empty desert. Sheer linen curtains and rich, pale-pink drapes framed the view.

My orange and black duffel bag seemed slightly offensive, like a smudge of dirt on a Persian rug. It sat on a heavy wooden suitcase rack next to a wide set of closet doors.

One closet door stood open, and I could see a few things hanging in there. However, the sixteen-hour flight—even though it was first class—had left me feeling both parched and greasy, so I decided on a shower first.

I pulled a plastic trash bag and a roll of tape out of my bag. Then I shed my clothes on the thick, creamy carpet and carefully encased my left hand in plastic. I padded into the marble bathroom.

It took me several minutes and a blast of water in the face before I figured out how to operate the shower. Once, I covered the Home, Condo, and Outdoor Show at the OC convention center for the *Weekly Breeze*. I saw displays with wide rain-shower heads and shower stalls that sprayed water every which way—but those were only displays. I had never seen one in operation. Now I was stepping into a steamy marble cubicle with water coming at me from every direction. Eyes closed, I fumbled around and located a bottle of shampoo that smelled of dark, exotic spices, and a chunky, square bar of soap with the same scent.

Eventually I found the right spot in the shower where I could stand without water shooting up my nose—and I felt my body relax.

The idea of flying all the way to Dubai to be the guests of these strangers, with or without Zamina, was insane. I mean, this was the Middle East: I was brought up knowing that this was the scariest, most dangerous place in the world. Now I was taking the best shower of my life. The only thing that really scared me so far was committing a fashion faux pas or accidentally flooding the apartment.

46.

ORTY-FIVE MINUTES LATER, I was seated in a buttery-soft leather armchair in the spacious living room. The room was modern but comfortable with its mix of antique and new furniture. I wore an ankle-length skirt made of multiple layers of fine soft-blue Indian cotton, and a crisp white cotton shirt with tailoring that nipped here and flared there to fit every curve.

Even the new shoes fit perfectly: cork wedges with chunky, natural-colored leather straps. If Mrs. Allyev had picked these clothes out for me, then Zamina did come by her fashion sense honestly. I felt fabulous in these clothes: feminine, confident, comfortable.

I was carefully holding a tiny cup of coffee that smelled almost like gingerbread, but not quite.

"Do you like the coffee?" Gita asked as she came in with a fancy dish of what appeared to be small brown prunes.

"I really do. What's in it?"

"It is typical Arabic coffee, made with a mixture of coffee and cardamom."

She put the plate on the coffee table and said, "These are fresh dates, flown in from this year's harvest in Saudi Arabia. The finest dates in the world."

"Saudi Arabia?"

"Yes, from the Al-Hasa region. This is the world's largest oasis, on the north side of the great Empty Quarter."

I had never tried a date before, but they looked wrinkly and unappetizing. I gingerly bit off one end of the sticky, light-brown fruit, about twice the size of a purple grape. The skin was thick and papery, but inside was sweet and almost creamy. It was much softer than I had expected. I smiled at Gita in surprise.

"Do you like?" She indicated a small empty bowl. "You can put the seed here."

I popped the rest of the date into my mouth, sucked the seed clean, and dropped it into the dish.

"Wow. Those are delicious, addictive. Not what I was expecting."

"Many people only know dried dates. Fresh dates are better. And Arabian dates are best of all."

I took a second date. "Yum! I can't believe these grow in Saudi Arabia. Can't believe anything does. I thought it was all oil wells and terrorists." I winced and covered my face at that dumb remark.

"I know. It's okay. In the Middle East everyone thinks America is all bikini girls and gun fights."

"It is, you know," I said, winking. Her eyes lit up with her smile.

"One more thing you did not know about the Al Hasa oasis: they even grow a special kind of rice there."

"Rice? In Saudi Arabia? Now you are joking."

"It's true: Al Hasa rice is red color and has a nutty flavor. Not many people know of it outside of that region—not even other Saudis."

"You've tried this rice?"

"Yes. Before I came to Dubai to work for the Allyevs, I worked for the prince who governed Saudi Arabia's Eastern province."

I gazed at this polished but approachable woman. "Where are you from, Gita?"

"India," she said. "All my family is there, my husband, our parents, our children."

"How long have you been away?"

"Ten years."

"Ten years! How awful to be away from your family all this time."

"I miss them every day. It is hard, but you will see many, many Indian workers in Dubai. We are everywhere in the Middle East, making money to support our families back home."

"I've heard the money is good. That's why everyone comes here, right?"

"It's true. Because of my work, we have a large family home in Kerala, and my husband owns an auto repair garage. Soon the house will be paid off and I will have enough for all of my children's education. Then it will be time to go home."

Lindsey came in then, wearing a slinky, charcoal-gray jumpsuit and a string of coral-colored beads around her neck.

"Ah, beautiful, Lindsey!" Gita said.

Lindsey executed a perfect model twirl and twisted the beads around the fingers of her usable hand.

"You two are different but both so beautiful," Gita said, walking back to the kitchen.

"I must be dreaming," Lindsey said. "I slipped and fell into heaven."

She sank onto a plush velvet sofa. "Jamie, you look great. That's the kind of clothes you would wear if you knew how to pick out clothes."

"Thanks," I said, rolling my eyes. "You say the sweetest things."

Gita brought a gold-rimmed tray with a tiny cup of coffee for Lindsey and a ceramic pot. "More for you, Jamie?"

I held out my cup. "Yes, please."

"Do you enjoy Middle Eastern cuisine?" she asked while she poured.

"I think so," I said. "I haven't had much of it, but I like almost every kind of food."

"Lebanese Taverna is pretty good," Lindsey said to me. "There's one down at the harbor in Baltimore. They have great falafels."

Gita left the pot on a small stand and went back to the kitchen. She returned with the tray loaded with a bowl of hummus swirled with thick, green olive oil. She also had a bowl of tabouleh, bright green with fresh parsley; a basket with triangles of still-warm flatbread; and several dishes of small olives, some green and some black.

"The green olives and the olive oil on top of the hummus are from Lebanon," she said, nodding to Lindsey, "and these black olives are Syrian."

We thanked her.

"I know you are hungry after your flight," she said, and it was true, despite the multicourse meals and desserts and after-dinner drinks that we had enjoyed in first class. "Please enjoy. Dr. and Mrs. Allyev will be home shortly."

We watched as dusk fell over the city. The apartment was quiet, except for the occasional sound coming from the kitchen. Dinner smells soon began wafting from the direction of the kitchen, but the swinging door prevented us from seeing what Gita was up to.

"I could get used to this," Lindsey said.

"Don't," I said.

47.

THE ELEVATOR CHIMED gently, and the doors slid open. A tall woman swept in wearing a drapey, billowing dress that somehow managed to conceal everything below her neck but still convey a sexy, curvy body underneath. She slid a silk scarf off of her long, dark hair as she walked in to greet us.

"The August sisters! You beautiful, brave women. You are my heroes," she said, dropping her giant leather purse and a Bloomingdale's shopping bag, and gathering us both into a hug. She kissed each of us on both cheeks. Then she stood back, a manicured hand on each of our shoulders. I was nearly overpowered by her strong, spicy perfume, though I loved the scent. She gazed at each of us in turn.

"Jamie, you are even more marvelous than I imagined. The clothing suits you," she said. "And Lindsey. From what Zamina told me, I knew you could pull off the jumpsuit. Retro but still fresh. Absolutely smashing." Her accent was more British than Russian. "Mashallah, praise God! Ladies, there are no words to express my gratitude for everything you have done for my daughter, or my regret for your suffering in trying to protect her."

We both murmured thanks, bowled over by Mrs. Allyev's intensity and glamour.

"Thank you for coming to my home," she said, clearly sincere.

"Thank you, Mrs. Allyev," I said.

"Please call me Kamala. I'm sorry Zamina wasn't able to make the trip, but these things happen." A gentle shrug. "Gita, I see you have been taking good care of these ladies, spoiling their dinners nicely."

Gita smiled and said, "It was a small snack only." She cleared up the remaining dishes.

"My husband will be here soon," Kamala said, checking a diamond-encrusted watch. "I have some things to take care of, and he usually needs to finish up a few loose ends when he gets home. Let's meet for dinner in one hour."

We all wandered off to our respective corners of the vast penthouse apartment, now softly lit by the glow of the Dubai night sky, and the lamps and discreet spotlights that Gita had switched on.

I e-mailed Sam to tell him that oh, BTW, I flew off to Dubai on a lark, back soon, miss you! There was no way not to make it sound preposterous. He'd told me I should travel, so I did.

Then I e-mailed Donald and told him the same thing, but I used slightly more businesslike language. Well, slightly: I had to describe Zamina's fable about André's precision-timed car accident using appropriate verbiage. Any other employer would fire me for dashing off to Dubai unannounced—but I knew for a fact that Donald the fashion maven would have done exactly the same thing in my shoes. Maybe this week one of the Weekly Breeze freelancers would catch their big break.

Finally, I e-mailed my mom to let her know Lindsey and I had arrived safely, sans Zamina, and were staying in the biggest, fanciest apartment I'd ever seen. Even nicer than Donald's, and his North OC penthouse is pretty swank. Mom doesn't check her e-mail too often, but that's all my parents were going to get after Dad's outburst. My anger flared up all over again, just thinking about it.

I freshened my makeup, brushed my hair, and slid my shoes back on, then knocked on Lindsey's door. We walked together to the dining room, where a long, highly polished table reflected the glow from the city and the gold leaf-patterned ceiling.

Kamala was standing with a short, slightly paunchy man with gray hair that was getting a little shaggy and thick glasses. He wore a pinstriped suit that looked expensive and a clearly pricey striped shirt that didn't really go with the suit. His tie was slightly askew. She was straightening the tie when we arrived.

"Ladies!" Kamala beamed. "Please allow me to introduce my husband, Dr. Abdulmajid Allyev."

He transformed from a rumpled, slight little man to a tycoon in an instant, I swear, when he squared his shoulders and smiled at us. He advanced with a confident stride and shook each of our hands warmly.

"Welcome to our home," he said. "I am delighted that you accepted our invitation. I felt it important to thank both of you in person for all you have done for my daughter. I only wish she were here to join me in thanking you."

Once again, Lindsey and I murmured an awkward but sincere thanks. I mean, if I had to do it over again, I still wouldn't choose to get roughed up by a bunch of scary Russian dudes. But the rewards for doing so were really starting to add up.

Judging by Lindsey's expression as she and Kamala put their heads together in conversation, she'd probably stick her arm out for another minor bullet wound in order to get back here.

48.

T HE FOUR OF US sat at one end of the long table. Gita brought in seasoned rice, delicate vegetable fritters, green salad with figs and pomegranates, and lots of kebabs—chicken, lamb, and vegetable. I was still wiping my plate with a piece of flatbread when Gita carried in a dish stacked high with squares of sticky, honey-scented baklava.

We talked into the evening. Kamala and Lindsey got along like a house on fire, of course. Kamala wanted to know all about Maude's Vintage Boutique and Lindsey's interest in classic couture. Lindsey wanted the scoop on the local shopping scene.

Meanwhile, Dr. Allyev, who insisted I call him Majid, asked me to tell him all about the *Breeze*. "It's an unusual situation," I said. "The *Weekly Breeze* is this tiny arts and entertainment paper, but we're the only independent in town. We have no ties to the big media conglomerates that have pretty much taken over American journalism. So when there's news happening, we've got the local connections, we know the backstory, and nobody in DC or New York is directing the coverage. No big commercial interests, no profit-hungry board of directors. And none of our advertisers is big enough to exert any real influence. We are truly an independent press. It's great."

"How does the paper finance its operations?" Majid asked.

"Not particularly well," I replied. "We have advertising revenue, but really, it's a labor of love for our editor, and I think he bankrolls it himself when he has to."

"That is not wise."

"No, but I suspect that's how it is."

Majid gazed out the window, thinking.

"It's interesting as a reporter, too," I continued. "We have maybe eight thousand full-time residents, so the core of the city is small. It's easy to learn who's who and what all the major issues are.

But on a good summer weekend, we get sometimes over three hundred thousand visitors. With that comes all kinds of interesting stories—and crime, too. As you know."

"Unfortunately, yes."

One of those conversational lulls happened, where the whole table fell silent at once. Then Majid said, "Please talk to us about what has been happening with our daughter. It is difficult, but we want to hear about this from both of you."

I began at the beginning, describing the unlikely pair of girls at the Kohr Brothers stand: cheerful, hard-working Leyla... and Zamina. "She, uh, didn't really take to the job," I said charitably.

"She doesn't like to work," Kamala said affably.

"Oh, but she showed some hustle at my shop," Lindsey said. "And you should have seen her at the estate sales I took her to in Washington. She had been with me at Maude's for only one day, but she was instinctively drawn to the right things. She knew quality, and she knew what would sell."

"Amazing," Majid said. "Maybe our daughter has found her calling. I suppose I could buy her a boutique. ..." He drummed his fingers on the table thoughtfully. Lindsey's eyes bulged.

I told them about my chance meeting with them at the Poolside Lounge, and Zamina's boyfriend, the rap star.

"This is André, yes?" Kamala asked.

"Yes."

"Tell us about this André."

Oh boy. "You know, I only met him that one night. He seemed a little, uh, tough to me. But if you know anything about the American music scene, then you can understand that a rapper has got to maintain a certain attitude."

Lindsey nodded. "Like, the guy may be a marketing genius who knows how to create the right image—which is a real skill, actually. But if he's doing rap shows, he must appear to be living the thug life, you know?"

Majid and Kamala appeared confused and distressed.

"You mean, he must act like a pimp and a drug dealer?" Majid said.

"Kind of," I said.

"Yes," Lindsey said, shrugging helplessly. "He calls himself Sniper Trigga."

Kamala seemed like she was going to cry.

"Go on," Majid said, like an executive getting through a difficult meeting.

I described the scene at Zamina's apartment when she and I found it on that first morning, and Zamina giving me the slip to avoid going to the police.

"I can understand this," Kamala said. "Police cannot always protect you. Sometimes they can do more harm."

"And the apartment had been searched?" Majid asked.

"I think so. It seemed like a bigger mess than it would have been if they had simply come in and grabbed Leyla. What would the kidnappers have been looking for?"

"It's hard to say." Majid shrugged. I saw Kamala's eyes dart to her lap. "Please continue."

I explained that the police initially suspected that gang violence was behind Leyla's disappearance and her death because the girls had been seen with André and his crew.

"But now evidence is starting to point in a different direction," I said. "Leyla was responsible for the death of an unidentified man found nearby the morning after she disappeared."

Majid nodded dispassionately.

"She was Zamina's bodyguard, wasn't she?" I asked.

"Yes. How did you find out? Even Zamina didn't know."

I told them about Terry, and how he had discovered the role she was playing.

"Leyla told this man she was guarding Zamina?"

"She didn't tell him, but he figured it out."

"So this man Terry knows who my daughter is?"

"No. He knew Leyla was guarding her, but he didn't know why."

"Perceptive."

"Yes, but not as incredible as you might think. Zamina's friend André had assigned Terry the same job. Leyla and Terry were both serving as Zamina's bodyguards. Between the two of them they had her pretty well covered, it sounds like."

"Why would André want this Terry to guard Zamina?"

"A rap star's girlfriend can sometimes get unwanted attention."

"I see."

"Terry is now being held for Leyla's murder," I said.

"Why?" Kamala asked, incredulous.

"Back to that gang thing. People saw them together the night she was killed, and the police jumped to the wrong conclusion."

"You see? What good are police," Kamala fumed.

"My dear, the police might be more effective if people like our daughter would cooperate with them," Majid pointed out.

"Achh," she said, waving a dismissive hand.

"He could use a good lawyer," I said.

"I will handle this," Majid said.

There. I didn't recommend a lawyer, did I?

I told them about Yuri and company's multiple trips to the Kohr Brothers stand in search of Zamina and about Sam's frightening encounter with him.

"Oh no! There was another victim of these Russians?" Kamala broke in.

"Well, yes, actually. They burned my friend Sam's chest with a cigarette—"

Kamala buried her face in her hands.

"This must stop," Majid said.

"While all this was going on, there was another incident on the boardwalk that was clearly a clash of young white men and young black men, which may have focused the police even more tightly on the gang theory—and away from the idea that the Russian Mafia could be behind some of the city's recent violence."

"Now tell me about what happened in Baltimore at the parade," Majid said, turning to Lindsey.

She described the day's events. "Here's what I don't understand. Why were they trying to shoot her? They could have killed her! I thought she was a kidnap target, for leverage against you in the oil deal."

"I think they did not mean to kill her, only to scare her—and scare me," Majid said. "Was anyone else hit by the gunman?"

"Not that I'm aware of," Lindsey said. "There were a few other injuries, though, if you count the cyclists who fell over when our car hit the human-powered pink poodle in front of us."

"America!" Kamala said, her voice full of wonder.

49.

THE MERCEDES SLID up to the entrance of Dubai Mall: the largest in the world. Lindsey, Kamala, and I piled out. Kamala wore a black, floor-length, embroidered silk dress that flowed around her like water, and a filmy scarf loosely draped around her head. Lindsey and I wore the clothes we had been given the day before. They were way better than anything in our luggage. Lindsey draped a scarf around her head.

"I don't think I'm wearing this right," she said. Kamala rearranged the scarf in an elegant drape around Lindsey's jawline. Her dark hair peeked out above her forehead, as it did with some of the other women I saw.

"Kamala, I thought women in the Middle East wore burqas because they had to, but you make it seem so glamorous," I said.

"This is not a burqa, darling," Kamala said sharply—clearly she threw the "darling" in to soften it. "Burqas are ugly, heavy things, and they cover the whole face. Women in Afghanistan must wear them. Never here. This is called an abaya. Sometimes Muslim women wear them, sometimes not. It depends on the country and the occasion."

"Oh," I said, beginning to realize what a cultural minefield I had stepped into.

We followed the crowd in through the doors, breathing in the icy air conditioning with relief. Some women wore abayas and some wore designer jeans and platform sandals. I didn't see too many shorts, but I did spot the occasional minidress.

"It seems more formal here than in the US," Lindsey said, and Kamala nodded.

"Yes. A woman would never wear athletic clothing for fashion," she said.

"In that case, I don't think I could make it here," I said.

Thousands of voices echoed on the vast marble floor. Kamala guided us to the mall's enormous aquarium, over 160 feet long and nearly 40 feet tall.

Its ghostly blue light tinged the crowd milling around in front of it.

"It's a shark!" I said, approaching the glass and locking eyes with the big gray creature. "I live at the beach, but I'm getting my first close-up with a shark in the desert."

"Haven't you been to Shark Alley at the Baltimore Aquarium?" Lindsey said, scanning the shops opposite the aquarium's glass wall. She was more interested in fashion than fish. She was like a kid at Disneyland.

We strolled past Tiffany, Cartier, and Rolex stores, past clothing stores I had never heard of before—and then I spotted a familiar one.

"Hey, let's go to the Gap!"

"No!" Kamala and Lindsey said in unison.

"The Gap's in my price range." I shrugged.

"Jamie, you and Lindsey are my family's guests. I will take care of everything," Kamala said. I began to protest but she cut me off.

"Please. We are forever in your debt. We are not even trying to repay you—that is ridiculous, is impossible. A few little things from the mall are nothing compared to what you have done for my daughter." She gestured with her elegant hands, and her exquisitely made-up eyes grew moist.

Lindsey and I gaped at each other.

"Thank you," we both said.

"I will take you to some of the best shops here, and we will give you a whole new, elegant look," Kamala declared, shifting the mood and cheerfully sizing me up.

"Okay, sure," I said amiably. "You're not the first to try."

Four hours and many stores later, all of us were loaded down with shopping bags. Kamala had whipped out her platinum card and outfitted Lindsey and me in silk shirts, tailored jackets, pencil skirts, sandals, boots, lingerie, and matching Coach duffel bags.

"I thought you girls could use an upgrade in your luggage," Kamala said. She must have heard about my orange and black duffel bag.

I felt a little unsettled, thinking about how much money had been spent in so little time, on clothes I'd be afraid to wear while eating pizza. I now owned brands that had Lindsey suppressing orgasms—but I'd never heard of them.

Shopping completed, we went outside for an early evening stroll to see the Burj Khalifa. The skyscraper was still hanging on to its claim to fame as the world's tallest building, towering like a comic book illusion over the Dubai Fountain, which

had its own notoriety as the world's largest chore-
ographed fountain. I was getting the idea that Dubai was working hard to have the biggest and most
extravagant of everything. And nobody seemed to
be snickering about any of it. I felt way too snarky
for this place.

Hundreds of people milled around in the choking evening heat, many of them women covered in
black from head to toe. They glided past me in
clouds of perfume, checking the time on chunky
gold watches, reaching manicured fingers into
elaborate handbags. My insides felt like they were
starting to cook, but most of the people in the
crowd seemed unfazed. They oohed and aahed to
the fountain's splashy interpretation of "All Night
Long."

"Is that Lionel Richie?"

"Who is Lionel Richie?" Kamala asked.

"Yes ma'am," Lindsey said. "Listen, it's so hot
my mascara is running." Indeed, her makeup appeared to be melting. We retreated to the arctic air
conditioning of the mall, and Kamala asked if we
were hungry. I'm always up for food, but Lindsey
was jet-lagging hard. Kamala called the driver, and
we returned to the apartment.

"Girls, please be comfortable," Kamala said. "I'm
happy we could spend such a nice day together.

Now I need to make some calls, order an ice sculpture, take care of a few details." She breezed off down the hallway, leaving me only mildly puzzled about the ice sculpture comment. I supposed that was a normal to-do list item in this bizarrely monied world. I felt grateful for the day, but also out of sorts. Is this what people got rich for? The philosophical problems I had with such profligate spending aside, it was kind of... boring.

50.

INDSEY WENT STRAIGHT to bed. The housekeeper, Gita, made me a plate of curried chicken salad with grapes on a bed of greens. Then I sat in the living room, exhausted but not quite ready for sleep, staring at the Dubai skyline, with hundreds of shiny skyscrapers, each vying to be taller, glassier, sparklier than its neighbors. Majid joined me, making himself comfortable in an armchair. He got down to business right away.

"You are an intelligent and capable women, Miss August, and I would like you to work for me."

I carefully set my plate on the coffee table.

"Work for you? Doing what?"

"I have controlling interest in two newspapers in the UAE. I need someone like you on board here in Dubai to write and to do some training in western-style journalism."

"You are involved in a lot of different businesses, Dr. Allyev—"

"Please. It's Majid. And I have a lot of interests. The oil business has been good to me and has given me the resources to pursue other things that I consider to be important."

"I don't know much about the Middle East, but one thing I'm pretty sure of is that there is no freedom of the press here."

"Is there in the United States, really?"

"Less and less, it's true. But at least at the Weekly Breeze, I'm pretty sure I won't end up getting sentenced to death for, like, criticizing City Hall."

Majid chuckled.

"The world is changing, and the Middle East is changing even faster. Azerbaijan is, too, but that's a different story. I wouldn't invite you to Azerbaijan, not right now."

He paused, collected his thoughts, adjusted his thick glasses and leaned forward earnestly.

"In Dubai, though, we need people like you to guide our newsroom toward more robust standards of reporting."

"I'm flattered, really, but—"

"The compensation would be quite generous." He named a sum that I couldn't make in ten years as an American reporter.

I was tongue-tied. Was this guy serious? I opened my mouth to speak, but at first no words came out.

"Wow," I finally choked out. "Why would you pay me that much?"

"I could pay you less." He smiled gently.

"That's not what I mean."

"When you do your research, and I assume you will, you'll discover that my offer is generous, but not out of line with the scale of pay in this region for people with specific skills like yours, skills that are at the moment in short supply here."

"But I'm just a small-town reporter."

"Yes, but you understand the principles of journalism, yes? How to verify and corroborate facts, how to question and critically think, how to structure news stories."

"Of course, but any reporter knows those things."

"If you will indulge me for a moment," he said. "I am a new resident here, but I have been doing business in various capacities in the Middle East for years. This is an area rich with resources—oil,

323

of course, but many other things too. In my opinion this region's biggest resource is its young, educated population. These young people are returning home from universities all over the world, and they are bringing with them a desire to create a society with more rigorous standards in business, science, academia. They want a more open—though not necessarily western—cultural experience. They are creating new standards.

"Media is one of the most rapidly growing and evolving industries here. Young Arabs have been exposed to the western style of journalism in their travels and their education abroad. Technology—new media in particular—is being used here to pry open doors that simply will not be closed again. Things are changing.

"This region may lag behind the West in some areas, but it is gaining ground at lightning speed. Look out at the city, Jamie."

I gazed out at the sea of glass towers, the brightly lit grid of traffic hundreds of feet below.

"Fifty years ago—even thirty years ago—this view would have been of sand. The window is closing fast on the need for western subject experts like you in the Middle East. You'd be wise to jump in now, while you're still needed and can command such a civilized rate of pay."

I nodded, weighing his words.

"Don't answer me right now. It's a big decision," he said, standing up. "And a big opportunity. Very big." The razor-sharp billionaire oil tycoon had once again replaced the rumpled nice guy. He gave me a friendly but formal nod and wished me a good night.

I tucked myself into bed soon after. Even with Majid's words swirling in my head, the cool silence of the penthouse apartment lulled me into a deep, comfortable sleep.

The next few days passed in a pampered fog of spa treatments, ladies lunches, afternoon chats with Gita about life in India (which were my favorite), and five-star dinners.

On Friday morning I joined Lindsey in the dining room for coffee. She was already several cups into the sharp cardamom brew, and full of plans.

"Majid and Kamala have already gone out to some kind of charity event, but Mark has offered to take us to brunch."

"Mark?" I said, rubbing the sleep from my eyes and pouring myself a cup of coffee.

Lindsey's eyes twinkled. "You know, Mark. Sexy security guy Mark. The guy who met us when we first arrived."

"Oh, right." The mental fog was lifting. "Great. So we're going to brunch."

"Yeah, apparently it's a thing here."

"Well, sure. I mean, what's not to like about brunch?"

"No, I mean, it's really a thing here. Five-star hotels have them every weekend, with open bars, deejays, dancing girls, bottomless Champagne. People have brunch all day in Dubai." Lindsey sounded really excited. Or really caffeinated.

I swallowed some coffee and shrugged amiably. "Lead on, sister."

An hour later, we met Mark in the lobby. I wore a nautical, striped tank dress and red sandals with dark wooden heels that did wonders for my legs, if I do say so myself. Lindsey swept in wearing a floral, one-shouldered maxi dress that hugged every curve. Mark couldn't stop staring at her. He led us out the glass doors to another Mercedes, this one in shiny white.

Lindsey sat in front, and I climbed in the back seat. As soon as the doors were closed I said to Mark, "I guess you knew Leyla Dovzhenko, didn't you?"

"Of course. I sent her there to shadow Zamina. Leyla Dovzhenko's real name was Darya Vetrov.

She was one of the toughest and smartest agents I've ever known. It was a great loss," he said.

"I'm sorry."

"Thank you." He paused. "Ladies, I want to tell you something before we go. Today is my day off, and I am asking you to join me for brunch as my new friends. Just because this is a social event, though, does not mean you're going out without protection. We are being followed, and I have a team already in place at the hotel. You're in good hands, so please enjoy and don't think for a minute that because I am relaxed, your security isn't being attended."

Lindsey's jaw hinged open. "Were we supposed to be worrying?"

"Mark, we went to the Mall of Dubai yesterday," I said. "If somebody was gunning for us, don't you think that would have been their golden opportunity?"

"Yes, quite. That's why I was there with a team of seven operatives surrounding you the whole time."

"You were?"

"Indeed."

"We didn't see you," Lindsey said.

"Exactly."

51.

WE PULLED UP TO the lavishly landscaped glass-and-steel Belmond Hotel, and Mark handed the keys to a valet. With every turn, the hotel's massive revolving door dispensed big drafts of air conditioning onto the furnace-hot sidewalk.

Inside, we ascended a curving marble and glass staircase to an enormous banquet hall. Lavish food stations were spread out among at least fifty large round dining tables. We passed towering displays of sushi, dim sum, Thai curries, Lebanese kebabs, trays of French cheeses, pasta salads, pastries, cookies and cakes, and tropical fruits arranged like floral displays on long skewers. I could tell there

were even more food options—many more—
arranged around the room, but Mark was leading
us quickly through the crowd to a table with several people already seated.

"Brilliant, my mates are already here."

"His accent is fabulous," Lindsey murmured to
me.

I agreed. "Is he British?"

"South African."

I'd never met anyone from South Africa before.

We weaved past a series of mirrored columns. I
glanced up and was startled to see a woman on top
of each one. They were Thai, or maybe Filipina,
draped in short, filmy dresses and dancing to the
deejay's trancelike Indian and techno mix.

I was already starting to go into sensory over-
load as we sat down and Mark introduced us to his
friends. They included one guy who was an editor
at Majid's Dubai newspaper. We were a regular
United Nations around the table: American, South
African, Lebanese, British, Irish, German, Swiss,
and Turkish.

Lindsey sat next to Mark, and the two of them
immediately leaned together in conversation. It was
sweet to see Lindsey so obviously smitten. Usually
she's the cool one, the femme fatale, the pursued
and not the pursuer.

I managed to catch her eye, gave her a little smile and a wink, and turned my attention to the others at the table.

I would love to report on the urbane conversation, the international witticism, the illuminating cultural exchange among the group of us. But the truth is, we all got smashed. The waiter kept the Champagne flowing, and I lost track of how many mojitos I drank. At one point, I recall giving Majid's editor some advice on self-defense tactics. He seemed interested. Or maybe I was flashing a whole lot of cleavage.

Several hours later I woke up on a velvet sofa in an alcove over by the elevators. As I opened my eyes, the elevator doors slid shut. Bad guy? Another of Majid's security operatives? I sat up quickly and took inventory. Purse: check. Wallet: check. Shoes: check.

I stood up carefully, waited for the floor to stop moving, then made my way back to the banquet hall. Mark and Lindsey were the only ones left, and she was sitting on his lap.

Mark glanced over and saw me, and stood Lindsey up.

"How are you feeling?" he asked me, grinning. He had nice dimples.

I blushed. "Wonderful, thanks. How long was I out there?"

"Oh, not more than two hours or so. I carried you over there after you attempted a nap under the table."

Lindsey rolled her eyes.

"Oh yeah. But no, see, that was me demonstrating my investigative reporter restaurant surveillance-techniques."

"I see. At first I thought perhaps you were demonstrating another kind of technique with my mate Ian."

"I don't even know who that is."

"Ian sat next to you at brunch. You talked to him for the better part of an hour."

"Hmmm. Must have been an interesting guy," I said, suddenly not caring about any of this and wanting to go back to the apartment and sleep for a week.

Lindsey gave me a giant, tipsy hug. "Jamie, Mark was telling me about this crazy Indian club he knows about. Let's go!"

"I don't know, I'm pretty tired."

"How often do you get a chance to go to an Indian supper club? In Dubai?"

"But my head's going to explode."

"Oh come on. You slept the afternoon away. You're going to miss your entire trip!"

Mark leaned back in his chair, crossed his arms, and watched us, amused.

"Do I have to?" Lindsey could reduce me to powerless little-sisterhood with the merest gesture.

"You do. Yes."

Mark caught the eye of a waiter clearing the last of the salad buffet. "Coffee please?"

I lounged in the plush back corner of a velvet banquette, my breathing even and shallow, my eyes at half-mast. The day's back-to-back buffets and bottomless drinks had made me glassy-eyed and antisocial. Just as well: I was too out of it to feel like Mark and Lindsey's awkward third wheel. They propped me up in a corner and got on with their increasingly amorous night.

A velvet curtain opened with a flourish at one end of a high-ceilinged dining room that was pungent with the smell of curry. A line of women in spangly saris danced across a stage. I giggled at the Bollywood-style dance numbers with their high-pitched Hindi warbling. I couldn't really follow the action on the stage—presumably there was a plot that involved some sort of royal family and a beautiful princess, or something. My eyes slid closed.

"Oh, shit." Lindsey sounded alarmed and thrilled.

"What, what?" I sat up and opened my eyes. Lindsey grabbed my shoulder and pointed. The stage was full of dancers in bright, shimmering dresses and matching, shiny suits. The princess was sitting in some kind of gilded box, and Mark was—

"What's Mark doing up there?"

Lindsey burst into giddy laughter. "I don't know!"

He jumped into the front row of dancers, bare-chested and wearing the princess's crown. He executed a few of the dance moves, then began shouting above the recorded tune. "Lindsey August is the most beeeaauuuutiful woman in the world!"

Lindsey's eyes grew wide. I clapped a hand over my mouth.

"Never has there been a more beautiful woman than my sweet Lindsey, from Baltimore in the USAaaaaaay!"

"Quite a voice he's got," I said, laughing and staring. "What happened to his shirt?"

"Oh, that's right here," Lindsey said, holding up a fine cotton dress shirt. I checked to confirm that Lindsey still had all her clothes on.

"He is so fine." Lindsey stood and weaved through the cocktail tables to the stage. She whispered something to a man in the front row of tables, who promptly stood up, took Lindsey's hand and helped her stand on his chair. From there she delicately stepped onto the stage and into Mark's arms.

The crowd cheered wildly, and the dancers modified the number so that they were moving in an artful circle around them. The music swelled, and the show culminated with the happy couple being lifted offstage in the princess's jewel-encrusted sedan chair.

52.

THE NEXT MORNING WAS awkward, to say the least. We had come in late, and drunk. Lindsey knocked a lamp on the floor in the bedroom hallway, waking up the household at 3:45 a.m. Then she slept through breakfast. Probably a wise move.

I sat at the dining table, squinting in the bright morning sunlight, and tried to act like my head wasn't sore. Majid was even quieter than usual.

Kamala gazed at me and sighed. She excused herself from the table and met Gita in the doorway as Gita was coming in with a fresh pot of coffee. Kamala whispered a few words, and Gita came back a moment later with a small bowl of dates and a glass of what appeared to be some kind of smoothie.

"Have a few dates, my dear, and some laban," Kamala said. "It's similar to yogurt, and you can drink it for, er, jet lag."

They were gracious and kind hosts, and I would have been even more mortified if I had been awake enough to muster the will for it.

Oh well. I don't know what they were expecting, turning the August sisters loose on a Dubai weekend with a hot South African and a Mercedes Benz.

Majid called me into his study after breakfast.

"Your sister has made quite an impression on my head of security."

"Ah, you've heard."

"Of course. There was a security detail with you yesterday."

"Ah. Well, it was clearly mutual."

"This creates an unfortunate situation."

"I'm sorry if my sister did anything inappropriate," I said, having visions of her being dragged out of the apartment and arrested for wanton behavior or something. Crap, what if Dad was right? We should never have come to the Middle East.

"It's not your sister's behavior that concerns me," Majid said, and I breathed a little sigh of relief. "But their... antics lead me to question whether

I can trust Mr. Boshoff to oversee my family's security arrangements any longer."

"Oh no! You're not going to fire him, are you?"

"I haven't decided yet. Reports from other members of the security detail lead me to believe he showed poor judgment last night, and a level of indiscretion that he has never displayed before. I can't afford to trust my family's safety to a head of security who is suddenly behaving irrationally."

"Good grief."

Majid scowled. "The Shell deal happens in a few more days, so the timing of this could hardly be worse."

I dropped my eyes to the floor. "We'll leave today. I need to get back home anyway."

"Jamie, I really don't think that's a good idea. It's not safe for you yet, with this oil transaction so close. Maybe you could talk to your sister?"

"When will the deal be signed?"

"Well, the attorneys are still finalizing the documents, but they tell me—"

"There's not a firm date yet?"

"Only a few more days."

"Majid, no. We need to leave. What would I say to Lindsey? I can't tell her what to do—nobody can. If she is distracting your head of security, then it's time for us to go."

"I'm sorry, Jamie. I simply want to follow the safest course of action. Until the issue with these Russians has been solved, I will see to security arrangements for you and your sister back in the United States."

"In the US. How?"

He gazed at me mildly through his thick glasses with a hint of a smile.

I sighed and shrugged.

"Let's move past this," he said, straightening up and facing me across the desk. "These things will pass, and they have no bearing on the job offer I made you. That still stands. Whenever you are ready, there is a place for you at my Dubai newspaper."

"I appreciate that, Majid. I love Ocean City, and I can't imagine leaving it. Well, I couldn't have imagined leaving it before. Now I can imagine it. But I'm not sure if I could do it."

"You must follow your passions," he said. "Sometimes you can find them without leaving home but not usually."

"I will think about it. I promise."

"You are a strong woman. Never decide against something because you're afraid. Maybe a job in Dubai is not the thing for you—but find a way, somehow, to follow your passion. That is how to be truly alive."

I nodded and smiled.

"And now, please go back there and try to keep my daughter alive."

"If I can't rein in my sister, what makes you think I can have any influence on your daughter?"

"I think you must be a good influence on her."

"I hope so. But she's going to do what she wants."

"I'm afraid you're right. At any rate, I imagine your paths will cross again," he said vaguely. "Thank you for coming." He turned his attention to some papers on his desk. Meeting over.

53.

WENTY HOURS LATER, our Emirates flight landed at Dulles. Lindsey and I stood and stretched in the wide first-class aisle, and each of us opened the compartments over our respective seats to retrieve our carry-on bags.

I heard a familiar voice say to Lindsey, "Help you with that?"

I turned as she squealed and threw her arms around Mark. "What are you doing here?" she said, laughing and planting kisses all over his face.

"You think the Allyevs would put you ladies on a commercial flight with no security onboard?"

"Why couldn't you fly up here in first, with us?" She solicitously smoothed Mark's rumpled shirt.

"Certain sacrifices must be made in my line of work," he said. "Plus, I think Mr. Allyev was expressing his displeasure with me by booking me in coach. I had to bribe a flight attendant just to get a seat up near business. My ticket was for the center seat at the rear of the plane, in the row that doesn't recline because it backs up to the toilets."

I snickered and was grateful to Majid for making good on his promise to take care of our safety even back home. I was guessing that Lindsey was going to get 24/7 protection.

Mark took both of our bags, and we walked off the plane back into the lush green East Coast summer. My skin drank in the damp air, and I felt the sweat collect—and stay—on my forehead.

The phone rang and woke me out of the soundest sleep I think I'd ever had in my life. I was in my own bed, back home in Ocean City after the car service dropped Lindsey—and Mark—at her place in Baltimore. He promised he'd have eyes on me. Whatever that meant.

First-class flight aside, there's nothing quite as wonderful as hitting your own sheets after a vacation. If that's what my Dubai junket could be called.

I stretched an arm out and knocked a Sue Grafton paperback from my bedside table onto the floor, finally grabbing the phone.

"Hello?" I said, sounding like a smoker with a head cold thanks to the long flight and the drastic flip-flop from swampy humidity to desert and back again.

"Jamie, it's Terry."

"Oh hey, Terry. I'm back from a few days away, and my sleep schedule is kind of—well, I have no idea what time it is," I confessed.

"It's around eleven. How was your trip?"

"What?"

"Your trip? How was your trip?"

I swung my feet to the floor and ran a hand through my hair.

"Oh, uh, it was nice. Hey, are you out of jail?"

"Yeah, that's why I'm calling you. I just got out."

"That's great, Terry. So they dropped the charges?"

"Nah, they still haven't done that. But I made bail."

"I'm glad to hear it." If I recalled from my story notes, Terry was being held on a $500,000 bail.

"Yeah. Hey, I heard some Russian dudes got to you and your man down at Ocean Gateway."

"You heard all that, did you?"

"I'm up on the news, baby. Listen, you got my number in your phone now. You see them dudes again, you call me up. I'll be around."

"I appreciate that, Terry, but I'm sure you're going to want to keep a really low profile until your court date, right?"

"Don't worry about that. I'll be a'ight. And I'll be right here. Can't leave town anyhow."

"Oh, right, I guess you have to stay until your court date. Well, at least you'll get some more time at the beach," I said with a sarcastic chuckle.

"Man, fuck this place. Next summer Imma go to Dewey Beach."

A couple of hours later, I was dressed and awake, if a little bleary-eyed, and presenting myself at the front counter of the police station, notebook in hand. I wore a white peasant blouse with a pair of cream-colored pencil pants and a pair of simple, hand-tooled slip-on sandals, all from Dubai. Mrs. Allyev thought it strange that I chose these flat shoes rather than the blinged-out platforms and stilettos that women wear there. However, I thought the sandals were one of my most exotic purchases. I'd never seen anything like them in the States.

I was feeling jittery and out of sorts from the three big mugs of coffee I'd had already that morning.

Detective Morrison came out to greet me at the desk.

"Any further news that you can share for publication?"

"Yes, in fact," Morrison said. "We found new evidence that Leyla Dovzhenko was present in a hotel room on the boardwalk, next door to the Haunted House."

I feigned surprise. "Really?"

"Yes. Evidence suggests that Dovzhenko was killed in the hotel room, then dumped over the railing onto the terrace of the Haunted House."

"Who rented that hotel room?"

"We don't know," she said. I remembered the snapshot that I had taken of the hotel register, with plain-vanilla "Tony Jones" as the cash-up-front renter of apartment 2D. Not exactly helpful information.

"Right," I said.

She eyed me suspiciously. "Work with me, Jamie."

"I am," I assured her.

She watched me thoughtfully as I tucked my notebook in my purse. I met her gaze and offered a bland smile.

54.

ARE WE RUNNING A nail salon now?" I gazed around the redecorated newsroom, hand on hip. Donald was lounging behind a large Lucite desk, an aqua-colored polo shirt beautifully accentuating his summer tan.

Three smaller, matching Lucite desks were lined up on the left side of the room. The space had fresh, candy-striped carpeting, and an individual vase of shasta daisies graced the corner of each desk. The front window and door had been replaced with tinted glass, which actually was nice on a hot day like this.

"Welcome back, Jamie!" he said, ignoring my outburst. "How was Dubai? Did you love it? Did you shop? Take lots of pictures? I want every detail. After I give you an update on some new police information and you finish all the stories you left hanging, of course."

I ignored that jab, having no words of defense to offer.

"Dubai was, uh, I don't even know how to describe it. But Donald, where's my desk? Where's my stuff? I can't work on this thing! It's transparent, and it has no drawers."

"Minimalism, sweetie," Donald said. "It's very freeing. When you streamline your workspace, you streamline your mind."

"But what about my notes? My files? My emergency high heels?"

"I'm sure you'll find a creative solution."

I sat gingerly at my desk, trying to get comfortable in its delicate, matching office chair.

"Now let me fill you in on some pretty big news. You remember the body that was found in the Dough Roller dumpster?"

"Of course."

"Pending DNA confirmation, the police are naming Leyla Dovzhenko as the killer."

"Leyla killed two people?"

"It appears so. The victim's neck was broken. He had blood and skin fragments under his fingernails, and Leyla's arms had heavy scratches consistent with someone trying to fight her off."

"Do we know the victim's identity?"

"No, still no IDs on either body."

"Wow. This explains what happened that night. Three bad guys came after Zamina. They had the unfortunate luck to find only Leyla at home. Leyla dispatched one with a kitchen knife. The other two managed to get her into a car and drive over to the hotel on the boardwalk."

"Yes, that works. One to drive and the other to hold a gun on her."

"Exactly. They got her up to the hotel room—"

"How'd they get her through the lobby?"

"I think the lobby attendant was studiously ignoring them." I told Donald about Tammy's and my peek inside the old hotel and Tammy's anonymous tip to the police.

"Life is like a Dana Girls sleuthing adventure for you," Donald said.

"Well, yes! So they got upstairs, and somehow Leyla got the upper hand long enough to kill goon number two. But the last man standing shot her dead and threw her body across the Haunted House tracks—which would be fairly quick and easy because the hotel-room balcony is right there, and Leyla's small. He hauled henchman number

351

two back downstairs and through the lobby to the first dumpster he found."

Donald thoughtfully rubbed his chin. "That works. At the moment, though, OCPD is reconsidering the remaining three homicides of the summer: the two shootings outside that teen dance club in late June and the stabbing victim from around the same time."

"Who was that victim?" I asked. Both of us turned to our computer screens to check press releases and notes.

"Unidentified male, Caucasian, midforties," I read from my screen. "Dollars to doughnuts, this victim was Russian Mafia too."

"Leyla was a busy girl."

A few hours later, my stories were updated, my notes were archived in the new grass-green file cabinets lining the back wall, and my heels were stashed behind a potted plant. My desk was clean.

"You know, this is kind of liberating," I said to Donald.

"I knew you'd think so if you gave it half a chance," he said, smiling.

"I get it now. The real reason you drove your Acura through the window wasn't to save me from

Russian Mafia hit men. It was an excuse to collect the insurance money for a renovation."

"It was a happy coincidence, I assure you."

"But listen, you really should consider installing a pedicure chair up front."

"Watch it, Jamie. I might set you up as the nail tech."

Donald spent the next hour grilling me on every shop I visited in Dubai, every bite of five-star brunch I ate (well, the bites I remembered), and all the other sights, smells, and impressions I had of the shopping mecca of the world.

I didn't mention Majid's job offer, which made me wonder: was I sort of considering it?

My tummy started grumbling around seven p.m., as Donald was packing his canvas messenger bag to go home for the evening. As soon as he left, I called Sam. Privacy was as lacking as storage space with the chic new office layout.

"Good evening, Ocean Gateway International Student Services," Sam said. His voice was like a caramel in my mouth.

"That's an awful lot to say whenever you answer the phone," I said.

I could hear him smiling. "It is, but I don't want to be confused with Ocean Gateway Plumbing or Ocean Gateway Termite and Pest Control."

"Mmm, I see what you mean."

"Are you back?"

"I am."

"I'd like to see you," he said.

"I'm glad to hear that. I wasn't sure."

"The last couple of times we've met have been kind of... dramatic," he said.

"Yeah," I concurred. "I'm wondering, do you want to have dinner with me? A nice, normal dinner? I'll take you to my favorite place."

"What's your favorite place?"

"It's a surprise."

"If you insist." He chuckled. "Where shall I meet you?"

"Corner of Coastal Highway and Forty-Third, oceanside, eight o'clock. I'll be at an outside table."

55.

THE CROWDS ON A SUMMER Saturday night in Ocean City are monstrous. I knew there would be no hope for a table at eight if I went home first. I rooted around in my bottomless purse and pulled out my favorite faded cutoffs, stashed there in case I spilled ketchup on my fancy new pants. Know thyself.

I ducked into the back room and switched out the pencil pants for the shorts. A swipe of mascara, a spritz of hairspray, and a kiss of sparkly lip gloss, and I was out the door.

I hopped on a crowded southbound bus and hopped off near Forty-Third. I crossed the street at a light with a mob of other pedestrians and made my way to the line for On the Bay Seafood, the best damn crab shack in Ocean City. Best in the world, quite possibly.

After waiting in line for half an hour, I put in an order that would be perfect for two: all-you-can-eat steamed crabs, plus cole slaw, fries, and a pitcher of beer. It set me back more than a full day's salary, but it would be worth it.

Then I found the perfect spot for us at the far end of one of On the Bay's long, hand-built picnic tables. I was practically vibrating in anticipation— of Sam and of a crab feast.

I scanned the pedestrians crowding the sidewalk along Coastal Highway and did a double take when Terry Montgomery walked past. He clearly noticed me, but he kept walking. Coincidence? It's a fairly small town, but I was skeptical. Majid's got someone new on the payroll, I thought. I wondered if Terry was going to be tailing me all night. I wondered who else was.

I examined the crowd at the picnic tables around me. Had someone been placed in the crowd to protect me? Searched it again, because I knew I should also keep an eye out for someone trying to kill me. A voice spoke behind me with a heavy accent, and I jumped up with a yelp.

"What happened?" the waitress said, stepping back.

"I'm sorry. You startled me."

She smiled quizzically at me and unrolled a length of brown paper across the table. She set down the beer and a couple of cups. I poured a beer and told myself to knock it off.

At eight on the nose, the first load of hot crabs was dumped in the middle of the table, permeating the air with steam and Old Bay Seasoning. I breathed it in with delight, then glanced up to see Sam.

He was more impossibly handsome than I had remembered, wearing jeans and a faded sky-blue T-shirt. His dark hair was tucked behind his ears, and his eyes were dark and a million miles deep. Now he was looking disturbed. Dismayed, even.

"Sam! Hi! Hey! What? What's the matter?"

He opened his mouth to speak but couldn't find the words. He pointed at the crabs.

"What's wrong?" I picked up a crab and began pulling the legs off its body.

"I'm sorry."

"What?"

"I can't eat this."

"Oh no! You're allergic?"

"No."

"Don't know how to pick a crab?"

"No, I—"

"Wait, you don't like crabs? Not possible!" I snapped off a pincer on a meaty crab claw, and drew out a fat, juicy segment of claw meat.

"I'm a vegetarian." His eyes cut away from the table.

"Oh." My heart dropped into my shoes. "Oh no."

The pile of crustaceans steamed on the table, caked with pungent, orange Old Bay. I imagined myself in Sam's shoes.

I dropped the crab.

A family of five sitting farther down the long picnic table had stopped eating and was staring at us. I blushed to the roots of my hair.

"I'm sorry," he said. "I thought I told you. You know, when we had vegetarian pizza?"

"No." My eyes filled with tears of embarrassment. I willed them not to spill over. "You didn't. We just talked about how much we both like veggie pizza."

"Oh shit," he said, equally distressed.

"It's okay," I said, standing up from the picnic table. I plastered on a big smile. "Here!" My voice shook as I addressed the family. "You want some more crabs?"

The three kids yelled, "Yeah!" They scooped all the crabs over to their end of the table and dug in.

I turned back to Sam. I wanted to vanish. To die.

He bit his lip, then smiled at me resolutely. "Let's go," he said. "I'll make dinner."

56.

THE STAIRWAY LEADING UPSTAIRS from OGISS was dimly lit, but it was clean and freshly swept. I was completely tongue-tied, mortified, as I followed Sam up the stairs and he unlocked the door at the top. As we went through and he flipped on the lights, though, my face broke into a grin and our desperate awkwardness dissipated.

"I love this place," I said.

The apartment was tiny, but everything fit perfectly. One whole wall was lined with bookshelves, and a futon sat in front of them, with bedding and pillows tucked underneath. A heavy, low, round coffee table sat in front of it, with big cushions placed on either side instead of chairs. This was, apparently, the dining table. A surfboard leaned against the wall behind the front door.

"This reminds me a little bit of my old houseboat."

"Cool. Where was that?"

"Docked at the old cement plant."

"By the inlet?"

"Yes. A big housing development is going in over there now."

"Yeah, I've seen it. So you had to move when the developers came in?"

"Well, no. I had to move when somebody blew up the houseboat."

"Blew it up? On purpose?"

"Mmm-hmm."

"You lead an exciting life, Ms. August," Sam said, handing me a glass of wine. I took a sip, then he leaned in and kissed me. I kissed him back, relieved as hell that I didn't have Old Bay breath. I willed myself to keep it calm, keep it light. I was completely frazzled by the crab disaster and frightened by how much I cared what this guy thought of me.

After a moment he pulled away and gave me a gentle kiss on the nose. He walked over to the kitchen, which was simply a row of cabinets and appliances on the far wall. A counter-height table divided the space from the living room.

Sam put a pot of water on to boil and pulled out a box of linguine from the cupboard. A wide bowl of bright summer vegetables sat on the counter. He quickly chopped onions, tomatoes, peppers, zucchini, and garlic, then heated some olive oil in a cast-iron frying pan on the stove. He sipped from his wine glass as he worked.

I forced myself not to stare at his compact, slender frame as he chopped and stirred. I couldn't think of anything to say. My head was completely empty. Everything I could think of sounded ridiculous to my lovesick mental censor. What a mess.

I focused instead on his books. Most of them tugged at the part of my brain that catalogs items I ought to know about but don't: Stephen Mitchell's translation of The Bhagavad Gita, a Noam Chomsky omnibus, Thomas Friedman's The World is Flat, several travel narratives by Jan Morris, and a bunch of titles by Michael Pollan. Something about food.

Rich, oniony smells started wafting from the kitchen.

"So, tell me about Dubai," Sam said.

Finally! Something to say.

As Sam drained the pasta and dressed it with the fresh, simple vegetables, I recounted my Middle Eastern adventures. I even told him about the job offer.

We sat on the cushions at the low, round table and served ourselves from the big pasta bowl.

"It's a completely crazy idea, to go become a reporter in Dubai," I said, gesturing with a fork full of pasta. "This is delicious, by the way."

He grated Parmesan cheese over his plate. "Why do you think it's crazy?"

"Taking a news job in the Dubai? Seriously? My dad flipped out at the idea of me even setting foot in the Middle East. Can you imagine how he would feel if I moved there?"

"I can't really see you making decisions about your life based on what your dad would say."

"This is true. But seriously? I like my life here. I like my job. I love Ocean City. Why leave it?"

Sam tipped his head to one side and squinted a little, thinking. "It's hard to fully appreciate a place until you've experienced something different. Like I didn't appreciate the seasons until I lived somewhere without them. I didn't really get the natural beauty of the Eastern Shore until I saw other places. Maybe you know what I'm talking about."

"Yeah, maybe so."

He paused for a moment and took another bite. "Even with my family background, I didn't really see the freedoms we have in this country—or recognize the problems here, either—until I had spent some time somewhere completely else." His dark eyes were soft and serious.

"Thing is, Dubai doesn't exactly seem like a center of interesting cultural activity. Unless you're into shopping. It also doesn't seem like a place where I'd have much freedom as a reporter."

"That may be true, though you'd probably find that all kinds of cool things are happening somewhere over there. Somebody is doing something great pretty much everywhere," Sam said. "But regardless, it's a new experience. You'd learn about a culture that's completely different from America. Better or worse—who's to judge? And anyway, that doesn't matter. The point is, it's different. You'd learn about Dubai, and in the process you'd get a new perspective on America—and on journalism. So it would be a good thing."

"You've given this a lot of thought," I said, taking another sip of wine.

"Plus, maybe this thing in Dubai is a real reporting job. A chance to move on from the indignity of writing about church bake-offs for a freebie, weekly paper."

"That's what you really think of my job?" My buzz dropped away.

"I'm not insulting you, Jamie. You could just be reaching so much higher. You know what I'm saying."

"Nope," I said crisply, sitting up straight and tossing my napkin onto my plate. "Most of my stories are about small-town life and tourist events, but that is news here. You live here. You should know that. I write about the stuff that's actually happening around us, stuff people can relate to and use. I'll admit, for every real news story that comes along I have to cover a lot of damn charity bake sales. But that's what's happening here—current crime wave notwithstanding. And I love it."

I carried my plate to the sink.

Sam stood up from his cross-legged seated position in one fluid motion and cleared the remaining dinner dishes from the table.

I scooped up my purse. Hand on the doorknob, I said, "Thank you for dinner."

"You're going?"

"Long day tomorrow."

"Jamie. Stay for a while. I'm sorry for what I said about your job."

"Don't apologize. You said what you think. No shame in that."

I opened the door.

"Wait." He walked over and gently pushed it closed again. "Of course you can leave if you want. But first please let me try and explain."

We stood close. I felt every possible physical symptom of arousal and was really annoyed with my body for betraying my brain so completely.

"Why?" I said faintly.

"I don't understand."

"I don't get why I'm here. Why you want me here."

"Because I like you."

"Why?"

"Because you're beautiful. You're strong," he said, cupping my chin in his hand and kissing me.

"I come from a blue-collar Baltimore family, and my uncle is your slumlord," I said, taking a step away from him. "My favorite food is crabs, my favorite band is Bon Jovi, and my favorite beer is Coors Light. That's who I am, and I'm pretty cool with that. I'm learning new stuff all the time, but I'm never going to measure up, Sam. I'm never going to be the girl you want."

He put his hands gently, carefully on my shoulders. "Please don't go yet. Okay? Please?" He took my hand and led me to the futon, where I sat.

He went to the fridge and rummaged around. I heard bottles clinking, crisper drawers opening, and a few muttered curses.

"What are you doing?"

"I'll be right there."

Finally he plunked two cans of National Bohemian beer on the coffee table and sat next to me.

"I don't have any Coors Light."

I burst out laughing.

"Will this do?" He popped open one can and held it toward me for a toast. I popped the other one.

"They don't even make Nattie Boh in Baltimore anymore," I said. "You know that, right?" I clinked my can against his and took a swig.

"I think I've heard that."

"This is hipster swill," I said and put the can down.

"Can I please pour you a glass of white wine instead?"

"I guess."

He hopped up and pulled a bottle of white wine out of the fridge, quickly rinsed out our glasses from dinner, and carried everything back to the round table.

"Screw top! Now I'm starting to feel at home," I said, smoothing the fringes on my cutoffs against my bare legs.

"Actually, screw tops have a much lower failure rate than corks," Sam replied. "Plus, did you know that there is a serious shortage of cork trees? They're being overharvested."

He was focused on pouring our glasses, but I could see that he was trying to stifle a laugh.

I snickered.

He picked up the wine glasses, handing me one. We toasted again and sipped. Delicious. I drank the rest of it. Then I kissed him.

57.

THE CAST ON MY LEFT hand made me lean in awkwardly. Sam noticed and carefully raised the arm to kiss the inside of my wrist. "I'm so sorry you were hurt."

I used my right hand to begin pulling his shirt up over his chest. He pulled it off, and I traced a circle around the burn mark on his chest with a finger. I carefully kissed it. "I'm sorry they got you, too."

Sam lifted the billowy white blouse over my head and enfolded me in a warm, long, slow embrace. Our breathing synchronized, my inhales lining up with his exhales, our bellies rising and falling into one another. I became aware of every

inch of my skin in contact with his. When we
kissed again, our mouths opened and our breath,
teeth, tongues merged together. I didn't understand
why our bodies felt so easy and right, when everything else was such prickly drama.

He unhooked my lacy cotton bra and tossed it
far away, then lay me back on the futon. I reached
for his belt buckle as his fingers found the button
on my cutoffs. It felt like everything was moving a
mile a minute—I couldn't get to this man fast
enough. And at the same time, my brain was permanently registering every kiss, every touch, every
sound, recording it frame by frame by frame, forever in my memory.

He paused when we were down to panties and
boxer briefs.

"Jamie," he said.

I murmured something as I kissed him again.

"Jamie," he said again, rising up on one elbow
and gazing down at me.

"Sam," I breathed.

"I want to make love to you," he said.

"Yes yes yes yes," I said, encircling his neck with
my good arm and drawing him toward me again.
He resisted.

"Jamie."

I forced myself to stop. "Yes?"

"We've been drinking. Kind of a lot. Including some Nattie Boh."

I giggled.

"I don't want to take advantage of you. Are you sure you want this?"

"I do. It's stupid how much I want you. Right now. I will want you again when I'm stone sober at two tomorrow afternoon. I promise."

"Good. Tomorrow at two," he said. "Now, stand up."

"Wait, what?"

"Get up for a second."

He had gotten to his feet and extended a hand to help me up. I stood awkwardly. Sam walked over and turned the light switch off. A little bit of light from the street filtered in through the window blinds. I watched the light glance off the muscles in his back and his arms as he quickly unfolded the futon to its flat position and spread the sheets into place. He lit a candle, sat on the futon, then held out a hand to me.

"Come to bed with me."

I stood by the side of the futon and watched him watch me as I slowly, slowly slid my panties down the curve of my hips, smooth and tight from all that running. I lowered myself onto him, and

373

the single candle cast a shadow of our naked bodies joining together.

58.

ZAMINA STRETCHED AND YAWNED, *relishing the feel of the snowy, one thousand-thread-count sheets on her bare skin. She glanced out the window at the New York skyline, sparkling in the late morning sun.*

"André? André, habibi, where you go?" she called plaintively, using the Arabic version of baby. She didn't speak much Arabic, but it was the sexiest term of endearment she knew.

"Hold up, Z," she heard him call from the living room of the hotel suite. A crescendo of video-game gunfire echoed off the walls and into the bedroom, then subsided.

André sauntered into the bedroom, jeans riding way lower than his Calvin Klein briefs. The heavy rope of gold around his neck emphasized the worked-out bulk of his chest.

"Whatchu want, baby?" he said, sitting on the edge of the bed and running a finger along her jawline.

"You know what I want," Zamina replied.

André smiled and began to unbutton his fly. "You want some Sniper Trigga."

"I want breakfast," she said.

"Oh, Imma give you a real nice breakfast," he said, dropping his jeans and crawling under the sheets.

Zamina rolled her eyes. "No. Breakfast. Smoked salmon, caviar, Champagne, like every day."

André reached for Zamina and tried to pull her on top of him.

"Stop your hands! You think I am Russian whore?" she yelled.

"No, baby. You're from Azerbaijan." He threw her a brilliant white grin.

"Don't touch me!" she shrieked. She stormed out of bed, threw her shoulders back to present every inch of her perfect, naked self, then flounced into the master bathroom. She heard André's languid chuckle.

Zamina slammed the door and turned on the taps to fill the soaking tub. She also picked up the remote and clicked on MTV, loud. The wall-mounted flat screen vibrated over the tub, and Beyoncé echoed off the marble walls of the massive room.

Half an hour later, André opened the door and rolled a room service breakfast cart into the bathroom, together with three dozen red roses.

Zamina was arranged prettily in the tub, in a sea of fragrant bubbles. She dropped her eyes and gazed up at André through thick lashes. "André! For me?"

"For you, baby."

"Habibi..." She stood up in the tub, a queen rising from the bubbles. She embraced him, kissing him hotly. "Come into bath with me."

A moment later, the rap star and the oil tycoon's daughter were entwined in the soaking tub. André popped the Champagne cork, while Zamina beheaded the roses, one by one, sprinkling the petals in the bathwater.

59.

"OGISS IS LEGIT, Uncle Abe," I said, leaning back in a blue vinyl easy chair that had probably been tossed out during a dental clinic renovation in the mid-'80s. "It's a busy office that's been in operation for several years, and the tenant is keeping the property in good shape."

Abe sat behind an enormous, battered wooden desk. Late morning sun spilled across its vast surface, which was littered with files, receipts on a spindle, a giant plastic pen in lime green ("for signing big deals," the barrel read), an aging PC, and a framed picture of a much younger Abe leaning against a boxy, gold Lincoln Continental.

The office was on the second floor above Beach Getaway Rentals, a tableau in threadbare low-pile carpet and fake wood paneling. It hadn't been updated since any of Abe's rental properties had been. Which was to say, never. Well, except for Merv and Dot's favorite, Sunrise Paradise. Burn one of Abe's buildings to the ground and he might consider renovating.

"Huh. Did you check this Ocean Gateway outfit with the Better Business Bureau?"

I guffawed. "No. Are you aware of what the Better Business Bureau has to say about Beach Getaway Rentals?"

"Yeah, well, people complain about everything," Abe complained. "I mean, what do they want from me, fer crissake? Valet parking and solid gold bathroom fixtures in every bayside shack? Huh?"

"I don't know," I said, hoping this wouldn't turn into an extended bitchfest about the never-ending string of damages and vandalism that tarnishes Abe's otherwise faultless portfolio of real-estate holdings. "Anyway, Uncle Abe. I, uh... I've gotten to know the owner of Ocean Gateway."

"Oh yeah?"

"Yeah." Did I really want to go there?

"I think I'm falling in love." Ah shit. I went there. True Confessions with Uncle Abe.

Abe's weathered, sun-spotted face creased into a nicotine-stained grin that would have frightened a small child. "Jamie! Seems like you've always got some lucky guy on the hook, sweetheart, but I've never heard you throw around that word."

"I know. Maybe it's not love yet, exactly. ..." I felt my face flush. I stared down at my lap, fussing with the hem of my floral sundress.

"So who is this guy? He's a business owner. We know that—that's good," Abe said, leaning back in his executive office chair with a deafening squeak.

"He's a first-generation American. His father is Lebanese and his mother is Lithuanian. He grew up in Rockville."

"Rockville. Hmm, okay." I could see Abe's brain calculating, his worldview revolving around zip codes and property values.

"He's ... I don't know. He's smart."

"Well, I would hope so."

"No, I mean, come on Abe. I date lifeguards and firefighters. They're all superbrave and hot, and I'm not saying they've all been idiots, but we don't sit around drinking wine and having discussions about international politics. You know what I'm saying?"

He reluctantly shrugged acquiescence.

"But this guy makes me think. Sometimes he makes me really mad, too. He kind of drives me nuts. But he makes me wonder about the world, consider things in ways I never have before."

Abe reached across the desk, the chair screeching, and patted my hand. "Sounds like you're in it deep, my girl. Meanwhile, don't you worry. I won't evict the guy."

From Abe's office I went directly to Sam's. His eyes raked my body with undisguised lust as the bell jingled on the door. I walked straight up to his desk, my high-heeled sandals clicking on the wood floor. Every student's head turned to stare, but I didn't take my eyes off Sam.

"It's two o'clock," I said, leaning on his desk.

"We're closed for lunch," Sam announced. A couple of students groaned in protest. "You can Skype later. Go outside. Get some sun." He briskly ushered several stragglers out.

When the last of them had packed up and left, he flipped the sign on the door to "Closed," and we rushed up the stairs to his apartment. The fingers of my right hand fumbled with his button fly as he unlocked the door. He put an arm around my waist and held me tight, backing me into the room. We must have looked like a couple of hot-blooded ball-room dancers.

He kicked the door closed behind him and guided me across the floor to the coffee table, pushing me gently down onto it. He kneeled in front of me and discovered that I had completely failed to put on panties that day. Only a swingy cotton sundress separated me and my birthday suit from the big, wide world.

He ran his hands up the insides of my thighs and lowered his head to me. I sighed with pure pleasure. My mind, my body, my whole self let down every defense. I thought, this is the real thing. This is the guy.

The intensity of our lovemaking would have col-lapsed a lesser coffee table, but this one held up well. Afterward, Sam made us cucumber and cheese sandwiches, and we sat and ate them right where we'd done the deed.

60.

SAM AND I PARTED WAYS with a long kiss on the sidewalk. The bell tinkled on the door as he went back to work and I began walking toward the bus stop. An OC police cruiser drove slowly past. The Russian-speaking Peter Lapin sat behind the wheel. His eerie blue eyes followed Sam through the door, then bored into me as he rolled past. The Crown Vic continued down the block and turned the corner.

Was this a coincidence? Was he following me? Watching Sam or the OGISS office, hoping to get his hands on Zamina? Detective Morrison may have thought I was crazy, but I suspected Peter Lapin was the rotten apple in the OCPD barrel.

A black Yukon with tinted windows passed me as I walked around the corner. My brain was swirling with police-corruption conspiracy theories until I heard the huge, coughing thuds of automatic gunfire and window glass hitting concrete. I pressed myself against the side of a clapboard apartment house in terror, my heart banging in my chest.

The low rumble of the idling SUV echoed down the quiet street for what seemed like an eternity, but was probably three minutes, max. Then the crunch of sneakers on glass, and Yuri's voice—which would be imprinted forever into my brain after the finger-breaking episode—barking some kind of order in Russian.

I heard a couple of preteen girls chatting, and I turned to see them sauntering up behind me. They were laughing and eating ice cream sandwiches. I swept them up against the wall with my casted arm, shushing them with a quiet, urgent sound. My expression must have told them this was serious. One of them dropped her ice cream.

I heard a heavy car door slam and tires pealing out, then silence.

I turned to the girls. "Run back the way you came, and call 911."

"About what?"

"A drive-by shooting, black Yukon, three Russian guys in their forties. Call from a pay phone, give the information and then hang up. No names."

"For real?" Both girls gasped. Their initial excitement was replaced by mortal dread. I could see it in the girls' eyes. They knew I was telling them to make sure nobody could trace the tip back to them.

The girls ran off the way they had come.

I peeked my head around the corner and saw glass all over the sidewalk in front of Ocean Gateway. I ran over and yanked on the office door. The bottom of its frame had swung shut against so much broken glass on the sidewalk that it was wedged closed. I pulled so hard that the bell on the hinge fell off with a clank.

Glass shards glittered in the sunlight and bullet holes riddled the back wall. Sam's computer had been tipped backward onto the floor, the screen smashed. The afternoon breeze blew in through the open front of the office. It was eerily quiet.

Abject terror drove me through the doorway into the small kitchenette and storage area in the back. It was empty. A fresh carafe of coffee was gurgling; the back door was open. Sam's Subaru was parked neatly in the small parking area.

A hot breeze ruffled my hair, and a seagull cawed. Where was Sam? Had the Russians taken him?

I heard police sirens in the distance. I stepped down from the back stoop and ran away from the building. Some kind of autopilot led me blindly down the alleyway between the buildings behind Ocean Gateway. I was vaguely aware that I was weeping as I ran, taking in gulps of air so big that I was beginning to see stars in front of my eyes.

Suddenly, arms grabbed me and pulled me into a doorway. A hand closed over my mouth, blocking my scream. I was pushed against a wall in a dark back hallway. I squeezed my eyes shut. This was it: death at the hands of the Russian Mafia.

"Jamie," I heard whispered in my ear.

I opened my eyes, saw Sam's beautiful face, and moaned with relief. "We have to stay quiet, okay?" I nodded. I covered his face in wet, teary kisses.

"How did you get away?" I whispered.

"I was making coffee, heard the bullets, and ran out the back door before they even finished driving by."

"It wasn't a drive-by," I said. "They trashed your office."

"Oh, great." He leaned against the wall and ran a hand through his hair. "What the hell do they want with me?"

"Maybe they wanted the file you have for Zamina?"

"For what? They've already got her address. What the hell?"

"Who knows? Could be they're trying to clean up loose ends. You and I are loose ends."

We stood in the hallway until I caught my breath and we were ready to venture back into the alley. We eased out into the sunlight and began retracing our steps to the back of Sam's office—and his car.

We got halfway down the block and heard the crunch of tires on gravel, a vehicle turning into the alley behind us. We ducked behind a couple of dumpsters. A glimpse through the narrow space between the two metal boxes revealed a flash of blue and white. An OCPD cruiser was inching past the dumpster. I felt Sam shift but tugged urgently on his arm and silently shook my head.

The low rumble of the heavy car continued down the block and around the corner.

"That cop rolled past me as I was leaving your place," I said. "Peter Lapin is his name. He speaks Russian. I don't trust him."

"You don't trust him because he speaks Russian?"

"He speaks Russian, and he slowed down to watch you walk into OGISS, then a minute later an SUV full of Russian Mafia shot up your office."

"Those things may be unrelated," Sam said, but he didn't sound convinced.

"Coincidence, my ass."

"Maybe Zamina was right not to trust the cops," Sam said. "Maybe that wasn't knee-jerk former-Soviet paranoia. Maybe she actually knew something about an OC cop—or cops."

"Shit. We've got to get out of here."

"Where should we go?"

I paused, squinted in thought, then inspiration struck. "I have an idea."

61.

THRIFTY-BUY LOOMED before us, and Sam groaned in dismay. "I'm not going in there."

"Come on. We don't have a lot of options right now."

Sam radiated outrage and fumed from the front door (where he scowled at the greeter) to the Sporting Goods section. "Thrifty-Buy is the embodiment of everything that's wrong with this country."

A young mother passing us with a toddler in her shopping cart glared at Sam.

"Yes, I know, you told me that already," I said, moving Sam farther down the aisle. "How about this tent? It's an igloo. Those are nice."

"Well, it bears repeating. Aren't you afraid we're going to get shot in here?"

"What? How could Yuri have tracked us here? I'm sure we gave them the slip when we caught the Park & Ride shuttle over the bridge to West Ocean City."

"I'm not talking about Yuri. Idiots and young children are always picking up guns in Thrifty-Buy and accidentally shooting people in the head."

Fortunately the woman was at the other end of the aisle and seemed to have missed that last remark.

"Then let's get this done, okay? You choose the camping stuff. I'll go pick out a change of clothes. I'll meet you over by the food."

I chose a pair of green terry-cloth running shorts and a three-pack of tank tops, along with a pair of knockoff Converse low tops.

I pulled out my phone behind a rack of teddy bear-themed sleep shirts and called Uncle Abe.

"Abe, there's a little problem over at OGISS."

"I don't like the sound of that."

"You're not going to like any of this. Some Russian mobsters are gunning for one of Sam's stu-

dents, and they shot up your building this afternoon."

"Ah Christ. Did I call this one or what? I knew
that place was gonna be trouble."

"It's not Sam's fault. It's about the girl. I know
her parents—"

"This the family you and Lindsey went to visit
in Dubai? Your mom and dad were real worried
about you."

"Yeah, that's them. And the trip was fine—I was
safer there than here, that's for sure. Anyway, I
know they're good for the cost of a replacement
window."

"I would say so."

"Right. So Sam and I are getting out of town for
a few days."

"Are you safe?"

"I'm fine, Abe. Don't worry about it. But you
might want to get down there to make sure the
cops don't make an even bigger mess of the place,
and get some new glass in the window."

"I'll call Donny, my glass guy. I don't want that
place sitting open all night."

"Thanks, Abe."

I found Sam losing his mind in the cereal aisle.
"Hey, good news—"

"They're all GMO," he said, stretching his arms wide and glaring at the rows of cereal boxes.

"Maybe not the best selection, but hey, I spoke to—"

"Not the best selection? Really? Every cereal here has genetically modified ingredients—and look! Only this one has no sugar."

He was hot and all, but the guy was really starting to get on my nerves. "Then get that one."

"Do you really want to eat genetically modified wheat?"

"You are losing it, Sam," I said, dropping the box of unsugared cereal in the cart. "Let's get you out of here."

He stopped and seemed to catch himself and laughed ruefully. "I guess I'm a little stressed."

"You are a hot mess," I said and kissed him hard. He pulled me to him. I wrapped my leg around him and instantly felt the start of a hard-on against my thigh.

"Do you people mind?" The woman with the toddler trundled her shopping cart past. The child stared at us.

In a dented toilet stall in the Thrifty-Buy bathroom I changed out of my sundress and high-heeled sandals, marveling at the difference a few days could make. This time last week, I'd been trying on haute couture with an oil tycoon's wife in Dubai.

Sam and I figured out how to put together the tent and stake it. Then Sam built a fire and opened cans to put together a stew in our new Dutch oven. As the sun set over Frontier Town campground, water park and family-entertainment center on the Sinepuxent Bay, we set up the rest of our new camping supplies. We were lucky: there was a last-minute cancellation that allowed us to squeeze into a spot by the water's edge. Our site was shady and felt a little secluded from the busy campground.

Sam dumped our stuff on the ground, not even noticing the pretty view.

"It's the first time I have ever spent a single dime in that place." The man would not shut up about Thrifty-Buy.

I rolled my eyes and stuffed our new sleeping bags into the tent, scratched a mosquito bite on my hand, inside the top edge of my cast, and tucked a bra strap back onto my shoulder. "Baby, we're not going to save the world tonight. Let's just get out of this alive."

Sam stared through the leafy canopy at the last of the sun glinting on the water, tension etched on his forehead. He had been quick and smart at putting together all the gear we needed and squeezing it into backpacks, and cheerful about hiking through cornfields to avoid the roads between the shopping center and the campground. Once the urgency had passed, though, his sour mood returned. Still, I knew a good thing when I saw it: I couldn't have made it there without him. I knelt down next to him on the ground by the fire and kissed him on the cheek. His face softened fractionally, and he turned and kissed me back.

I stood up and crossed to the other side of the site, away from the food Sam was preparing, and squirted myself with bug spray. There is nothing more lovely, or mosquito-infested, than a Maryland sunset in the summertime. I opened up a couple of beers—Coors Light, thank you very much—and handed one to Sam. He was still a little cranky, but I could see he was easing up.

After a vegetable and bean stew dinner at our campsite's picnic table, I pulled out my cell phone and dialed the long string of numbers to connect me to Majid Allyev's Dubai office.

"Jamie, how are you?" Majid's deep, calm voice sounded stressed.

"I'm doing okay, but things aren't going so great here in Ocean City."

I told him about the drive-by shooting at OGISS, and how Sam and I had been reduced to hiding out from Russian mobsters in a western-themed campground on the outskirts of town.

"I am sorry, really. I assure you, I have people working on this right now," Majid said, sounding genuinely pained.

"Yeah, I know who you have working on this. Terry Montgomery might be good security for a rap artist in a club, but can he really go up against the Russian mob?"

"Terry has military experience—and he was good enough to inspire Leyla's trust."

"And Mark is working with him from Baltimore?"

"They're working together, yes."

I sighed. "Okay, Majid. Listen, we seem to be safe for the moment. But my friend Sam has a business to run, and of course I have my work too. We can't walk away from our everyday lives. This has got to stop. We are in way over our heads here, and none of this business has anything to do with us."

"I understand, Jamie, and I'm sorry. The dates have firmed up. The deal will be signed in three days. After that, my daughter will no longer be a target. The Russians will have no further interest in her, in you, or anyone else associated with this entire unfortunate incident."

I threw up a hand in exasperation. "So we need to lay low until... when? How will we know when it's safe?"

"Watch the news."

"Can you be a little more specific here, Majid? I mean we're—" My phone beeped, the sound indicating the call had ended.

"Did he hang up on me?" I stared at the phone, then redialed the number. An electronic voice informed me that I had exceeded my monthly credit allowance and invited me to go online and select an enhanced plan. Huh. I guess cell phone calls to Dubai really add up quick.

I sighed, feeling completely defeated. I chucked my useless cell phone into my purse and put my head down on the picnic table. The crickets and cicadas started up their evening racket, and the bay lapped gently at the shoreline.

62.

LATE IN THE NIGHT, long after Sam's breathing evened into a gentle, quiet rhythm, I lay awake next to him, listening to the night noises. The August family had never been into camping. Whenever we came down to OC for our summer vacation, we'd stay at a motel or one of Uncle Abe's rentals—which was roughing it, maybe, but in a different way.

I listened for footfalls, or vehicles rolling into our section of campground. I stared out the tent screening, but all I saw was the occasional firefly. I heard a baby crying somewhere, and the squeak and echo of the bathhouse door, softened by the leafy trees between here and there. I couldn't get comfortable, with every stick and pebble under the tent grinding into my spine. As the night wore on, my eyes and ears started playing tricks on me. I was sure I heard a rustle in the underbrush near us. I knew they had found us. They were coming for us. They'd break the rest of my fingers, then move to the more essential parts of my anatomy.

"Wake up, Jamie."

My eyes flew open and I gasped, blinking in the bright morning light.

"You were having a bad dream." Sam reached over and pulled me tightly against him. "You were kicking me."

"I thought they were coming after us."

"Shhh. It's okay. It's just me and you."

The sounds of a squalling child and some quarreling teenage siblings drifted in from the next campsite. Didn't sound like just us to me.

I buried my head in his shoulder, exhausted.

"How do people do this?"

"Do what?" Sam smoothed my hair behind one ear.

"Camp."

"What do you mean?"

"I mean, I didn't sleep at all."

"Yes you did. I just woke you up."

"Yeah, but I fell asleep five minutes before that. And there's a big rock under my ass."

Sam made a big production of feeling around on the ground and then groping my ass. "I don't feel any rocks."

I felt about as sexy as a trucker on day six of a long haul.

"I need to brush my teeth." I dragged my hands through my hair and unzipped my sleeping bag.

"I'll make us some coffee."

"Oh thank God."

Later, fortified with unsweetened cereal that tasted like shards of cardboard, with boxed almond milk and lots of strong coffee, I felt I might survive the day.

We tidied up camp and went for a walk around the campground. Every other campsite seemed to be filled with families, mostly with young children. The roads around the camp were swarming with squadrons of kids on bikes and trikes, while parents chatted across from one site to the next: extended family or friends taking their summer vacations together.

I remembered that our Ocean City trips usually happened at the same time as our Pittsburgh family's vacations. All of us kids roamed the streets and the boardwalk in packs, usually with me and my cousins Sarah and Jennifer trailing around behind Lindsey and their ultracool older brother, Scott. The two of them were supposed to be watching us, but usually they would park us in front of Skee-Ball at one of the boardwalk arcades and sneak away to hang out in front of the Purple Moose Saloon. I knew this because once I followed them. (My investigative instincts started early.) They were too young to get in so they hung out front on the boardwalk, smoking cigarettes and listening to the bands playing inside.

It was still early enough in the day for Sam and me to stake out two poolside lounge chairs. I made sure they were strategically located next to the bar.

"Wake me when it's noon and I can start drinking." I cranked my lounge chair flat and promptly fell asleep.

Several hours later, I was stuffing fried appetizers into my mouth and downing them with strawberry margaritas.

"Cheese stick?" I offered the plate to Sam.

"No thanks," Sam said, typing away on his smartphone.

"What are you doing?"

"Answering e-mails."

"Oh. Not me. It's my policy: when I'm on the run and being chased by Russian hit men, I don't check e-mail." My straw made a rude slurping noise as I hit the bottom of margarita number three. "You gotta draw the line somewhere or people take advantage of you." Sam glanced over at me, eyed my cup.

"I'm getting another. Want one?" I stood up, slightly unsteady.

"No thanks. Hey, go easy, okay?"

"Why? We're in exile at Frontier Town. Drinking seems like our best option."

"Well, I'm trying to run a business here," he said irritably. "Not so easy when I can't go to my office. Anyway the place was probably looted and trashed last night, with the window broken wide open."

"Oh, did I forget to mention? Sorry 'bout that. Your window was fixed last night."

"What?"

"I took care of it. No worries."

"What do you mean, you took care of it?" He sounded even more agitated. Guy seriously needed to chill.

"I mean, you got a new window. My uncle is your slumlord now, remember?"

"Oh, great. How much is that going to set me back?"

"Nothing. I told Abe what happened, and he said he'd cover it. I'm sure I can get Majid to reimburse him."

"When did you do this?"

"Yesterday afternoon, while you were having a meltdown in the cereal aisle. I tried to tell you, but you were flipping the fuck out about genetically modified wheat."

Sam sputtered for another second, then shook his head. He smiled at me, shading his eyes against the afternoon sun. "Thank you."

"You're welcome. Margarita?"

He stopped resisting. "Yes please."

63.

WE SPENT THE REST of the afternoon on the waterslide and the lazy river. We goofed off with the mostly under-ten crowd, and got a little frisky in the shade of the giant covered wagon that's beached in the middle of the swimming pool. We spent two hours over dinner at the Lazy River Saloon restaurant and shot a few rounds of pool in the arcade. When the ten o'clock news came on, we abandoned our table midgame and sat in front of the television.

A third of the way into the newscast, we heard what we were listening for.

Shell Oil will be concluding a deal to purchase oil rights in a large, strategically valuable portion of the

Caspian Sea, in Azerbaijan, a former Soviet state. The current rights holder, Azeri businessman Abdulmajid Allyev, will pocket $15 billion in the deal. Russian business leaders are outraged that an American oil company will control such a significant portion of Caspian Sea oil reserves. However, the government of Azerbaijan has approved the deal, which is scheduled to be signed at Shell's headquarters in Houston two days from now.

"Fifteen billion dollars," Sam said, whistling.

"No wonder the Russians were so hot to get their hands on Zamina."

I pointed again to the screen, as the newscast turned to more local events. "Hey, that's André."

Atlantic City is bracing for an appearance late tonight by rap artist and music producer Sniper Trigga. Three shootings and a stampede marked his last appearance two nights ago at a concert venue in the Bronx, and officials in the beach resort of Ocean City, Maryland, say that he is a person of interest in a murder investigation there. Meanwhile, local authorities in Atlantic City are preparing for the worst.

The newscast cut to a shaky-cam clip of the tall, chiseled André. He was strutting across a large club stage, his neck and fingers heavy with gold, gesturing and encouraging an audience that was already clearly out of control and beginning to stampede.

The newscast cut to an interview with André in a tour bus. "My shows can get a little wild. The club gotta be ready for my fans. They already know this. If they ain't ready for it..." He waved his hand dismissively and shook his head.

People are lining up now to get into Sniper Trigga's sold-out show in Atlantic City tonight, but so far the crowd has been orderly. We'll keep you posted as things develop.

"What an asshole," Sam said.

"He and Zamina make the most perfect, horrible couple."

We finished the game of pool, then walked back toward our tent, holding hands in the darkness under the trees. About fifty feet from the campsite, I froze in my tracks, squeezing Sam's hand tightly. A figure all in black stepped out of the stand of trees by our tent, leaves and twigs snapping underfoot.

"They found us," I breathed.

We backed into the woods and made our way quietly out of the campsite. When we reached the main road, we followed it south. We stayed off the blacktop itself, keeping back in the tall grasses and cornfields, the silence crackling with our tension and fear. Once, we spotted headlights and flattened ourselves to the ground until the car had passed. It was a white sedan, heading back the way we had come, but still.

After what felt like forever but was probably more like an hour, we reached a bridge across the water.

"This is the bridge to Assateague Island," I said.

Sam pulled up short. "Should we go?"

"Sure, I guess. There's nothing else around here."

"There's nothing on Assateague, either."

"Sure there is," I said brightly. "Wild ponies!"

We set out across the bridge at a quick pace. I felt exposed out in the open, in the moonlight. Soon enough we had crossed the span of the Assateague bridge. Not a car had passed us in either direction. The Atlantic surf pounded against the far shore of the wild barrier island, and the sand dunes glowed in the moonlight. I felt oddly safe here, sheltered. Sam seemed to be feeling a different vibe too. He put his arm around me as we walked.

Soon we slowed to a stop on the road. I was so tired it felt like my knees would buckle.

"What are we going to do now?"

"We're going to sleep," Sam said decisively.

"Where?"

"In the dunes." He took my hand and led me off the road and into the sand. We practically fell onto a soft spot behind a clump of dune grass, and I sank into a deep, black, dreamless sleep.

64.

WOKE UP with a yelp. A wild pony gently snuffled at my foot, his mane brushing against my leg. It gazed at me with mild brown eyes, then wandered off. I got to my feet and shook the sand out of my hair and clothes. But I couldn't shake the grains wedged inside my cast. My eyes felt gritty. The early morning sun was already beating down on us, causing sweat to trickle down my back, despite the relentless ocean winds. I swatted at a fly that seemed determined to enter my right nostril. My hair tangled and whipped at my face.

Assateague felt so much more wild and exposed to the elements than Ocean City, even though you can see the shores of Assateague from the Ocean

City inlet. Even apart from the wild ponies wandering around all over the place, the city girl in me always got a little panicky there. I never did well with the island's voracious mosquitoes and other swarming, buzzing creatures. There were no buildings to block the wind, no nightly beach grooming, and no annual sand replenishment to keep the shoreline smooth and flat. Made me nervous.

Sam was nowhere in sight, but I followed his footprints toward the sound of the surf, and found him on the beach. He sat lounging in a canvas chair in a circle with five campers, drinking coffee from a tin cup. He seemed surprisingly rested and carefree. I tried to smooth my greasy, sandy hair off my forehead, but it was hopeless. I must have looked like Medusa.

"Hey, you must be Jamie." As I approached, a white guy with massive dreadlocks stuck his hand out. "I'm Lars." I shook his hand uncertainly.

"Here, babe, have some coffee," a wild-haired blond woman said, handing me a cup. "I'm Melinda."

"Thank you," I said, taking the little mug in both hands like it was the Holy Grail. I drank the rich brew, suddenly oblivious to the sand flies and the wind.

The sliding door on the side of the group's VW bus screeched open, and a deeply tanned girl with a short, choppy haircut jumped out, a griddle and a plastic Tupperware container in hand.

"Pancakes?"

Her friends cheered as the girl knelt down to the camp stove, a massive, dented army surplus thing. One burner was already fired up and keeping the coffee warm. She expertly lit another burner, set up the iron griddle, and a few minutes later, began pouring circles of pancake batter.

A guy with dark, buzz-cut hair sat on the sand strumming a guitar. A heavyset woman in a peasant-style sundress smiled peacefully as she sat in a camp chair and gazed at the surf. Melinda sat on Dave's lap and they shared a giant, smelly spliff.

Had we hit some kind of time warp when we crossed the 611 bridge to Assateague?

We chowed down on warm and fluffy—if slightly gritty—pancakes on the windy beach. After breakfast, more stogie-sized spliffs got passed around the circle of camp chairs.

I got higher than I'd ever been in my life—though that wasn't saying much. Pot wasn't usually my style. I preferred to party with fruity cocktails.

The guy with the buzz cut and the guitar, Fidel, strummed what I guessed must be Grateful Dead tunes while Heather, the woman in the sundress, sang soulfully and wildly off-key. Or maybe she wasn't off-key. I'm a Bon Jovi girl. What do I know about the Grateful Dead?

A white pony ambled past us, his mane sparkling and bright in the sun. A single horn glowed at the perfect center of his forehead. My mind broke into a blissful smile. I took another hit and passed the spliff, then stood up and swayed with joy in the perfect morning.

The group clapped and cheered. "You're a beautiful being," Heather called out. Fidel's strumming grew louder. I pulled Sam, laughing, out of his camp chair to sway with me on the beach. We plunged into the surf, and I pulled off my tank top, hurling it out to sea. Sam put his arms around me—for modesty, or maybe it was a gesture of pure love.

"You got your cast wet," he said, turning his head to look at my hand on his shoulder.

"Oops."

We both cracked up.

He carried me out to where the water held most of my weight. I felt light and in love. I released my hold around Sam's neck and pulled his shirt off. He tried to protest but was laughing too hard to fight the amorous sea monster I had become.

I locked eyes with him as I threw his T-shirt out to sea. We shared a deep, salty kiss. I hooked one arm around his shoulders and used the other to pull off my shorts. I eased away and threw these out of reach, Sam trying unsuccessfully to stop me.

"I'm free like a sea creature!" I lay naked on the surface of the water. I was a starfish, feeling the sun on my wet skin and gazing at the perfect blue sky. I smiled and inhaled the beauty of the day.

Then a little ripple washed over my face, and I sucked seawater into my nose and mouth. I sputtered and choked. Sam pulled me to him and carried me out of the water as I coughed and hacked uncontrollably.

Our new pals howled with laughter. Then they raided their backpacks and gave me some new clothes.

A couple of hours later, I regained consciousness on the sand, feeling the sun dry my hair into endless brackish knots. The salt on my skin itched, and the sand flies buzzed and bit incessantly. I lay there. I couldn't think of any reason to move.

"Hey."

Somewhere, I imagined someone was trying to get my attention. I felt a fly land on my nose. Fascinating.

"Hey, Jamie. Hey, Sam." Vaguely, I noticed that someone was nudging my leg with their foot. I heard Sam stir beside me. I considered the possibility of opening my eyes.

"Oh, hey. I guess we fell asleep," Sam said. The other voice chuckled, and finally I recognized it as belonging to Dreadlock Lars. I opened my eyes into tiny, squinty slits and peeked at Sam. He seemed pretty rough, with sand stuck in his two-day stubble. He was still shirtless and his nose was sunburnt and peeling.

"You guys were so baked," Lars said, flopping on the sand next to us.

I struggled up to my elbows and forced my eyes into focus. "What the fuck did we smoke?"

"Purple Passion, man," he said, giggling.

I noticed red welts rising on my arms and legs: angry, itchy bug bites. I had on a pair of threadbare board shorts and a macramé halter top that looked like potholder squares.

The cast on my hand was soaked through and ruined. Some poor sea creature was probably out there choking on my polyester running shorts.

"Thanks—I mean, to all of you guys—for the clothes," I said, stumbling over my words and blushing an even deeper red than my skin must already have been.

Lars giggled again. "It was our pleasure."

65.

HAT AFTERNOON, SAM tried to talk me into negotiating a trade with these guys: our apartment keys for their VW bus.

"That's a pretty good deal for them," I said, eyeing the ancient vehicle, vividly decorated with what seemed to be house paint.

"We could just drive off together," Sam said to me as we sat in the sand, the wind keeping the flies down to a somewhat tolerable level. "We'll head to the Florida Keys and get lost." He pulled me into a warm, mellow hug.

"Nah, that wouldn't be safe," I said. "I have an ex-boyfriend down there with a gambling problem.

He's got a history of ratting me out to the bad guys if the price is right."

"Canada?"

"In that thing?"

"You're no fun," he said, playfully pushing me onto my back. I pulled him down on top of me for more gritty kisses.

In the end, we didn't have the resources or the brain power to come up with anything clever at all. I called Donald on Sam's phone once my head was clear enough to string sentences together, and Donald insisted we come to his penthouse apartment in North Ocean City. It was the only place where we hadn't already been tracked down, threatened, tortured, or shot at. But hey, there's a first time for everything.

We tumbled out of the VW bus in a cloud of patchouli and pot smoke and stood in a dazed funk at the front entrance of Donald and his partner Wesley's apartment building. The bus clattered away, and we stood on the tarmac, completely exposed.

The afternoon sun flashed in the building's big glass doors as they swung open. I turned and squinted into the glare, terrified and mesmerized. Sam and I clung to each other. The doors opened further, and the blinding reflection vanished. Terry Montgomery stood in the entryway. He urged us inside with a single wave, his eyes sweeping the lot.

"Would you all get in here?" he called. "Y'all are crazy."

"Oh hey, Terry."

"Girl, I don't even know how you do it."

"Do what?"

"Stay alive." He scowled at me and gave Sam a critical once-over as he stood shirtless in the entryway. Then he hustled us through the lobby and into the penthouse elevator.

"You made it!" Wesley said when he opened the door to us. "I wish you had come here in the first place instead of risking your life out there, camping in the wilderness, you poor things."

He ushered us inside, shaking Sam's proffered hand, clucking over our dangerous predicament and making no reference at all to the fact that Sam and I were both wildly underdressed. Also, my wet cast was starting to give off an unpleasant odor. Again. Our camping gear was neatly stacked in a corner of the entryway.

"What?" I pointed.

"How?" Sam sputtered.

Wesley ignored us and continued with his soothing patter: "Sam, when I heard you're a vegetarian I pulled out some recipes I've been meaning to try, and I'm pretty excited about today's menu." He dispassionately sized up our disheveled state. "I'm trying a new eggplant parmesan recipe, which will be ready soon. But don't worry. You'll have plenty of time to relax, catch your breath, get yourselves cleaned up."

Short and hairy everywhere but on his head, Wesley looked like an Italian butcher—with a taste for pastel designer casuals. Cooking was his passion and, having retired from a career importing European wines, he now spent his time whipping up feasts to pair with his jaw-dropping wine collection.

The tension in Sam's shoulders visibly released as we followed Wesley through the large apartment and into the kitchen.

Donald, Lindsey, and Mark Boshoff sat around the granite breakfast bar. As I let out an astonished cry and Lindsey broke into a big, relieved laugh, Donald did a double take, choked on his coffee, and banged down his "Better Gay Than Grumpy" mug.

"Jamie, what on earth—"

"Everyone, this is my friend Sam."

Sam stepped in smoothly with handshakes all around, and a hug for Lindsey. Donald and Lindsey were as polite as they come, but I could see both of them checking out Sam's trim, muscular body. How could they help themselves? So much of it was on display. My shirtless boyfriend remained calm and confident, like he was relaxing on the beach. Dang, he was hot. I slung an arm around his waist.

"Jamie, I cannot adequately express my relief that you are safe," Donald said. "Truly, I am overwhelmed. But perhaps you can explain how it is that you came to be wearing... that."

I glanced down at the board shorts and macramé tank top, and my salty, bug-bitten skin. "I'll tell you that story if you guys tell me how it is that you're all here—and Terry's downstairs, too."

The group shifted to make room for us, while Wesley bustled around the kitchen.

"Once you abandoned your campsite, we knew you would be low on resources," Mark said.

"It was only a matter of time before you showed up at Donald and Wesley's," Lindsey said. "It's what you do."

I blushed. "So, Majid must have told you that we were at the campground," I said to Mark, who nodded.

"But then somehow you gave us the slip. Where did you go?"

"Well, we were coming back to our tent from the campground's restaurant, where we had watched the nightly news. As we approached we saw someone in our campsite. Somehow they tracked us down. So we had to bail out of there in the middle of the night."

"That wasn't a Russian," Mark said. "That was Terry."

I groaned. Sam looked at the ceiling. "That man needs some more training," he said. "Any Boy Scout would have made less noise than he did."

"Noted," Mark said, cutting that line of conversation short.

"So we walked all the way to Assateague and fell asleep on the dunes," I continued.

Donald recoiled.

"It was kind of comfortable. Actually better than in the tent on hard ground," I reflected.

"The ground wasn't that hard," Sam said, nudging me playfully. "Actually, tent camping can be really great." The rest of us stared at him blankly.

Lindsey giggled. "Tough crowd," she said.

"At least one of us knew how the hell to put up a tent and build a campfire." I squeezed Sam's waist. His arm went around my shoulder. Lindsey studied the two of us with a small, happy smile.

"Anyway," I continued, "this morning was kind of amazing and surreal. We met the nicest group of people on the beach at Assateague."

"Way down the beach where people get naked?" Wesley piped up from the oven as he pulled out the eggplant parm.

"How do you know these things?" Donald asked. Wesley winked. Then he poured two mugs of coffee and handed them to Sam and me.

"They shared their pancakes with us, and then they shared some other stuff, too." I snorted.

Donald scrutinized me. Sam carefully studied the floor. "Jamie, are you stoned?" My boss sounded like a stern parent.

"A little," I said. What was the point in denying it?

"Well, you're probably starving then," Wesley said brightly. "Come on, I'll show you two where to get cleaned up and find something for you to wear for lunch."

66.

THE SHOWER FELT AMAZING. I put on a simple white linen dress I found folded on the bed in our room and was back at the dining table in twenty minutes flat.

Everyone else was already seated, Sam having showered in the bathroom across the hall. He wore a pale-yellow button-down cotton shirt and a pair of shorts in a jaunty plaid.

"I love this dress," I said, twirling the wide, smock skirt. "But why is your apartment stocked with women's clothing?"

"Honey, this is not the first time you've arrived at our door in need of a wardrobe change," Wesley said as Donald rolled his eyes and shook his head.

"I keep you in mind when I hit the outlet malls up in Delaware."

"Thank you." I gave Wesley a squeeze as I passed his chair and sat beside Sam.

"So, why didn't you guys call the police after the shooting at OGISS?" Donald asked as the salad bowl was passed around.

"Because we think there could be at least one dirty cop," I said.

Mark looked at me with interest.

"I've heard many of your conspiracy theories, Jamie, but now you think the OCPD is mobbed up? You're really spreading your wings now," Donald said.

I explained the odd timing of Peter Lapin cruising down the street in the squad car and spotting us on the sidewalk, and the SUV full of Russians showing up so soon thereafter. Lapin's search through the back alleys afterward seemed to indicate that he was working in concert with the guys in the SUV in their efforts to round us up.

"His presence there could mean a lot of things," Donald said.

"It does sound unlikely," Sam chimed in. "But hiding in that alley after my office had been shot up, and seeing that officer creeping through there, solo. ..." He shook his head. "That guy was hunting for us."

"Pete Lapin is part of my team," Mark said.

"Oh! Well shit," I said.

"He's the nephew of one of Majid's business partners. He's been a Pittsburgh cop for almost twenty years. We brought him on the team, and he easily got hired as one of Ocean City's seasonal officers."

"Wait, Zamina told me she was here because the niece of Majid's business partner worked here at the CVS last summer," I said. "And that's how Majid knew about the summer work-away programs."

"That's what Majid told Zamina, yes," Mark said. "When she got into the OGISS program, we moved Pete into place."

"So we ran off to Frontier Town for nothing, and then we ran off to Assateague for nothing," Sam said, throwing his hands up in exasperation.

"I'll say this: you managed to elude our team twice. I'm impressed."

"Your team needs some refresher training," Sam said acidly. The chatter around the table clammed up fast. Someone clinked a piece of cutlery against a plate.

"You're right, of course," Mark said. He gave Sam a nod of acknowledgement.

"Dig in!" Wesley broke the tension by serving out generous helpings of eggplant parm with fresh basil and goat's milk ricotta, while Lindsey passed the garlic and olive bread.

Donald told us that the police this morning had issued a new statement. The unidentified homicide victim who had been knifed to death in late June—before I'd even gotten tangled up with the two girls from Azerbaijan—also had DNA evidence implicating Leyla Dovzhenko.

Mark nodded. "That was the first guy the Russians sent for Zamina," Mark said. "Leyla intercepted him trying to grab Zamina off the street late one night."

"Are you sure he was going to kidnap Zamina? How do you know what he was going to do?" I asked.

"Clearly they sent their second-string guy down from New York first, thinking Zamina would be an easy mark. Leyla confiscated his ID—which he never should have had on him—as well as a taser and a roll of duct tape. That ID helped us pinpoint exactly which organization we were dealing with."

Donald had further news: Zamina called the *Weekly Breeze* offices with a message for me, saying

Sniper Trigga was going to play a surprise set at Seacrets tonight, and Zamina wanted to see me after the show. Seacrets was the biggest club in Ocean City, an island-themed compound with several stages and dining in the sand. It also happened to be the place where I won that freezing bikini contest last winter.

Zamina said she had something she wanted to give me. Very important. Anyone watching would expect Zamina to be at Seacrets, under the careful protection of Sniper Trigga's security. Therefore, our rendezvous point was to be Trimper's on the boardwalk. Midnight.

"You're not going to go, are you?" Sam asked, alarmed.

"Well, uh—"

"Wait, let's talk about that in a second," Donald said, gesturing with a baton of garlic bread. "Let me tell you the rest. She also said to make sure the police are at Seacrets tonight, because there will be trouble. Quite the drama queen, that one."

"She's got the gift," I said. "The cops ought to be all over Seacrets if they want to control the mob that's probably going to show up for Sniper Trigga. I'm not even talking about the Russian Mafia." I recounted the news segment that Sam and I had seen about the violent crowds at André's shows.

"So maybe she's playing the role of André's publicist," Donald said dubiously. "Or maybe they're trying to create some kind of distraction that will allow Zamina to get away and see you. Either way, it sounds like kind of a harebrained scheme."

"Exactly. It's insane," Sam said.

"I already have manpower lined up, if you do choose to go," Mark said. "Sniper Trigga's team is probably going to be stretched thin at Seacrets. With intel like this I know I've got to cover Zamina at Trimper's, whether or not you're there."

"Donald, what did the cops say when you talked to them?" I asked.

"I reached Detective Morrison, who assured me there would be police presence at both Seacrets and Trimper's."

"The oil deal gets signed tomorrow," Sam said. "Those mob guys have one more night—only one more chance—to get to Zamina. Tonight of all nights, Jamie, you have got to stay away from that girl."

"I have an idea," Lindsey said.

"I've heard that line before from an August girl," Sam said dubiously.

67.

THRIFTY-BUY LOOMED The group of us sat around the table and hatched a plan for the evening. It was so crazy that it just might work, as they say.

Then I worked in Donald's study for a couple of hours, making phone calls to confirm statistics from a recent county budget hearing and following up with an Ocean Pines resident who wanted me to do a story about a high school girl who had raised $5,000 for the local animal shelter with her own dog-walking business.

I retrieved my dead cell phone from our pile of camping stuff in the living room and added a bunch of minutes to it. Time is money.

Sam was napping. I shed my clothes and climbed into bed with him, and within minutes his boxers dropped next to my undies on the floor. Soon he was warm and hard inside me, and I was frantically reaching for a pillow to bite back the sounds of my pleasure. He came with a long, deep sigh, then held me quietly.

He quenched a longing in me like nobody ever had. I loved him. And I wasn't at all sure this was going to work. I listened to his soft inhales and exhales for a while. A few tears slid from my eyes, but my breathing remained steady.

Eventually he shifted away from me in sleep. I heard the quiet voices of Donald and Wesley in the living room and felt restless. I silently slid out of bed, eased the linen dress over my head, and tiptoed out of the bedroom.

"Hello, bright eyes," Wesley said. He wore cargo shorts and a black Orioles T-shirt.

"Nice shirt," I said.

Wesley sighed and shifted uncomfortably. "I really don't care for this outfit."

I smiled and sat with them.

"I like your friend," Donald said.

I dropped my eyes, hoping to avoid a discussion of my love life.

"Are you serious, or are you going to break the guy's heart?"

"Me? Break his heart?"

"You have been known to do that. He seems much more, shall we say, worldly than most of the guys you date."

"He's not a summer fling," I said. "I like him a lot. I mean, really a lot. He also bugs the shit out of me sometimes. He makes me feel like an idiot, and I probably give him a harder time than I should. I'm probably going to screw everything up."

"This sounds big."

"But how do you know? I mean, when did you know Wesley was the one for you?" I asked. Wesley grinned and leaned forward in his chair.

"It was definitely that night at Tracks in DC—"

"Oh my God, you mean that night when Miss Shirley lost a heel up in the dance cage?"

"No, no," I quickly interrupted. "I mean how soon after you met him? Did you know right away?"

Donald's eyes softened, and he smiled. "Jamie, are you falling in love?"

"Yes." I sighed deeply.

"I like him, though he seems so serious. Not like your usual suspects."

"I'm not sure what he sees in me. And I know I'm going to ruin it."

"What do you mean? You're smart, you're beautiful, you're brave—"

I grinned, in spite of my gloominess. "Keep going."

"I drive through plate-glass windows for you, honey, you know that. Anyway, knock it off," he said dismissively. "You're fabulous."

Around eight o'clock, Sam joined us in the living room. A few minutes later Mark and Lindsey strolled in, hand in hand. Lindsey's hair was now shoulder-length and honey-blond, and she wore knee-length khaki walking shorts and an Old Navy T-shirt.

"Holy shit, you're my own sister and I barely recognize you." She did a sporty little curtsy.

The doorbell rang, and Mark went to answer it. A moment later he and the blue-eyed cop walked in, together with Terry, who, we learned, had been on guard outside the door all day.

Peter Lapin noticed the camping gear in the corner. His brow furrowed, then he grinned almost imperceptibly and shook his head.

Mark introduced Lapin to each of us. "Pleasure to meet you all," he said in a low, gravelly voice.

"Thanks for helping us out." His eyes lingered on mine, and my spine tingled.

"Quick review," Mark said. "Lindsey and Wesley, you're the happy couple strolling through the arcade. Lindsey, your idea to disguise yourself, but not so thoroughly that Zamina wouldn't recognize you, is a good one. But if it backfires, you could be in danger. You're okay with this?"

"Sure. This is so different from my normal look, so boring, that even with this stupid cast no man will recognize me, mobbed up or not."

"Okay then. You two are Plan A. You're on the lookout for Zamina. When you see her, you make contact and try to get her to come with you. We'll have a secure vehicle standing by. We want this meeting to take place in a more controlled environment than Trimper's."

"Of course. And if she doesn't want to?" Wesley asked.

"Which she won't," Lindsey said.

"Right. If she won't, we move to Plan B. Jamie will enter Trimper's, shadowed by Pete."

"I don't like this," Sam said. "Zamina is going to do something stupid tonight and get herself killed. Sounds harsh, but that's how I see it. Anybody near her is going to get caught in the cross fire."

"I'll be there every step of the way," Peter said, the thought of which felt like icicles in my veins. Get a grip, I mentally scolded myself.

"Jamie connects with Zamina," Mark continued. "Zamina gives Jamie whatever this thing is. Jamie walks out, Pete by her side. Nobody gets hurt. We all come back here, full stop."

"And where are you?" I asked Mark.

"I'm on the scene from start to finish, ready to pull all of you back at the first sign of trouble."

"Why can't you call Zamina, talk to Sniper Trigga's security people, make a better plan?" Sam asked.

"I already tried that. Zamina is convinced that I'm here to grab her and return her home at the first opportunity. She refuses to talk further and insists that she and Jamie meet alone. She also informed me that she was getting rid of her UAE mobile number, having no further need for it. Indeed, the number has been nonoperational for the past several hours. It was my only line of connection to her."

"But you're not really going to try and grab her," I said, scrutinizing him.

"No! I'm not. Majid and Kamala hope Zamina will come home, but they're not going to force her. However, without going into further detail, I can tell you that Zamina is in possession of items that Majid urgently wishes returned."

"That's why her apartment kept getting tossed, isn't it? The Russians know, or suspect, that she's got something."

"Exactly."

"And Pete, is that why you seemed so edgy when I showed up at the apartment saying I knew something about the tenant? Were you searching for this thing, whatever it is?"

"Yes," he said.

"However, Zamina has assured her father that she is still in possession of the materials," Mark said.

"Does Detective Morrison know about any of this?"

"No, she's not involved," Peter said.

"What's my role in this?" Sam asked.

"You're to stay here," Mark said. "Nothing personal, my friend, but you have the distinct disadvantage of being known to the Russians but of no interest to Zamina."

"I think Zamina might be very interested," I said, eyeing Sam lecherously.

"Oh!" Wesley said. "Since you'll be here, Sam, would you mind turning the oven on to 350 in about thirty minutes? I have some nice little canapés that I'll pop in the oven when we return home. We can celebrate with some bubbly and a little snack."

"I am really not happy with this. If I can't convince Jamie to stay out of this—" he shot me a pleading look "—then at least I want to do something constructive."

"I understand what you're saying, Sam, and I'd feel the same way if I were you," Peter said, his deep voice settling like a fog over the room. "But there's a chance that whatever Zamina wants to give Jamie might have relevance to Dr. Allyev's pending transaction."

"Not our problem," Sam said. "I'm sick of that obscene oil deal. How many people have died in the run-up to this thing?"

"I agree, really," I said. "But, if whatever this is helps to get the deal signed and done tomorrow, then let's do it. It's not about helping Majid. It's about getting this thing finished."

"To clarify: Majid does not know what Zamina wants to give Jamie?" Peter asked Mark.

"He does not," Mark said. "Zamina's a bit of a wild card."

"There's an understatement," I said.

"And that's what makes this potentially quite significant," Mark said.

Sam stood and faced Mark in the center of the room. "You keep her safe."

"You have my word."

"Um, hello," I said, waving my hand between the two of them. "I'm right here. No need to talk about me in the third person."

Wesley jumped up and said, "Okay, everyone, tension is high but we have a plan. Let's get a move on."

Donald gathered together his reporter's notebook and his keys. "It's showtime down at Seacrets."

68.

OUT ON COASTAL HIGHWAY, I caught a crowded southbound bus—exactly as if I wasn't on a secret mission to foil a Russian hit squad—and soon was chugging past Seacrets. I counted six squad cars and three news trucks, along with a mob of people swarming around the front door. The antennae and satellite dishes gleamed purple and green from the building's neon.

As the view slid south, I worked my elbows to create some personal space. I could feel Pete's eyes on me, though of course I didn't turn around.

A round of "Ninety-nine Bottles of Beer on the Wall" started at the back of the bus, and soon the whole crowd was singing. I was wound up so tight I could barely manage to join in, but it seemed like the appropriate thing to do. The OC bus on a summer night often turned into a jolly sing-along.

Finally the bus swung into the depot at the inlet. We had reached eighty-six bottles of beer on the wall. As I filed past the driver, he was slumped in his seat, massaging his temples.

I moved with the late-night crowd toward the boardwalk, natural and normal. I carried my phone in my hand, and it vibrated with a text message.

Plan B, it read. I could see that Mark had sent the same words to Peter and me. So much for Lindsey talking Zamina out of there.

Copy. Jamie covered, proceed when ready.

The carnival rides were all in motion, the whirr of engines blending with the squeals of the riders. A blur of Tilt-A-Whirl arms, swinging pirate ships, and flashing lights barely registered as I made my way through the night. My white linen smock dress ruffled in the ocean breeze, offering peeks high up on my legs. I thought the loose style was prim and girlish until I wore it outside.

My goal was the boardwalk entrance of Trimper's, where the ornate, antique carnival rides lent an air of respectable nostalgia to the boardwalk's riot of plastic schlock and junk food. My head was on a swivel as I searched for Zamina but also for Yuri and his henchman. I was shaking with fear. I needed a cigarette so bad. I spotted a candy vendor and bought a Blow Pop. If there had been a cigarette girl, I would have chosen a smoke instead, but this was OC, not Vegas.

After several minutes, I saw a head of frosty-blond hair in the crowd. My view was obstructed by a group of guys wearing Harley Davidson gear from head to toe. They paused in their stroll toward the inlet, thinning hairstyles blowing majestically in the night breeze, allowing the frosty-blonde to more into view. She wore a neon-pink miniskirt and a halter top of spandex and lace in a death match. Her back was turned to me. She seemed to be Zamina's height, and the tousled hair had clearly been accomplished with a careful combination of styling products. Definitely Zamina's style.

Then the woman began rhythmically punching a hand in the air and doing an a cappella rendition of "Sweet Home Alabama" (with a little butt wiggle to indicate the pause for the guitar part). The accent was pure southern Virginia.

I walked through the vast indoor arcade. It was deafening, with video games, racing simulators complete with authentic-sounding mufflers and backfires, the dings and pings of old-school pinball machines, and the knock of wooden balls on Skee-Ball lanes. On another day this would have been my idea of the perfect date: a pile of tokens and a growing string of paper tickets representing prizes waiting to be collected at the end of the night.

Tonight, though, I was afraid for my life. My pinky finger, swaddled in dirty, damp plaster, began to throb painfully. The flashing lights and noise were disorienting, and my eyes darted around in search of a meaty bald head or an Adidas tracksuit. I walked through the arcade, scanning every face. I swore to myself, when I found Zamina I would give her such a smack.

A hand grabbed my shoulder roughly and spun me around.

69.

ZAMINA STOOD BEFORE ME, completely transformed. Her hair was a shiny russet color, cascading smoothly down her shoulders. She wore a vintage black satin cocktail dress and a diamond choker. The crowd seemed to give her space, deferring to this glamorous creature in their midst.

I gaped, nearly dropping my lollipop. "What happened to you? You look amazing." I had to shout to be heard over the arcade's roar.

"I get good style from Lindsey. I get shopping trip from André."

"Well, that worked out nicely for you."

"Yes."

"We've gotta get out of here. I can't believe you didn't trust Lindsey; she could have taken you to a safe spot for us to meet. It's insane for both of us to be standing out in the open. Those hit men are going to find us for sure."

"Lindsey is beautiful, is wonderful, she save my life. But Mark Boshoff, I cannot trust."

"Mark swore to me he was not trying to force you back home to your parents."

"This is what he say, of course. Is okay, don't worry. We are safe." Zamina languidly gestured to one side, where a massive man in a beautifully tailored suit stood a step back and watched us impassively, one hand hidden inside the jacket. "This is Jamal."

I nodded at the man. He stood, impassive, continuing to scan the crowd.

"He is big, no? He protect me."

Jamal's face suddenly registered shock. His eyes grew wide, his mouth moved soundlessly, and he dropped on his face like a felled tree. A bullet hole cut through the fine wool of his suit, a dark stain spreading across his back. Someone in the crowd began to scream.

Before either of us could react, Yuri grabbed Zamina and another guy grabbed me: Peter Lapin. "I knew it!" I shouted. He wrenched my left arm behind my back, perhaps to reemphasize that point. I could feel the cool metal of a gun barrel against my ribs. "Be quiet and walk."

They led us away from Jamal's body. We speed-walked through the children's rides, past the classic kiddie cars, the saloon shoot-out game, and the ornate old carousel. I noted that one of the intricately painted menagerie was a camel. Then I noted that my brain was focusing on details that were not at all helpful.

We continued our grim march out a door into a narrow alley behind the amusement hall. Glass crunched under my feet, and I looked up to see a darkened security light high on the wall, a few jagged shards of glass still hanging in the frame. The Russian's grip tightened savagely on my arm, and I bit down on the Blow Pop in a reflexive pain response. I felt blood on my tongue.

Peter threw me against the wall, pinning me with one hand and holding his gun on me with the other. He looked me up and down with malice—and lust. His eyes glittered in the dim light.

"That dress makes me think of schoolgirls," he said. "I'm going to teach you a few things, and then I'm going to kill you."

"No you're not," I said, willing my voice to stay calm. "If I don't report back to Mark soon, he's go-

ing to find us back here and blow your head off."
This was mere speculation on my part.

"Not so," Peter said. "I told him we're on foot
with Zamina. He's heading north in the armored
vehicle to pick us up several blocks away."

His eyes glittered as he grinned at me, his gun
hand never wavering an inch.

Yuri, meanwhile, had Zamina backed up against
the grill of the Yukon, which was so wide, its side
view mirrors nearly scraped the walls on either side
of the alley. He was getting ready to haul off and
punch her.

Suddenly Peter's body jerked violently to one
side and he pitched to the ground, his gun clatter-
ing against the concrete.

A silhouetted figure came running up the alley
toward us, shouting "Police! Drop your weapon."

Yuri pulled Zamina against him as a human
shield, and she screamed. In a rage, I hurled myself
against the two of them. Meanwhile, Zamina raised
a knee and drove a sharp heel backwards into
Yuri's leg. Our combined forces topped Yuri,
knocking us all to the ground. I took the Blow Pop
out of my mouth and jammed the sharp cherry
shards into his eye. I felt it pop like an over-easy
egg yolk.

Yuri bellowed as he grabbed for the lollipop stick. The eye was squeezed shut, and blood dripped down his cheek. I rolled off of Zamina, and she lurched away from Yuri.

Our rescuer, still only a silhouette, was racing up the alley toward us. Yuri struggled to a seated position, a gun in his hand. He turned his face at an odd angle and took aim with his good eye.

Two shots rang out.

Yuri was knocked flat on his back. The other figure fell to the ground and lay still.

70.

THRIFTY-BUY LOOMED I jumped up and ran to the other shooter. Detective Morrison lay bleeding on the concrete. Sirens squealed in the distance. Morrison's eyes slid closed.

"Hang on, Morrison, help is coming. You're going to be okay," I said, fearing she wasn't.

"What kind of weapon did you use on that man's eye?"

"Blow Pop."

She blinked, her brow furrowed in confusion. "I'm sorry? I don't... Huh." Her eyes drifted out of focus. I took her hand.

Her breathing evened out a little. She wore a black T-shirt, but I could see even in the dim light that blood was spreading across her abdomen. I wanted to let her rest, but I was afraid that if she closed her eyes once more, she'd never open them again.

"Talk to me, Morrison. What are you doing here? How did you know we were back here?"

"Terry Montgomery."

"Terry? I don't understand."

"Reached me at the station an hour ago. Told me about your meeting with Zamina."

"Why?"

"Didn't trust the cops, but... trusted me. Don't know why."

"Maybe because Zamina trusted you a little."

"Yeah." She paused and focused on her breathing. I squeezed her hand. "Terry said there was a guy from Allyev's team in the OCPD. Didn't like him. Said if a man could be bought once, he could be bought twice."

A cell phone broke the tense quiet of the alley. Zamina and I glanced around. Not hers. Not mine. Not Morrisons's. Zamina walked over to Yuri's sprawled-out body, gave him a kick—I guess to make sure he had no fight left in him—and bent down to reach into the pocket of his suit jacket.

She came out with a ringing phone. I cried out, "No! Don't answer that!" But Zamina had already hit the button.

She spat something in Russian, then threw the phone onto the pavement, where it broke into pieces.

"What did you say?"

"I said 'fuck you. I am not dead.'"

"Was that really wise?"

"Those shits cannot kill me."

I clenched my jaw and returned my attention to Detective Morrison.

A vehicle turned turned into the alley down at the other end, blocked from our view by Yuri's Yukon. High beams flashed on as it rolled up to the SUV, throwing its boxy shape into brilliant silhouette.

At the same time, a black limousine turned into the alley on the end closer to us, blinding us and illuminating a spray of broken glass and the three bodies down.

Car doors slammed on the far side of Yuri's SUV.

The limo slid toward us, and the back door opened. Bass-heavy rap echoed down the alleyway.

André leaned out. "Get in the car," he said, all business.

Zamina hopped right in. The sound of sirens grew louder.

"I can't leave Detective Morrison out here on the ground," I said.

"Ambulance almost here. Gangsters coming at you. You need to get the fuck in the car."

"Help is on the way, Detective Morrison." I squeezed her limp hand and jumped into the limo. André pulled the door closed, and the car did a quick reverse out of the alley, tires chirping. Shots rang out, but no one followed. Yuri's giant SUV blocking the narrow alley may have saved our lives.

The limo made a few more turns, then slipped into the late-night, northbound traffic on Coastal Highway.

André handed each of us a drink. I downed mine—vodka, naturally—in one gulp, then relaxed back into the plush leather upholstery.

Crisis over, Zamina turned the drama all the way up. She held onto André for dear life, weeping into his shoulder. He held her close with one arm and draped the other one across the top of the seat.

"Where you want us to drop you?" he asked, casual.

I told him Donald and Wesley's North Ocean City address. He lowered the window to the driver and repeated it, then pressed the button to slide the glass back into place.

"Zamina, you have something for me?"

Zamina pulled her head up from André's shoulder. "What?"

"You know, the reason we all came out tonight and got shot up? You were going to give me something?"

"Oh," she said, reaching into her purse for a tissue. She dabbed at her eyes and carefully wiped her nose. She touched up her lipstick, then faced me.

"I want to give you something to thank you for helping me."

"Nice of you, Zamina. Your family has already been really kind to Lindsey and me."

"That is my from my parents, but that is not from me."

"Well, but—"

"I am on my own now."

"Is that a fact?" André said, pulling her to him.

"Ach, you know what I mean. I choose you. I can un- choose you." She glowered at him, then turned back to me.

"I give you something from me." She removed the diamond Piaget watch from her wrist and fastened it onto mine. André leaned back and watched events transpire, bemused.

457

"What the hell, Zamina?" I said.

"You take."

"I can't use a diamond watch."

"No, but you can use a car."

I gaped.

"You take. You sell. You buy good car. When you drive, you think of me. So do not buy American shit car."

We were passing Seacrets. I glanced over at the satellite parking lot and saw Donald's Acura glowing brightly under a sodium light.

"Hey!" I knocked on the glass behind my head, separating me from the driver. "Stop! I need to get out!"

"Wassup, baby?"

"My editor is over there. I want to get out."

"You sure you want to go over there? All that security and shit? You got blood on your dress."

I looked down. The linen smock was streaked with dirt and sprayed with blood.

"Zamina. Give me your dress."

She looked at me, shocked.

"I give you my watch. Now you want my dress?"

I held my hand out. "I need."

The limousine pulled over and stopped. Zamina narrowed her eyes at me. Then she pulled at the side zipper and slid the dress over her head.

"Close your eyes," I said to André. I pulled off the ruined white dress and dropped it on the floor.

André tilted his head to the side and grinned. "You think I ain't seen bitches get naked in my limo before?"

I slid into Zamina's black satin number. "Don't call me a bitch."

71.

LURKED IN THE SHADOWS at the edge of the parking lot, searching for Donald among the media types. Finally I spotted him, chatting with the police-beat reporter from the Salisbury paper. She batted her hair coquettishly and laughed at something he said, touching his jacket lapel gently.

"Get your radar checked, hon," I murmured.

Finally they said their good-byes, and he walked back to the car. "Donald!"

He squinted at me. "Jamie? Get in."

I jumped into the passenger seat.

Donald revved the engine and sped from the parking lot, his face rigid with tension.

"What happened?"

I recounted the night's action, from Lapin's double cross all the way through André's right-on-time pick-up service. I choked when I told him about leaving Detective Morrison bleeding in the alley.

"We'll get an update on her condition as soon as we get home, Jamie, I promise. I'll call my gal at the hospital."

Somewhere in my brain it registered that Donald had "a gal" he could call at the hospital. That was impressive.

"Why are you wearing a Versace cocktail dress?"

"How can you tell it's a Versace?"

Donald looked at me as if I were a slow child.

"My dress had blood on it, so I took Zamina's."

"Good for you."

"How could you have spotted the dress but missed the watch?"

He glanced at my wrist and yelped. I reached over and grabbed the steering wheel to keep him from sideswiping a minivan.

72.

THE LIMOUSINE CAME TO A STOP on the
runway at Baltimore/Washington International
Airport, next to a private jet chartered by her father.
Zamina gazed up from the open door of the limousine
at the sweep of the plane's wing and the sky, growing light
and turning pink in the dawn.

"You will not come?"

"Nah, baby, you know I can't. I got three shows in Baltimore and two in DC."

"Forget these things. Come with me. I will be lonely."

André kissed her. "I can't do that, Z. You know that.
I'm a professional."

"Then I don't want to go. I stay here. With you."

"You know that ain't right. You gotta go do this thing. Ink that deal, baby. You gonna be richer than me!"

"Going to be?" She eyed him skeptically.

He dropped his eyes. "Aw, why you gotta be like that?"

"Going to be?"

"Yeah, all right, all right. You already richer than me."

"Do not forget."

"Not likely."

"Good."

"Listen, baby, I say that 'cuz I want to take care of you, you know? You my woman."

"I want you to take care of me too," she said, switching tactics and burying her head in his shoulder. "I need."

"So get on the plane. Take care of business in Houston, then get back here. I'll meet you in DC."

Zamina sighed. "Okay. Where you stay?"

"I don't know. They got me booked somewhere."

"I like Four Seasons."

"Is that right?"

"Yes. Royal Suite, please."

The engines of the plane roared to life, making further conversation impossible.

Zamina kissed André one last time, then turned and walked up the steps of the private jet in her black lace slip. She worked her trim calves in her high-heeled shoes and threw her shoulders back. Her deep-red hair blew in the wind.

Zamina reached the top of the stairs, feeling André's eyes burning into her back. She was acutely aware that he was waiting for her to turn around and give him one final glance. She walked straight onto the aircraft, disappearing from his sight.

73.

W E ALL SLEPT IN but Wesley. He must have gotten up early to start preparing the mountain of french toast that greeted us at the breakfast table, together with his own home-made strawberry jam and freshly squeezed orange juice.

"Good news," Donald said between bites. "I heard from my hospital contact. Morrison has come out of surgery at Atlantic General. She lost quite a bit of blood, but she was lucky: the bullet just grazed her ribs. She'll be in the hospital for a few days, but she's going to be fine."

"And what about the Russians?" I asked.

"Yuri was pronounced dead at the scene. Lapin died in surgery."

"That's five down," Lindsey said. "Is there going to be blowback from this?"

"Ocean City wasn't home turf for any of these guys," Mark said. "Will others come down here to avenge these deaths? Hard to say, but I rather doubt it."

"What about the guys who showed up after Yuri and Lapin were down?" I asked.

"We don't know. Probably never will. Always be careful. All of you. The Russian Mafia is not going away any time soon—and you've tangled with them," Mark said.

Yummy smells started emanating from the kitchen almost immediately after breakfast, promising an equally wonderful lunch.

Mark and Lindsey refilled their coffee cups and set up a Scrabble game. Wesley recruited Sam for a baking project.

I was under my editor's roof, so I had to work. When I popped my head in the kitchen later, Sam was kneading bread dough on a marble slab. I smiled at him, and he gave his head a little tip, calling me over.

"I'm glad you came home last night," he whispered in my ear. I kissed him from the other side of the counter. He cupped my face with his hands and kissed me slowly. "Wearing Versace and a Piaget."

I snorted.

Donald had set up on an extra laptop in his office. Donald and I worked all morning. CNN was turned on low, and we were keeping half an eye on it for the piece of news that would allow me to finish the big story.

At noon the story broke. "It's happening," Donald called out. Lindsey, Mark, Wesley, and Sam filed into the office.

The six of us watched, hardly breathing, as the business-news anchor announced that Azeri billionaire Majid Allyev sold all of his Caspian Sea oil rights to Shell in a $15 billion dollar deal. The sale represented a new American foothold in eastern European oil exploration.

"It's done," I breathed. "We can go home."

"I can have my house back," Donald said.

"But lunch is almost ready!" Wesley protested.

74.

A FEW DAYS LATER, Sam and I sat on the couch at Tammy's apartment. Dustin lounged in the recliner while Tammy poured a jar of cheese sauce, hot from the microwave, and a jar of salsa over some tortilla chips on a platter. She put the snack on the coffee table and Dustin said, "How come there's no ground beef?"

Tammy gave him a withering look. "It's vegetarian."

Sam squirmed. "Tammy, you didn't have to—"

"It's no problem, hon. Dig in!" She popped a chip in her mouth, punched Dustin in the arm, then sat on his lap.

Sam stared at the plate, glanced at me. I gave him a warning look. He picked up a chip with a little salsa.

"Thank you," he said. "This is nice."

I ate chip after cheesy, gloopy chip, a huge fan of the whole fake-cheese-in-a-jar concept. I was with Dustin, though: nachos needed beef. In fact, beef would maybe have been one of the healthier things on this particular plate—oh, wait, unless it was feedlot beef, which was full of antibiotics. So maybe not. Other than the drizzle of salsa and the corn in the chips, which was almost certainly genetically modified, there was probably no actual food here at all: only petroleum products. Oil! It's not just for cars anymore! Sam was teaching me well, and it was ruining all my favorite foods.

Dustin was asking Sam which Ravens player ought to be traded out next season. Sam clearly was on the verge of admitting he doesn't watch football—God knows how Dustin would've reacted—when Tammy spoke up.

"Okay, be quiet. It's on, it's on!" She kicked her heels into Dustin's leg.

"Ow," he said, poking her in the ribs.

Welcome back to Nightly News Special Edition. I'm Candy Holloway, and tonight we have a tale of intrigue and danger—and love, around the world and against all odds.

Candy's face was serious yet perfectly airbrushed.

This evening I will be speaking to the daughter of Azerbaijani oil magnate Abdulmajid Allyev, who has signed the largest deal in history granting an American oil company rights to drill in the Caspian Sea. Dr. Allyev's daughter played a critical role in sealing that deal, and tonight she's going to tell her exciting story. Please welcome the beautiful, the brave Zamina Allyev.

Candy's Eastern Shore accent made Zamina's name and her country sound even more exotic than they already were.

The camera panned out and Zamina walked in, devastating in a skintight black pants suit, her hair pulled up in a smooth twist.

Candy stood up and hugged Zamina, who responded coolly. Candy seemed starstruck and small-town.

Her enthusiasm won the day, though. The regional news anchor listened, rapt, as Zamina recounted her adventures, describing herself as a "conscientious Kohr Brothers employee."

"As if," I scoffed.

Actually, Zamina admitted, she was "a scared immigrant on the run."

"She wasn't an immigrant," Sam said. "She was a seasonal summer worker."

Zamina described how, by necessity, she "reinvented herself as a fashion buyer for an exclusive East Coast boutique."

"Maude's?" Tammy laughed out loud.

I didn't complain that she had "reinvented herself." I was glad she was leaving me completely out of the story. Why remind other East Coast Russian mobsters—those not already mowed down over the past few weeks—of my existence?

Zamina "fled in terror from a Fourth of July parade-turned-bloodbath."

"Bloodbath?" Dustin rolled his eyes.

"Into the waiting arms of her on-again, off-again boyfriend, the very hunky Sniper Trigga," Candy Holloway gushed.

"Hunky? Is that term still in use?" Tammy asked.

Zamina described how André and his entourage kept her safe against Russian Mafia men, who would stop at nothing to kidnap her and therefore stop the sale of the oil rights.

"Because your father would have given in to their demands?" Candy asked.

"Of course, yes. But also something else."

"Something else?" Candy's voice trilled upward at the end in a poor imitation of someone who doesn't already know the answer.

"Yes. Something else."

"The suspense is killing me," Candy gushed, turning to the camera. "Ladies and gentlemen, this breaking story is coming to you exclusively on Nightly News Special Edition. We'll be right back."

A string of commercials followed.

"How much you want to bet they're going to give Zamina a talk show?" Tammy said.

"Nah, she'd be a terrible talk show host," Dustin said. "She'd only want to talk about herself. But a reality TV show, now you're talking. Maybe about the lingerie modeling business."

Tammy made outraged noises.

Nightly News Special Edition returned to the screen. Candy turned to Zamina, eyes fractionally wider than normal, an eager smile stretched across her face. "Tell us, Zamina. Why else were you hiding here in Ocean City, right under our noses?"

"I had something with me."

"Yes?"

"A secret."

"A secret?"

"Yes, a big secret."

"Oh for God's sake," Tammy said.

Zamina paused, then reached under the coffee table, offscreen, and pulled out the blingy Valentino handbag she had been clutching to her chest all summer.

"Huh?" I said. We all leaned in.

"I carried the bearer bonds for my father's Caspian Sea oil rights. He had to give to Shell when he sign deal. I hid them in my Valentino handbag," she said. She opened the bag, now empty, and revealed a neat slice in the lining.

"So that's what everybody was after." I clapped a hand over my mouth.

"Holy crap," Sam said.

"She took those bonds from her father after he punished her by taking her credit cards away and making her get a job in OC," I explained to Dustin and Tammy. "He needed those to transfer the oil rights."

"Well, that's a very valuable handbag," Candy said, chuckling merrily.

"Yes of course. Is Valentino," Zamina said drily, crossing her legs and looking annoyed.

"Well, no, what I meant was—ha-ha! Well, well! Let's move on to your next amazing piece of show-and-tell! I understand you're now wearing another valuable piece..."

Zamina smiled graciously. "Yes, of course." She lifted her left hand and held it up, as if to be kissed by the studio audience. The camera panned in to show a gigantic diamond on her ring finger.

"From André." The audience oohed and aahed.

"That's horrible," Sam said. "A blood diamond, I'll bet."

"So tacky," Tammy said.

"I'm glad to hear you say that," Dustin said.

Tammy gasped at Dustin's remark. Dustin laughed, and the two of them whispered together on the recliner.

Meanwhile, André was strutting onto the stage in zoot-suit pinstripes, a rope of gold around his neck. Zamina stood and greeted him with a decidedly adult-viewing-style kiss. The audience went wild.

The happy couple announced their plans for an autumn wedding in Ibiza.

"I can't take any more," I said, picking up the wrecked nachos plate and carrying it over to the kitchen sink.

A moment later the music and closing credits rolled. Sam and I bid our farewells to Tammy and Dustin, who were already getting frisky on the recliner. Awkward.

75.

SAM WALKED ME HOME down a side street, the bay peeking between the houses on our right. He explained how the diamond industry was still horribly corrupt, even after the Kimberley Process was put into place to stop the sale of diamonds that support violent rebel movements in Africa. His brow wrinkled in fierce worry.

"I guess soon I'll be driving a blood car," I said, making a sick joke about the diamond-encrusted watch Zamina had given me. I'd opened up a safe-deposit box at the bank and locked it up there because I couldn't sleep at night with a $30,000 watch in my apartment.

"That's not funny," Sam said.

"You're right, that was inappropriate."

I was still hungry after Tammy's awful nachos. When we arrived at my place, I told Sam I needed to call it a night.

"I could stay," he said, smoothing a strand of hair behind my ear.

"If you stayed, I wouldn't get any sleep."

"I'll be good, I promise."

"You'll be so, so good. That's the problem," I said. "C'mon. I just need a night. I'll call you tomorrow, okay?"

"Sure, okay," he said uncertainly, kissing me.

Inside, I pulled a piece of cold sausage and pepperoni pizza from the fridge and took a greedy bite. I popped open a Coors Light, flipped up the laptop on my kitchen table, and logged into my bank account.

It was all still there in checking: $2.1 million. Nobody knew it was there but me. Not Sam. Not Tammy. I hadn't even told Lindsey yet, though I would soon: part of it would be hers.

"Consider this a commission, owed to you in consideration for your assistance in the recent transaction with Shell," Majid wrote in the note accompanying a check that arrived in a FedEx envelope the day after the Shell sale. "Remember: follow your passion. This should help."

Author's Note

Writing about Ocean City—real and imaginary, and believe me, the one slides right into the other—really keeps my home fires burning. Though I consider Maryland to be home, I spend most of the year in the Middle East because of my husband's work. So it scratches an itch, whipping up scenes involving real boardwalk businesses and all those trashy Ocean City foods I miss.

At the same time, because I've been living overseas for several years now it seemed only right to work in the stuff about Middle Eastern expat life. If the two settings seem strangely jarring next to one another, well, yes. That's how it feels in real life, too.

An army of talented and generous people helped me to conceive, write, polish, and publish this novel. Any errors are mine alone. Thanks to Brian Ashby, the man of endless great ideas, who pointed out the literary potential of the Caspian Sea's untapped oil, and those all-important bearer bonds. Development editor Paul Covington pushed Jamie to be smarter, sexier, more real—and, oh yeah, he wanted the plot to make some kind of sense too. If it still doesn't, it's not for his lack of trying. My husband the paramedic answered my questions about broken bones, gunshot wounds and emergency medical care, as well as keeping me well-fed and encouraged. My friend and Shakti sister Alison Gary (wardrobeoxygen.com) fielded my questions about haute couture with humor and good cheer. And speaking of haute couture, I offer a grateful nod to Mathurine Casside for ... the watch.

Big thanks are in order to Barb Goffman for her meticulous copyediting and for her wise and generous advice about all things relating to the mystery-writing community. J. Caleb Design delivered another knockout cover—and a big round of applause to the designer's wife, the live model who inspired Jamie's cover pose. Thanks, too, to my gracious and unflappable assistant, Nikki Forston. My dear friends in Dhahran literally delivered food to my door during several crunched writing weeks when my husband was away, so I raise a glass to them, too! I am a lucky girl.

ABOUT THE AUTHOR

Kim Kash is a freelance writer and the author of
the Jamie August novel series and *Ocean City: A
Guide to Maryland's Seaside Resort* (2009,
Channel Lake). She divides her time between
Maryland and the Middle East, where she lives
with her husband and a large black cat. Visit her
online at www.kimkash.com

CPSIA information can be obtained at www.ICGtesting.com
Printed in the USA
LVOW10s1027060715

445108LV00006B/135/P